"Didn't the nurse tell you you'll have to undress for the examination?"

Dr. Regina Lawton's gaze traveled over a trim waist and upward over a broad expanse of chest snugly fitted into a black polo shirt.

"She did, but . . ." He grinned at having caught her staring. There was a softness in her voice and manner that he hadn't expected.

Regina felt her flesh tingling in some uncommon blend of nervousness and reservation. There was something about the man that disturbed her. "I'll step out a moment while you change."

"Don't bother." He shook his head and chuckled, and Regina looked up in surprise. He stepped out of his shoes as he talked and was out of his trousers before she could leave the examining room. Then, whisking the polo shirt over his head, he took a seat on the examining table, clad in an immodest pair of black briefs.

"Ready, Doctor?"

Dear Reader,

The editorial staff of Silhouette Intimate Moments is always striving to bring new and exciting things your way: new authors, new concepts in romantic fiction and new ideas from favorite authors. This month we have once again come up with something special.

Emilie Richards is one of your favorite authors, as your letters have made clear, and this month she embarks on a project that will delight her current fans and undoubtedly win her new ones. Tales of the Pacific is a four-book miniseries set in Hawaii, Australia and New Zealand, and the cast of characters who fill the pages of these books will make you laugh, make you cry and make you fall in love—over and over again. Of course, each book stands alone as it presents one very special story, and in *From Glowing Embers*, the first book of the series, Julianna Mason and Gray Sheridan will capture your heart as they strive to mend the hurts of the past and rebuild their marriage. Theirs is a love story that will truly leave you breathless.

Also this month, look for delightful treats from Paula Detmer Riggs, whose first book was part of our March Madness promotion, Marion Smith Collins, and an author who's new to Silhouette Books but not to fans of romance, Andrea Parnell.

As always, Silhouette Intimate Moments is the place to find love stories *for* today's women *by* today's women. We hope you'll enjoy them as much as we do.

Leslie J. Wainger
Senior Editor

Andrea Parnell

The Silver Swan

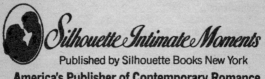

Silhouette Intimate Moments

Published by Silhouette Books New York

America's Publisher of Contemporary Romance

SILHOUETTE BOOKS
300 East 42nd St., New York, N.Y. 10017

ISBN: 0-373-07251-1

First Silhouette Books printing August 1988

All the characters in this book are fictitious. Any
resemblance to actual persons, living or dead, is
purely coincidental.

Printed in the U.S.A.

ANDREA PARNELL

says that writing gives her a license to daydream, and she's made daydreaming a serious business. She hardly misses the busy, people-filled days as a high school home economics teacher and instead relishes her quiet, solitary life as a writer. She hasn't completely eliminated teaching, however. She frequently speaks on writing techniques at seminars and conferences.

Aside from contemporary romances, Ms. Parnell writes historicals. She likes using universal characters, no matter what their time period. She believes she writes, to some extent, because she likes to study people. She writes about love because it is essential to happiness. No matter how you twist or bend it, she says, in the end love triumphs. By Ms. Parnell's philosophy, you can't say that often enough.

Prologue

The tall Frenchman, Jacques Marot, pulled his rented car into the narrow parking space outside a small chalet resting beneath the lofty, brooding peaks of the Swiss Alps. His muttered oath belied his expressionless face as he set the hand brake and stepped out of the car. He took a deep breath, filling his lungs with air so crisp and cool and fresh it ought to have been bottled and sold. That was the one impractical thought Marot allowed himself. A man in his line of work couldn't afford to be philosophical.

He moved slowly. The mountain dropped away steeply just beyond the nose of the car, and his eyes followed the incline to the green valley with its neat white buildings looking so small and unreal they might have been a child's toy. He snorted irritably, feeling a sudden tinge of queasiness in the pit of his stomach.

"Madness," he mumbled. "The Swiss and their mountains." He made a quick visual sweep of the chalet, then glanced back at the car. "Wait here, Larousse," he called to his companion, who had taken one look at the sheer drop and slid nearer the center of the seat.

Shuffling his feet on the rocky ground, Marot edged his way cautiously around the car to reach the flower-lined path that led to the chalet. He knocked on the sturdy wooden door painted too cheerful a shade of yellow. As he listened to the sound of footsteps inside, his hand went automatically to the handle of the gun holstered beneath his coat.

A moment later the door swung open, and he met the clear blue eyes of a middle-aged woman, who seemed to personify the Swiss countryside. Her coiled gray-blond hair was pinned high on her head. Her plain, scrubbed face was lit with an inquisitive smile Marot didn't seem capable of returning. In one hand she held a dust cloth, the other she quickly wiped on her checkered apron.

Marot didn't waste time with preliminaries. "You are?" he asked the woman in French.

"Mrs. Grunter, the cleaning woman," she answered.

"*Monsieur* is not in?" Marot pressed forward and the woman instinctively moved back a step.

"He is not."

"Do you expect him soon?" Marot's quick eyes combed the interior, noting the simple furnishings in the open room, the kettle steaming in a small kitchen at the rear, and the doors leading to a bedroom and a bath.

"Who can say?" Mrs. Grunter shrugged her shoulders and simply retreated into the room, since Marot had already made his way inside. "Monsieur Andrews comes and goes on no schedule."

Marot rolled up his eyes and gave a disappointed sigh. "I've come all the way from Paris to see him on a most urgent matter. Can you tell me where he's gone?"

"No." Mrs. Grunter rubbed the dust cloth over a polished tabletop. "Only that he said he'd be away a long while."

Marot frowned and reached inside his coat pocket to withdraw a small leather case. He flipped it open for Mrs. Grunter to see the papers that identified him as an agent of DESE, the Direction Générale de la Sécurité Extérieure de France.

"Is there anything you can tell me? An address perhaps?"

Her eyes widened. "You are French police?"

"Yes." Marot quickly pocketed the credentials. "I must find *Monsieur*."

"He was here only a day, packing, rushing about, making a mess of the house." A bit flustered, Mrs. Grunter laid her cleaning cloth aside and dropped into a high-backed wooden chair beside a tall secretary desk. "But he told me nothing of his plans." She wet her lips and paused in thought for a moment. "I'm sorry, I don't know how to reach him…" Again she paused as if searching her mind for a bit of information. "There was a package," she said, "which I mailed the day after he left."

"What was in the package, *madame*?"

"That I don't know. It was boxed already. I only packed it in a larger box for posting. I remember he first had it in his luggage but then he thought it had better go by mail. It was for his niece."

"His niece? Do you have her address?"

Mrs. Grunter turned, opened a desk drawer and lifted out a letter, which she laid on the desk top. "The same as this," she said.

For the first time a smile appeared on Marot's thin lips. He slipped a notebook from his coat pocket and copied down the name, Regina Lawton, and her address, while Mrs. Grunter went to the kitchen and poured boiling water into an earthenware teapot. She was about to offer Marot a cup when she glanced up and saw him hurrying out the door.

Without a word to Larousse, Marot slammed the car door and slipped the notebook into his pocket. He turned the key, bringing the engine chortling to life. A moment later his dark eyes were intent on the road, and he was driving at a speed that terrified his partner. Marot's mind raced as well. One diamond necklace, one elusive man, but he saw how they would come together.

"What did you learn?" Larousse asked.

"I have discovered the name of Andrews's accomplice." A satisfied smile spread across Marot's mouth. "We will be making a trip to the United States," he said emphatically. "We'll find what we're looking for in Atlanta." Triumph flooded into his eyes. "I'm sure of it."

In the chalet Mrs. Grunter shook her head and poured a cup of the fragrant, steaming tea. Cup in hand, she walked to the window and watched the car speed away.

"The French," she mumbled, "always rude." It was his loss, she thought. The tea was excellent and she had been about to tell him of the other package.

Chapter 1

Who had sent her a gift?

A sad, tinkling melody rang out before Regina Lawton completely unwrapped the little music box. She unfolded the last layer of newspaper, scarcely noticing the words written in French, and let it float to the floor as her eyes widened appreciatively at the exquisite bit of workmanship she held in her hands. It was a silver swan atop a porcelain base of hand-painted pink water lilies and delicate green lily pads.

The music box had been handcrafted in France, but she noted the package had been mailed from Switzerland. Uncle Blake must have sent it. Whom else did she know in Europe? But how uncharacteristic of him to send a gift for no particular occasion. He hadn't forgotten her thirty-second birthday six months back. She was wearing the gold necklace he'd sent her then. So what had prompted him to send the music box when he was due for a visit in a few weeks? Surely it wasn't an indication he intended to cancel their plans. In her last letter she had been insistent he come and had set the date for his visit. She would be crushed if he didn't come and had told him so.

Turning the carton upside down she shook it. Had she missed the card? Hurriedly, she rambled through the packing again, pulling newspapers apart and laying them aside. Nothing.

It had to be from Blake. If his plans had changed he would have mentioned it—wouldn't he? Regina picked up the music box, turned it in her hands and found the wind-up key underneath the base. She twisted the brass key several turns and set the swan on her dresser to watch the graceful, silver creature spin as it played. The melody was a French tune with the beautiful, haunting quality of a love song.

Combined with the music, the spinning swan had a lovely, hypnotic effect, and she found herself plunging into a pleasant, nostalgic trip somewhere far back in her childhood. The dreamy music sparked a faint memory. The tune had been a favorite of Aunt Sada's, one her aunt had learned in her girlhood in France.

Regina was smiling, humming, musing delightedly when the music stopped abruptly and the music box gave a pathetic little ping. Her smile faded as she lifted the box and tapped the key a few times. The music started again. Regina flopped down in the comfortable blue chintz chair by the window and began to absently twist the gold ring she wore on her right hand.

She let her head loll back dreamily, remembering carefree days growing up with Aunt Sada. She had never known her real parents. Both had died when she was an infant, and her father's brother had undertaken her support—though he'd left most of the child rearing duties to his widowed sister, Sada. Blake and Sada had been the only parents she'd ever known. Good, loving parents, despite Blake's sporadic presence.

She'd been legally adopted by her aunt and had grown up in Atlanta, seeing Blake a few times a year. Each visit he made had been a joy to her and Sada. Hers had been a wonderful, happy childhood, unshadowed by the situation. The single regret she had about her early years was that Sada's health had failed and she hadn't lived to see Regina complete medical school. The death of his elder sister had been a painful blow for Blake, too, and his visits to Atlanta had been less frequent ever since.

But he would be coming soon. A wisp of a smile settled on her lips, then disappeared as a loud ring overrode the music box's soft notes. Regina jumped up and dashed to the bedside table to answer the phone.

"Dr. Lawton," she said, running a hand through the thick wheat-colored hair that turned under smoothly on her shoulders.

"Regina!"

A bright glow lit her eyes. She recognized his voice even though it was accompanied by an interfering buzz on the transatlantic line.

"Uncle Blake!" She could picture him, silver haired and svelte, pacing the floor even as he talked. "What a surprise! I've just opened the gift," she told him. "I love the music box."

"Music box?" His voice rose in question while, frowning, Blake searched his pocket for his address book.

"Yes. The music box," Regina answered quickly, glancing toward her dresser where the little silver swan sat gleaming silently in the sunlight. "I got it this afternoon."

"Was it all right?" he asked, calming his voice as he hurriedly located the name and number he needed.

Regina's lashes fluttered. Did she detect an anxious note in his voice?

"It's perfect and beautiful," she said. "I love it. Thanks a bunch."

"I was afraid it might have been damaged in shipping." His voice sounded strained but quickly evened out as he continued. "It reminded me of you the minute I saw it."

"I'm glad to know my globe-trotting uncle thinks of me once in a while." She brushed the wisps of hair from her forehead, feeling a flash of sentiment start to warm her heart. Whatever had come over Blake gave her a comfortable sensation she liked.

"I think of you often." He paused and cleared his throat. "Though I suppose I haven't let you know. Consider the music box a peace offering for too long an absence."

"Where are you this time?" So he *did* realize how negligent he was about keeping in touch. He hadn't phoned in months and had answered but one of the half-dozen letters she'd sent to his Swiss address. "I thought you'd gone to the moon."

"I did." He laughed. "And now I'm on the way to paradise. Can you get a few weeks off and come along?"

"Me?" She hadn't been on a trip with Blake since she was a teenager. "You want me to go with you?"

"I do. You needn't sound shocked. Aren't I your favorite uncle?"

"My only uncle, and I *am* shocked." And he was the most unpredictable person in the world if she didn't miss her guess. "Aren't you coming here at all?"

"Not if I can talk you into meeting me elsewhere." His voice had returned to normal. He wished he hadn't agreed to do a favor for that impossible French girl, Nellie. Now it was interfering with his plans. Blake sighed and added a deliberate note of merriment to his voice. "Can you get away and go with me?"

"Where?"

"The Caribbean."

"Why?"

"Why?" he asked indignantly. "Because I want to treat my favorite niece to a real vacation."

"Your only niece." She laughed. "Are you serious?"

"I am. Indulge me. We'll go to Antigua. Can you?"

"Yes!" she almost shouted into the line. Not only was he unpredictable, he was psychic. She'd actually been thinking recently about sand and sea and balmy blue skies. "I've taken the time off for your visit, so it's no problem. Give me the details."

"Splendid," he pronounced as he hurriedly thumbed the pocket schedule he'd picked up in the hotel lobby. "I've checked the schedules. There's a Worldways flight from Atlanta that will get you to Antigua by 11:00 p.m. I'll meet you at the airport on the eighteenth."

"That's good," she responded. "I'll make the reservation tonight."

"Regina, what about you?" Blake asked. "You're being careful, aren't you? Locking up and looking out for yourself? I wouldn't want anything to happen to my favorite niece."

Regina gave a quick laugh. "Is this fatherly advice from an international playboy?"

Blake's voice softened. "All right, all right. I know. You're a big girl, a doctor. Though heaven knows why a beautiful woman would want to be a doctor," he rambled on, saying all the things he always said about her work. The conversation had become almost a ritual to be played out each time they talked. She heard him exhale a deep breath, then continue. "How are things at the clinic?"

"Everyone is fine at Fleetwood. Dr. Granger asks about you often."

Blake's gift to her when she'd passed the medical board exams and completed her residency was a partnership in the Fleetwood Orthopedic Clinic. She practiced there as a surgeon with three other doctors she both respected and admired. She considered the clinic an ideal setup for both patients and medical staff. Fleetwood was known for the quality of its medical personnel and care. The partnership had led to a very successful practice.

"I'm glad to hear it. Give him my regards," Blake said. "And Regina, be careful making the trip."

Regina shook her head, making a wave of sunlight dance across her blond hair. Eyes the cool soft color of the ocean, filled with laughter. Would Blake ever stop thinking of her as a child? She wrapped the telephone cord around her fingers and turned toward the window. Her face had an arresting classical beauty that could be forbidding, but the frequency of smiles like the one she had for her uncle made that look rare.

With amusement in her voice she answered, "I'll be fine. Just promise you'll show up. I wouldn't want to arrive in Antigua and learn you've decided to climb Mount Kilimanjaro instead."

"I'll be there. I promise." He laughed. "I've got a surprise for you."

"That's all I ever expect from you, Uncle Blake." She smiled. The Caribbean would be wonderful. Tranquility, peace. No cares, no worries. Yes, it would be much better than the two of them staying in Atlanta where she would be tempted to drop by the clinic.

She could hear Blake chuckling, but when he spoke again his voice had fallen to a low, throaty sound. "Oh, and Regina," he said softly, "bring the silver swan along. I've a friend on the island who's a jeweler. I want him to engrave an inscription on the music box."

"I will," she answered. Her smile widened. She wished they were face-to-face. It would be nice to see in his eyes the thread of tenderness she could hear in his voice. Blake wasn't much given to expressing affection, yet she'd always sensed the repressed warmth and love he held in check. A lump formed in her throat. She sat on the bed and fell back to the pillows, her voice going soft and gentle. "See you soon."

"Right. Bye, Queenie." A click sounded at the other end of the line.

Queenie? He hadn't used that pet name for her since she was twelve and had insisted she was too grown-up for it. Now it sounded good again. A tear surprised her by trickling down her cheek. She wiped it away and sat up wondering where Blake was. He hadn't bothered to say. Probably some elegant hotel in Paris or the house of one of his jet-set pals. What a life he led, bouncing about from one country to the other. And how different it was from her carefully scheduled one. She was glad they were going to have a chance to be together and get closer.

Her smile deepened. Had the music box reminded him, too, of Sada and taken him on a similar nostalgic trip? Was he becoming sentimental so late in life? Perhaps that was what the silver swan was all about. Could it be Blake was finally wanting to put down roots and tighten family ties as Sada had always said he would one day? She hoped so. She'd missed that kind of closeness since her aunt died.

Regina wound the music box once more and then replaced it on her dresser. It looked right at home with her collection of curios: a porcelain bell, a jade cat, a tiny ivory elephant. She leaned back and closed her eyes to listen to the sad-sweet melody. This time the tune played on without disruption.

A few minutes later the music stopped. Regina opened her eyes, and a page of the newspaper packing on the floor caught her eye. She scooped it up and glanced at a photo above an article about the opening of a new night spot in Paris. Her French was marginal but she could make out the caption. Nellie Thanet Brings Success to Opening of the Blue Butterfly.

The photograph featured the singer and a man who at first glance reminded Regina of her uncle. But it wasn't Blake. The man pictured was dark-haired and had a mustache. She laughed lightly. Nevertheless, a hot Paris night spot was precisely where she might expect to find Blake Andrews.

The hot, golden tropical sun shone through the open windows of the plantation house. Life on Dominica, an island in the West Indies virtually unknown to tourists, was generally quiet and calm. Inhabitants and the few visitors who came retreated from the world on the primitive garden island filled with rain forests, plants and animals unlike those that exist anywhere else.

If Dominica could be considered paradise, then a shadow had darkened it today. Pierce Buchannan saw both tension and worry in the face of his septuagenarian aunt, Monica Caravelle Whitechurch, as she dropped the black telephone receiver into its cradle and slowly lifted a nettling stare to him.

"Blake Andrews is my friend and I've invited him here for a visit," she said.

Pierce winced slightly. Aunt Monica's high-pitched British voice had an aristocratic quality that could make a man think he should bow. He had never known a more peculiar or difficult woman, and he'd rarely seen her flustered. But at the moment, head thrown back, eyes wide, she had the appearance of a nervous, gawking bird with ruffled feathers.

"Why does that make you look worried?"

"I'm not worried," she snapped.

"I think you are, and I want you to know I don't trust the man, Aunt Monica." Pierce eyed the fluffy old dowager dressed in mauve chiffon. The brief worried look was gone.

Straightening sternly to her full five feet, she tapped the tip of her carved mahogany cane on the floor.

"It is sufficient that *I* trust him, nephew." The gold handle of the cane poked him lightly in the chest. "And I do not require a keeper."

"I didn't mean to imply otherwise."

Pierce smiled as he pushed the cane away. Aunt Monica was still a hellion when someone dared to dispute her. He remembered that cane catching his backside a few times in his boyhood, and the fact that he stood more than a foot taller than his petite aunt didn't awe her now in the least. Not that he would want it to. He was fond of Monica. Actually he hoped that at her age he would be just as plucky and maybe only a little less stubborn.

"See that you remember it," she retorted.

Grudgingly admitting an appreciation for her aloofness and independence, Pierce ran his fingers through his thick chestnut hair and dropped into the chair behind the oversize desk in his aunt's office. When his uncle had died the plantation had been almost in ruin. Monica had single-handedly made it prosperous again. She wasn't a woman to be easily daunted, but it had been obvious for the past few weeks that something was bothering her.

Part of the trouble was that neither of them liked taking advice. Maybe they were too much alike. She'd always been a gambler where business was concerned, and he'd warned her about pushing her luck. She'd retaliated by telling him he liked sailing too near the wind himself since the breakup of his marriage. He admitted that experience had changed him and not completely for the better. He sighed dismissively. Thinking about that chapter of life wouldn't help the immediate problem.

"I've been looking over the books for the plantation," he said. "Those notations of payments made to Blake Andrews don't indicate what he was being paid for."

Pierce eyed his aunt shrewdly to gauge her reaction. His concern about the notations and Blake Andrews went far deeper than he was willing to let on. Already he had friends in France making inquiries about the man, and they were turning up more questions than answers. Pierce didn't like it. His aunt was old and wealthy—just the sort of woman some men considered an easy mark.

In one of Monica's notebooks he'd found another name listed with Andrews's—an R. Lawton. Was Monica making secret payments to this R. Lawton, too? Pierce gritted his teeth. Of one thing he was fairly certain, Andrews had a hold on his aunt that went beyond the realm of legitimate business, and he meant to find out what it was.

Eyeing her nephew, Monica Whitechurch drew her lips into a tight little bow and puffed out her cheeks indignantly. "Has it occurred to you, my boy, to get my approval before you go snooping through my business records?"

"Aunt Monica," Pierce said gently, rising and wrapping an arm around his aunt's thin shoulders and turning her toward the double paneled doors of the office, "I wasn't snooping. You gave me the books so I could familiarize myself with the business operations of the plantation."

A flush of pink stained her pale cheeks. She'd lived most of her life in the tropics and somehow managed to maintain a flawless English complexion.

"Well, so I did," she said indignantly. "But that one ledger was personal. I gave it to you by mistake, and now you're drawing conclusions that are unfounded." She stopped short and wagged a finger at him, her voice quaking with that air of authority that had wilted many a servant at Whitechurch Plantation. "Blake Andrews will attend the house party as he has in the past, and he'll be bringing a young woman with him. A Regina Lawton."

Pierce turned aside for a moment to hide the look of surprise on his face. So R. Lawton was a woman. One small mystery was solved.

"As you wish, Aunt Monica." Pierce nodded, facing her again. He could see that he was making her angry. Perhaps he'd said enough about Blake Andrews for a while. What he really needed to know now was how to decipher her bookkeeping system. Then he might be able to understand just what was going on. Taking one of her frail hands in his, he looked at her fondly. "Would you like to explain those figures to me? If I'm to take over the plantation someday, I need to know how you've shown a profit all these years." Pierce laughed and bent down to give her an affectionate kiss on the cheek. "I'm beginning to think you've been doing something illegal."

"Illegal!" Monica drew back as if injured. "I've got a good business head, that's all," she said shrilly, poking his chest with the cane again. "Something illegal, indeed. What dreadful thoughts, my boy!"

"Only teasing." He hugged her shoulders. "You've done a remarkable job running this plantation. No man could have done better. But it's time you eased up a little. Enjoyed life more. Let me take some of the responsibility here."

"Don't be in such a hurry," she teased. "I'm not dead yet."

"All right, all right." He backed off. She didn't need to know what he had in mind. Not if he meant to pull it off. "But someday before you are, you're going to have to explain these books to me."

"There's plenty of time for that, my boy. Plenty of time." She started out the door of the large office at the rear of the house. "Right now I have to see Thomas about the rose garden." She was mumbling as she picked her way through the thick tropical growth of giant ferns and tall poinsettias to reach the open area of the garden. "The man has gotten the soil so wet, the roses will rot before they bloom."

Pierce Buchannan watched his aunt stop and hover over a rosebush like a large, lavender butterfly. She stirred the mulch around the base of the bush with her cane, then thumped the path hard with the mahogany stick and strode off in search of the gardener.

He'd always thought his aunt the most capable woman he knew. But she didn't know when to quit. She was getting old. And vulnerable. And maybe swindled. Who could tell? The books for Whitechurch Plantation were like one of those elaborate mazes in an English garden. You could get lost in a thousand directions before you found the way out.

He wasn't fooled. She was upset by the call from Blake Andrews. The man bore checking out. The woman, too. There wasn't much to go on, but he meant to get to the bottom of it. He'd only met Blake once, and on the surface he seemed a nice sort, even a little more interesting than most of Aunt Monica's friends.

But Pierce had dealt with all kinds of men and he could be as ruthless as any of them. He'd learned to look for traits the ordinary person wouldn't notice, like the way the veins in the neck stood out when a man told a lie. Blake Andrews wasn't the nonchalant and harmless fellow he pretended to be. He was tied into some shady business involving the plantation. One thing Blake would learn fast was that nobody moved in on Pierce Buchannan's territory.

He closed the leather-bound ledger on Monica's desk and strode across the room. He'd need to make a trip to the States right away. By the time of the house party everything would be settled. Pierce stopped and crossed his arms over his chest as he stared out the open window at the green stretch of banana trees that filled the distance.

"Regina Lawton," he said aloud. "I'll start with you."

Chapter 2

A peculiar sound disturbed Regina's sleep, a bump, a rustle that shouldn't have been there. What was it? The cat?

She tensed and gripped the eyelet ruffle that edged her sheets. She'd awakened somewhat disoriented and with a vague sense of foreboding that something was wrong, and her pulse leaped from the slow, steady rate of deep sleep to an erratic pace. Taking a shallow breath, she eased her eyelids up, not wanting to see what she feared and sensed behind their security.

Was it Marley? Regina had always thought the white-furred creature moved like a wily thief in the night. He had the remarkable ability to glide silently across her bedroom, ease beneath the sheets and snuggle against her side without disturbing her sleep. So it didn't make sense that the padded thud of footsteps she heard had awakened her.

A moment later her reluctant lids were fully open, but her vision was still blurred by sleep. Around her she saw only the cloaking blackness of a starless night. Just briefly she felt the panicky terror of a child in the grip of a bad dream. Her breath caught roughly in her throat while her eyes frantically searched the layers of darkness.

"Marley," she whispered.

Outside a tattered, dark cloud floated away from the moon like a ship set adrift at sea. As she raised her head slightly, she could make out the familiar shapes of furniture and objects in her bedroom. She heard another sound, just a light thump.

"Marley?" she whispered again as wispy moonlight filtered in a faint glow through the partially opened blinds. The pale show of light was just enough to define the ogreish shadow of what appeared to be the hulking black shape of a man beside her dresser.

Regina dropped her head silently to the pillow, feeling a lump begin to swell in her throat. Dear God! What was it? Why couldn't she ever wake up with a clear head? Her teeth bit nervously into her lower lip and she tried to focus her eyes on the shadow. It loomed there so black and so much a part of the night, Regina wasn't terribly sure what she saw. In her drowsy state, she wondered if the man was real or a subtle trick of moonlight and darkness.

Dark rooms and half dreams didn't mix well in the wee hours of the night. But even as she tried to think that man-like shadow away, fear made her heartbeat an unsteady clatter and her breathing shallow and uncomfortable. Was he real? A small voice far back in her mind was telling her to scream, but she could only swallow at the tightening in her throat and wish she hadn't opened her eyes in the first place. Quick as the closing of a camera lens, she snapped them shut. The image remained, the burning black outline of a man framed in silver moonlight.

It could have been only a few frozen seconds before she found the courage to look again. When she did another cloud had blocked out the moonlight and the shadow was gone. Moving slowly, she reached for the bedside lamp and turned it on. It was a quarter after two. Regina collapsed to the pillow for a few seconds, listening for an unfamiliar noise, hoping she wouldn't hear one. Outside the distant, dull hum of an air-conditioning unit coming to life drowned out all sounds. Inside there was only the rapid, fitful pounding of her heart.

Sighing, she rubbed her eyes. Soon her heartbeat slowed to normal. The ripples of alarm in her chest died away and the cottony feel left her mouth. It was another still and warm Atlanta night, and there wasn't even enough breeze to rustle whispers from the leaves of the dogwood tree outside her window. And to her relief, there were no dreaded footsteps in the house.

She sighed again, more heavily. Was she having a case of nerves about being alone at night? Certainly she'd never imagined a man in her room before.

She really *did* need a vacation if just the contemplation of a sudden change of plans was this unsettling. Regina yawned and brushed a few strands of hair from her eyes. Had she really gotten that regimented? She rubbed her tired eyes and rolled to her side, trying to settle back to sleep. Tomorrow would be a busy day and a sleepless night wouldn't help her get through it. She reached out to press a button on the alarm clock on her bedside table. The alarm was set for six. Then she reached for the lamp. Her hand was on the switch, her eyelids already growing heavy, when she heard a wild and terrified wailing from downstairs.

"Marley!" she cried out throwing off the covers and jumping to her feet.

She'd reached the bedroom door when she heard a crash and the sound of a heavy object hitting the floor.

"Damn!" The voice was male and mad and followed by a jumble of sounds that rang in her ears like Chinese gongs.

Regina flew down the stairs, her satin nightgown tangling around willowy legs, her long blond hair bouncing wildly on her shoulders. She might have been paralyzed with fear for herself, but if someone was trying to kill Marley she meant to stop it. Her fingers missed the light switch as she rushed into the den. Marley's terrified sounds split the air. In the faint glow of moonlight from the window she could see a man crouched over him on the floor.

She could picture an angry scowl beneath the tight, ski mask that covered the intruder's face and hair. His head snapped around in her direction, and as suddenly the outline of his face seemed to disappear into the blackness of the mask. His clothing was dark and tight fitting, allowing him to blend in with the shadows.

Her only thought as she advanced on him was that he was hurting Marley.

"Damn!" the man swore and started to rise, shoving the hissing cat aside with a gloved hand. In his haste he dropped the penlight he'd been shining in Marley's anguished eyes. Regina made a dive for the man's back, an action as futile as foolish. He was enormous even in a crouched position and she regretted her impulsive attack before she hit him. The man anticipated her move and sprang to his feet before she reached him, but his escape was hampered by the closeness of the furniture in her small den.

He lunged toward the sliding glass doors at the back of the room. Regina slammed into his back and threw her arms up to catch his neck. He jerked roughly away, but she'd wrapped her arms around him like clamps.

He made a growling sound, his voice muffled by the mask. Before she had a chance to reconsider her rashness and retreat, he spun around and she found herself the one captured. He held her easily, the gloved hands tightly pinning her arms to her sides.

"Turn me loose!" she demanded, the choking sound of hysteria in her voice.

A surge of sheer fright swept through her with the shock of realization that she was completely helpless against this man. Why had she tried anything so stupid as tackling a burglar? He would have been out the door and gone by now. She knew the man could crush her, and the thought nearly made her numb.

At last she felt strength returning to her body. She tried lurching, throwing her full weight against him in an attempt to break free of his arms. Every try was useless. Surprisingly though, she realized even in the midst of her panic, that his grip was tempered simply to keep her under control and to avoid her kicks.

"Little demon," the man whispered, then broke into a low, rumbling laugh that she could feel vibrating in his chest.

His arrogance built up her anger to match her fear.

"Don't you hurt me!" she shouted, struggling to kick her way free.

"Hurt you?" He laughed again and thrust her out to arm's length to avoid her wild, flying feet. "I'll be lucky to get away alive."

Regina sensed something puzzling in his muffled laughter. This man was too sure of himself. He'd been discovered in a burglary but instead of showing panic or desperate rage, he seemed to find the situation humorous.

A moment later, he relaxed his grip slightly and started to push her away so that he could bolt through the sliding glass doors. Regina took the opportunity to connect one solidly placed kick. She couldn't tell where her foot hit him, but at the impact the man stumbled heavily back, colliding with the antique sea chest she used as a coffee table. She saw his leg buckle in what must have been a painful twist as a tall

crystal lamp hit the floor with a crash and shattered into a
thousand fragments.

Swearing, he caught himself but jerked suddenly and let
out a yelp as Marley clawed his leg and hissed.

"Damn cat," he muttered as he kicked at Marley and
gave Regina a shove that landed her in a heap on the sofa.
Like a lightning flash he was gone before she could get to her
feet.

She scrambled up, throwing the hair back from her eyes,
and flicked the lights on. Marley, fur ruffled and eyes wild,
jumped to a chair and sat licking a sore paw. Regina sank
down weakly beside the disgruntled cat and ran a soothing
hand over his bristly head. Marley arched his back appreciatively and, though still looking less than happy, started a
soft purr.

Regina let out her breath in a gush and reached for the
phone. She hoped she could settle down as quickly as Marley had.

The police arrived within a matter of minutes, and though
their presence made her feel safe, the investigation was almost as much an ordeal as her confrontation with the burglar. Lieutenant Langley, tall, trim and dressed impeccably
in a gray suit, started off by berating her for coming downstairs with a burglar in the house.

Langley rubbed a finger over his lips, then shook his head
disgustedly. "You say nothing is missing?"

"Nothing at all."

He brushed an offending speck off the lapel of his coat.
"Well then, Dr. Lawton, looks like you surprised him before he had a chance to locate your valuables."

The lieutenant noted a pulled-out drawer at her desk and
the spilled contents of her purse, the paintings and prints
thrown from the wall. The expression in his mild, gray eyes
and lined face again showed his opinion of her foolhardi-
ness.

Regina stiffened her back as he returned his attention to her.

"If he hadn't hurt Marley I'd have thought I imagined someone being in the house."

"Marley?"

"My cat."

The officer cocked his brow, setting his face into an I've-heard-everything-now look. One side of his mouth twitched as he scratched out something on his notepad.

"You say he was in your bedroom?"

"Yes. I think he was. At least I saw something and it must have been him." Regina had put on a terry robe and combed her hair. She was amazed at how calm she was, but she'd realized when it was all over that if the man had meant to harm her he could easily have done so.

Lieutenant Langley slipped the ballpoint pen into his shirt pocket, then eased up a hand to scratch the back of his neck.

"Must have thought you weren't home. No car outside."

"I'm having some work done on it."

"The grass needs mowing."

Her brows shot up. "I've been busy. I've been doing extra hours at the clinic while Dr. Wills is on vacation."

"Uh-huh." He frowned. "These guys usually can read the signs. Happens all the time. People go out of town, no car in the drive, newspapers pile up. They can tell." Langley tugged at the knot in his tie.

"Well, this one made a mistake," Regina said indignantly, her eyes firing up. She got to her feet and with one hand pulled the lapels of her robe together as if she were trying to seal them shut. Absently, she massaged her shoulder with the other hand. Her body still seemed to burn where the man's arms had held her, not from any pain but from the sensation of the forced physical contact.

"You ought to put in an alarm system and have better locks on that sliding door," Langley said flatly. "The man could have hurt you."

Regina frowned. Noting the lieutenant's eyes on her she dropped both hands and slipped them into the roomy pockets of her oversize robe. One more lecture on her stupidity would be more than she could stand. She'd refused a trip to the hospital, reminding the lieutenant that she was a doctor and nothing was bruised or broken—though a great deal of damage had been done to her pride.

"I think he just wanted to get away as quickly as possible." She tilted her head and met the lieutenant's steely gaze. "Once he realized someone was here."

One other thought she kept to herself, a thought she found vaguely disturbing. The man had been terribly sure of himself. She felt certain he wasn't an ordinary burglar— he'd been looking for something in particular. But what?

Lieutenant Langley raised both bushy brows and looked at her with obvious appreciation. "Yeah, he made a mistake. And you got lucky," he said bluntly.

She would've taken exception to that comment if she'd had the energy, but by now she was too tired to care. She'd given her statement, had her house searched and been told a dozen times they would probably never find the man and she should never have come downstairs. All of which was undoubtedly true, but surely the lieutenant could understand people acted instinctively in emergencies unless they were conditioned for a particular response. Give her a fractured arm or a sprained ankle to deal with and she knew precisely what to do, but burglaries weren't covered in her reservoir of knowledge.

It was half an hour later when the police left. Lieutenant Langley had insisted on keeping an officer in the neighborhood when she refused to spend what remained of the night with friends. Once the police were gone and she'd locked up, she felt a surprising sense of relief at being alone again. What had the man been after? she wondered staring at the rubble of the lamp on the hardwood floor.

She would probably never know. But he'd certainly ruined a good night's sleep and a very expensive lamp.

Thank goodness she wasn't scheduled for surgery in the morning. Later she would clear away the broken lamp, the only real casualty from the break-in. And she would be sure to give Marley some extra cream for breakfast. All she could think of now was getting to sleep.

Sitting on the edge of her bed, she reset the alarm to give herself another few minutes of rest. Minutes later she fell asleep, thinking what a shame it was that crime was spreading into the suburbs. Burglary was so commonplace now there probably wouldn't even be a mention of the break-in on the morning news.

As it turned out she wouldn't have known. She slept through the alarm and the early broadcast and had to rush to get to the clinic on time.

"Dr. Lawton." Nurse Marcia Wilson's friendly, round face peered around the edge of the door of Regina's office at the Fleetwood Clinic.

"Was that the last patient, Marcia?" Regina looked up from her desk and the medical file on which she was making notations. She smoothed the hair back from her temples. "I'm bushed."

"Sorry, Doc, there's one more, a new patient and he asked to see you." Marcia's eyes widened sheepishly. "I know you didn't get much sleep last night and I tried to steer him in to Dr. Gaines, but he was insistent that he see Dr. Lawton."

"Oh?"

"After twenty questions, that is. Guess he wanted to be sure you were the right Dr. Lawton. Said a Dr. Adams in

Arizona had recommended you and told him you were the best. Anyway he waited until you were through and . . ."

Adams. She'd worked briefly with a Joseph Adams from Arizona during her residency. She seemed to recall he'd planned on returning to Arizona to practice, but they hadn't kept in touch over the years. She was a bit surprised he would have remembered she lived in Atlanta. A quick glance reminded her Marcia was still waiting for confirmation she'd done the right thing.

"That's fine, Marcia," she said. "I'm sure I can bear up under one more examination." She managed a smile. "You have the chart?"

"Right here. Look, I'm sorry," she added. "The other nurses are helping with a cast. I've got to assist Dr. Granger for a few minutes, and then I'll be in with you." Marcia passed the folder into Regina's hands, then winked. "Anyway this one should be a pleasure. He'll be in 3."

Regina lifted her brows quizzically but Marcia had turned and started back to the reception area. Chuckling, she opened the folder to check the information requested of all new patients.

Marcia's remarks tended to stray from professionalism at times, but they did have a way of livening up the day. And it wasn't as if she wasn't used to them. The two of them had been friends long before she'd gone to medical school and Marcia to nursing school.

"Hmm," Regina mumbled reading over the data on the form as she walked toward examining room 3. Pierce L. Buchannan, age thirty-eight, height six feet four inches, weight 220 pounds, hair brown, eyes brown, blood pressure normal, temperature normal, no operations, no diseases. Reason for visit—leg injury.

Still looking down as she entered the examining room, Regina raised her head slowly, her eyes following the length of a pair of rather long, muscular legs encased in khaki trousers.

"Didn't the nurse tell you you'll have to undress for the examination?" Her gaze traveled over a trim waist and upward over a broad expanse of chest snugly fitted into a black polo shirt. The 220 pounds were nicely arranged on the six-four frame. She caught a glimpse of tanned arms sprinkled with crisp, coppery hair.

"She did, but..." He grinned at having caught her staring. There was a softness in her voice and her manner that he hadn't expected. He could see faint lines of fatigue in her face but none of it had seeped into her eyes. They were blue-green crystals and filled with what he couldn't deny was concern. He'd been prepared for a haughty face and a shrewish manner. This woman had the face of Aphrodite and hair with all the gold of ripened wheat.

Regina's eyes reached his face, and she concluded instantly that one learned very little by reading cold statistics. Still it was exactly what she would expect. It was a strong face, with smooth, bronzed skin and dark, compelling eyes. Only she wouldn't call them brown. They were a dark, rich umber. His hair wasn't truly brown, either, with its warm, auburn highlights. Cropped short and swept back from his forehead, it gleamed just a shade darker than his mustache. His nose had straight sculpted lines and his mouth formed a sort of crooked, tolerant smile that she was certain could just as easily take on a cruel twist.

She felt her flesh tingling in some uncommon blend of nervousness and reservation. There was something about the man that disturbed her. Certainly not his voice. It was smooth and mellow, a sort of sandpaper-and-silk voice that just suited him.

Oddly, she didn't feel the usual detached objectivity of a doctor observing a patient. She ran through his chart once more, trying to pinpoint exactly what she felt. Finding nothing to account for her uneasiness, she quickly attributed her unmedical thoughts to a case of jitters stemming from last night's experience. Mr. Buchannan was approximately the same size and body build as the burglar. That was enough to get anyone flustered.

Abruptly, she glanced up at him. Diagnosing patients often involved reading faces and eyes as well as test results. Her impression that Mr. Buchannan was harboring something just beyond the half grin and the smiling eyes annoyed her. And she didn't often get annoyed at patients. They had enough problems when they came to her and her job was to get them better. Sometimes she felt as if she needed a trench coat instead of a lab coat to find out just what was bothering a patient. Flipping the file folder shut, she gave Pierce Buchannan her best bedside-manner smile.

"I'll step out for a moment while you change." She breathed in slowly and deeply.

"Don't bother." He shook his head and chuckled. "I've been here exactly ten seconds longer than you, but I'll have them off in a flash." Regina's eyes followed his hands as he brought them to his belt and started to unfasten it. She looked up in surprise. He stepped out of his shoes as he talked, and was out of his trousers before she could leave the examining room.

He whisked the polo shirt over his head, and clad in an immodest pair of black briefs, took a seat on the examining table.

"Ready, Doctor?" he asked.

Modesty wasn't one of his failings. Arrogance apparently was. He was attractive. She acknowledged that. A fine specimen if she wanted to get back to objectivity. But it wasn't his appearance that disturbed her, it was the challenge she sensed as strongly as if it had been spoken. Perhaps there was a case to be made for bad chemistry between two people. A moment later she was chastising herself for letting frayed nerves alter her judgment. She didn't really know anything about the man at all. His dreams, his beliefs, his thoughts weren't covered on the medical chart, and she didn't have any right to draw hasty conclusions.

She sought a way to improve on an awkward beginning. "The Dr. Adams who recommended me, was that Joseph Adams?"

"Yes. Joe Adams," he said, meeting her eyes. "Actually, it wasn't exactly a referral. We were playing golf. He knew I was making a trip here and just happened to mention knowing a Dr. Lawton in Atlanta, and he said you were good. I never expected I'd need to see a doctor, but—well—when I did . . ."

"You thought of me," she supplied.

"I was glad I knew about you." She seemed to warm up a little after that comment. He wondered what she would think if she knew that he'd pumped an acquaintance for information about her. The result had hardly been worth a flight to Tucson. Dr. Lawton had apparently been a rather private person during her residency, and Adams hadn't been able to relate more than that she was an excellent doctor and in his words, "a real looker."

Regina put down the chart and began the examination. "Have you always lived in Atlanta?" he questioned as she made a visual comparison of the injured leg and the other one.

"Yes," she responded. "You seem to be moving relatively well, Mr. Buchannan. What's the problem with your leg?"

He smiled. "I've got some stiffness here." He indicated his left knee. "And a bad bruise." He paused as she bent over him. That hair shone like liquid gold and it wasn't what he needed to have his mind on. "Been with the clinic long?" he asked.

"Since it opened," she answered matter-of-factly as she pressed her fingers along each side of his kneecap and noted some minor swelling.

"And how long has that been?"

"Seven years, Mr. Buchannan." She ran her hand lightly over a deep purple bruise on the back of his leg just below the knee. It was ugly and obviously very sore. "How long have you had this?" There was a knot beneath the skin. She continued running her fingers over the length of his leg, trailing through the crisp, coppery hair like that on his arms. The muscles were hard as steel cables. It would have taken quite a blow to cause a bruise like that.

"Since yesterday. I've been using ice on it but it's still sore."

"Bend your knee." She stepped back and watched carefully as he complied. "Now straighten it out." He did, and she caught his leg just above the ankle with one hand and supported his heel with the other. "What happened?"

"I...ahh." He winced as she rotated his ankle. "Fell over some weights at the hotel gym. Didn't think any damage had been done until that bruise showed up."

"You've got a cut here, too." Regina leaned over to examine the small red slash on his skin. Releasing his leg, she dipped a swab in Betadine and painted the burnt-orange medicine on the wound. That done, she opened a cabinet drawer and took out a small rubber hammer. "I'm going to test your reflexes now." Gently she tapped his knee and then his ankle, getting a normal response. "Fine," she said, putting away the hammer and using her fingers to probe at his knee once again.

"I don't think it's serious," he volunteered as his eyes locked in on hers. "I just came in as a precaution. I'm in Atlanta on business, and since I'll be going out of the country in a few days I didn't want to take a chance on the injury getting worse once I'm away."

"That was wise," she said as she straightened up, unable to help noticing that he smelled good, of some expensive scent that was oddly familiar. Was it the same cologne used by her senior partner, the ancient Dr. Granger? Perhaps that was it. Well, it suited Mr. Buchannan much better.

Regina's brows knit together and she drummed a finger on the tabletop before she scrawled out some instructions and a prescription. That done she looked up at him.

The smile faded from Pierce Buchannan's face. It had held a look of wry amusement since she'd entered the examining room, but now his eyes were sparked with worry.

"Not serious is it, Doctor?"

"Hmm." Regina exhaled a long slow breath and ran her gaze over his well-shaped legs. "Not good. However, the bruise looks worse than it is. Your knee is sprained. Do you run?"

"Every day."

"Well, don't for a few weeks." She tore off the top page on the pad and handed it to him. "Stay off your feet as much as you can. I've prescribed something for whatever pain persists, and follow this program of treatment for a week."

She pressed her fingers into the side of his kneecap. "When the swelling goes down here you can start running again."

"Here?" he asked, touching the spot on his knee and inadvertently brushing his large, warm hand against hers.

"Yes," she answered, flinching as she quickly pulled her hand away. What was the matter with her? He hadn't done anything wayward, and yet she felt very definitely a little wave of heat in the room.

He stepped from the table and was on his feet, his thumbs unconsciously making an adjustment to the elastic band of his briefs.

"Do I need to come back?"

Her brows lifted suddenly. "I don't think that'll be necessary. Just remember, when you start running again, build your distance up slowly. The leg shouldn't give you any more trouble." She looked him directly in the eye and added, "Tell Joe hello for me." Then she turned to leave, grabbing his chart on the way out.

"Dr. Lawton."

Instantly, she spun around, her eyes meeting the dark, unreadable depths of his. Why did his voice stir a shadow of warning deep in her mind? Why did Pierce Buchannan make her think of danger? It made no sense. He was a stranger, a patient, and because he was in town for only a few days, a man she wasn't likely to ever see again.

"Yes?" she answered after a moment of hesitation and with an evident note of uncertainty in her voice.

Pierce smiled. She was clever, a woman who would make a good poker player. She'd called his hand there for a moment, making him think there might be serious damage to the ligaments. She knew the injury didn't really warrant seeing a doctor, and she knew that he knew it, and he wondered just how suspicious she was of him.

Perhaps he could make her think his interest was in her as a woman. It wouldn't be difficult to develop that interest if the circumstances were different. Not at all. He suspected there was a raging fire inside the cool Dr. Lawton and would enjoy finding out.

He smiled and gave her a look no woman could mistake for anything other than admiration. If there was one thing Pierce Buchannan knew, it was how to charm a woman.

The smile formed a dimple in one cheek and set a boyish twinkle in his eyes. At the least he would leave her confused about the reason for his visit. He spoke, only one word, but his voice carried the smooth-rough allure of rich, raw silk.

"Thanks."

Chapter 3

Pierce Buchannan sat in the plush seat of his rented Mercedes, grateful he'd parked in the shade. Did people think the tropics were hot? He could use one of the balmy ocean breezes from Dominica right now. Even Miami, where he based his resort development business, had cool ocean breezes to temper the heat. Here there was no relief other than keeping a cool head, and he was certainly having trouble with that. Leaving the door ajar, he got to his feet and stood beside the silver vehicle.

Damn it! He was going to have to reevaluate the whole situation. Where did the woman fit in with Blake Andrews? She didn't look like the type who would try to swindle an old woman out of her fortune. Or was he forgetting that looks could be deceiving? April, his ex-wife, should have made that fact an indelible memory. Some women never had enough money or enough power. April had turned what should have been a terrific marriage into a stepping stone to something better, for her. She had her count, her title—for what that was worth in today's world—and enough jewels to fill a swimming pool.

Hell! Why was he thinking of April? He'd quit being bitter about that disaster years ago. He suspected that today he was worth a lot more money than April's landed German, a man twice her age. Maybe he ought to thank her for fueling his success. She'd left him wounded and burning, but he'd used the fire to build a financial empire. He admitted to being ruthless when necessary. That had gotten him to the top. But money didn't take care of everything.

There'd been a few other women in his life since the divorce, but nothing serious. He'd soon discovered that the bedroom was a good place to learn what a woman was really like, what she wanted. He wondered what Regina Lawton was after?

She was a doctor, and that ruled out a list of possibilities. She worked hard, too, if today was any indication of what her life was like. She'd made hospital rounds at mid-morning and seen a steady stream of patients all afternoon, including himself. It was just possible that if Blake Andrews was a confidence man, as he thought him to be, Regina Lawton might just be another victim. A doctor might have dark secrets to hide. The other possibility was that she was his accomplice—or his mistress.

In any event he intended to find out. He still had good contacts from the years he'd spent in Naval Intelligence. Calling in some favors due ought to help him find out what he wanted to know about her and Andrews. Pierce wiped his sweaty brow and swore. If Regina Lawton was involved that would be her misfortune. He wasn't about to start developing a soft spot for a woman, no matter how beautiful or accomplished she might be.

His knee was getting stiff from standing around. He stretched and flexed it, wincing as a dull pain hit him, then turned to watch the private entrance to the clinic. She would be leaving at six-thirty. The nurse had told him the doctor's schedule without being aware of it. She'd also let it slip that Dr. Lawton was leaving for Antigua on the eighteenth. Pierce Buchannan would stake his career on the hunch that Blake Andrews would be there to meet her.

A cynical smile flickered on his lips. It hadn't been simple talking the receptionist into scheduling an appointment for him, but he'd managed. Actually he'd had easier times securing business agreements with foreign governments, an accomplishment that had earned him a sterling reputation as a negotiator. Gifts and entertainment for the right dignitaries didn't hurt, either. His company specialized in the procurement of land and the development of resort areas for private investors.

Getting inside the heads of the guys across the negotiating table was his specialty. You had to know everything about an opponent and what he was after before you could deal with him and come to an agreement satisfactory to all concerned. Getting that information required a thorough investigation, and he had the expertise to do just that. Blake Andrews, however, was proving to be one of his biggest challenges. The man seemed to appear on the social scene for a while and then just evaporate for a period of months. And there was Aunt Monica's intimidated reaction to even a mention of the man's name.

Pierce shrugged his shoulders. He was more and more convinced Blake Andrews had an illegal hold on his aunt. But if Blake thought he was going to have Whitechurch or milk it dry, he was wrong. The plantation had been in Pierce's family for years and it would stay there. He was banking on what he would learn from Regina Lawton's tie-in with Blake to guarantee that. She might be his best lead yet and was certainly the most interesting to check out. Now that they'd met, he intended to establish a relationship that would help him learn what he needed to know.

Relationship? Now that was a matter he would have to be wary of. She was an attractive woman and one worth admiring. It was a long time since he had felt more than physical appreciation for a woman. Such feelings could cloud his judgment and he couldn't afford that. She was simply a link to Andrews and the puzzle he wanted to solve. She wouldn't be more.

A slight, hot breeze stirred the oak leaves above him. With his elbows propped against the roof of the Mercedes and one foot resting in the open door of the car, he smiled again. She was coming out. It was time to put his plan in action.

He felt the welcome blast of cold from the car's air conditioner as he steered the vehicle around a row of parked cars. Her car was the blue Ferrari that had been delivered an hour ago by a mechanic from Hogan's foreign car service center. Either Dr. Lawton had an especially prosperous medical practice or she had some other means of augmenting her income.

When the man from the garage left the keys with Nurse Wilson while he was in the waiting room, Pierce had gotten an idea for another chance to talk to Dr. Lawton. Besides, if she could afford a Ferrari, she could afford a new tire. He pulled up beside her and rolled down the automatic window.

"Got a problem?" His voice was smooth and polite.

"Mr. Buchannan." Surprised, Regina looked up from where she was kneeling beside the front tire on the driver's side of the car. "Yes."

"Maybe I can help," he said as he turned off the ignition. "Lucky I was still around. I walked down to the pharmacy to get that prescription filled."

She stood and brushed the grime from her hands, thinking how amazing it was that a little problem could change a person's point of view. Only a short while earlier she'd been happy to see Mr. Buchannan leave her office. Now she welcomed his warm smile and offer of assistance. Why had she thought his manner antagonistic, or at least challenging, before?

"I can't believe it," she said with resignation. "A flat and my car was just returned from the garage."

"Uh-huh," he mumbled, far more conscious of the sound of her voice than the words she was using. Even in a state of exasperation her voice was clear and decisive, a way of speaking she'd undoubtedly developed for her profession. Begrudgingly, he liked that about her. Like her beauty, it was unaffected and all the more alluring because of it.

Her hair, dazzlingly light in the sun, was in a chignon snugly pinned at the back of her neck. She was wearing a slim beige skirt and medium-heeled pumps, which had been all that was visible from under her smock when he had seen her in the examining room. Her blouse was of oatmeal-colored silk with a scooped neck and short sleeves that just capped her shoulders. Her arms were slim, and her skin, all gold and peach tones, promised to be as soft as satin.

She twisted the gold nugget ring on her right hand, the only piece of jewelry she wore. The action drew Pierce's eyes to a pair of hands that looked both delicate and capable. She was tired, he could see it in her eyes, but they were beautiful in spite of the weariness. A soft, cool, blue-green like ocean water.

It occurred to him—and he didn't like admitting it—that she was one of the most enticing women he'd ever seen. What a shame she was mixed up in a scam that was going to cost her much of that decorum. His guess at this point was that Andrews was blackmailing Monica. If his aunt had one fault it was her overabundance of pride, and it was just possible that she would pay to keep secret some indiscretion of long ago.

Regina sighed resolutely. "They're probably closed for the day. Guess I'll have to call a garage."

"No." Pierce shook his head. "I can change it for you."

"No, you can't." She fixed those startling pale eyes on him. "It wouldn't be good for your knee and you'd ruin your clothes."

"I can have the tire changed and you on the road before you get to the phone," he said, getting out of the car. "Give me your keys."

Regina's brows lifted as he reached for the keys she still held in her hand. She must have assaulted his dignity, she supposed. Most men couldn't stand the implication that they were helpless or incapable, particularly imperious types like Pierce Buchannan.

"Mr. Buchannan," she protested as he slipped the keys from her fingers. "I can't let you change my tire, you're injured." She followed him toward the trunk. Of course he wasn't injured much. An athletic person could perform with worse injuries than that. And there was no doubt he was athletic, every muscle developed to tempting perfection.

"I'll live." He grinned. "You said so yourself." He lifted the jack and the spare out and headed for the front of the car, Regina dogging his tracks again. A few minutes later he had loosened the last of the lugs and was pulling the flat tire free. Ten minutes more and the spare was in place, the flat tire and jack secured in the trunk.

"You're limping," Regina commented as Pierce slammed the trunk lid down and walked back around the car. His trousers were smudged with dirt and grease.

He shrugged his shoulders. "The knee stiffened up on me a little."

She dipped her head slightly and frowned. "I knew it. I shouldn't have let you change that tire."

He smiled the crooked smile that gave his face a boyish look and his eyes an insistent twinkle. But behind the deceptive lightness she sensed a determined spirit hard as metal. Regina suspected in that moment there was no deterring Pierce Buchannan once he set his mind on something.

"Well," he said, pulling a crisp white handkerchief from his pocket and mopping his brow, "it wasn't much of a job." He used the handkerchief to wipe most of the dirt from his hands, then balled it up and tossed it in the open window of the Mercedes. "You ought to drop that flat off somewhere so you won't be without a spare for long."

"I will." She looked at him gratefully.

He smiled and opened the door of the Ferrari for her. Regina scooted under the wheel as he pushed the door shut. She looked back to find his hands resting on the window opening and Pierce leaning down to meet her gaze.

"Mr. Buchannan, you've been very kind and I appreciate your assistance. I really feel obligated."

"Enough, I hope, to have a drink with me. Something cool would go down like a glass of heaven."

"I guess I could do that after I drop off the tire."

He frowned, looking at the dirty streaks on his trousers and the grime under his nails. "On the other hand, I look like a grease monkey and my hotel's all the way across town. I wonder..."

"Look," she said, hesitating only a moment as she convinced herself Pierce wasn't a total stranger. Normally she wouldn't have considered what she was about to do, but they both *did* know Joe Adams, and Pierce had gone out of his way to help. "I only live a few blocks from here. And I've got a big pitcher of iced tea in the refrigerator. Why don't you just follow me home?"

"Sure," he said, a self-satisfied light shining in his eyes as he nodded and pulled back from the car.

Regina waited for him to back the Mercedes out of the way, then drove out ahead of him. The one good thing about being delayed by a flat was that the traffic had thinned to a trickle of cars and she would probably arrive home only a few minutes later than she'd expected to. Marley wouldn't appreciate having his dinner late, but that couldn't be helped. She felt a lot more guilty about letting a patient she'd advised to take it easy change her tire. But she couldn't deny being grateful he'd come along.

Thirty minutes later she'd dropped off the tire at a garage and was turning into the front drive of her house. Pierce Buchannan turned in behind her and parked his car beside hers. She waited in the driveway as Pierce limped toward her.

"Any problem about getting the tire repaired?" he asked.

"Yes," she answered, smiling resolutely and gesturing for him to come along to the house. "The mechanic said there were several punctures, probably nails. It can't be fixed, so I'll pick up a new one tomorrow." Heat seemed to radiate from the concrete and amplified the mugginess of the air as Regina paused a moment on the length of walk that led to the front door. "I'm surprised about Hogan's."

"Hogan's?"

"The garage that serviced my car," she said, starting up the walkway. "You'd think the guy would have noticed driving over anything that would flatten a tire so fast."

"Maybe you ought to give them a call."

"I'll do that. Somebody there isn't on the ball."

Regina stopped again to pick a handful of pink zinnias from the masses of blooms in the narrow beds that lined the walkway. The foundation of the house was flanked by azalea bushes, no longer in bloom but thick with rich green leaves. She'd planted a row of white whiskey-leaf begonias, which were blooming in front of the azaleas. As she paused on the front stoop and unlocked the door, she noted that the flowers were suffering from the heat and that she would need to turn on the sprinkler later in the evening.

"Come on in," she invited, pushing the door open wide and waiting for him to enter.

"Thanks." He stepped inside.

Regina closed the door behind him. "There's a bathroom there." She indicated a door just beyond the stairs. "You can wash up and then just have a seat in the den. I'm going to put these in water, make a quick trip upstairs and then I'll get some tea." Her voice was gentler and softer than before. "If it were a little later we could go out on the patio but I believe we'll be more comfortable in here now." She swept through the kitchen door as she talked, sounding as if she'd known Pierce Buchannan all her life.

Pierce watched her departure appreciatively until she was out of sight in the kitchen. She moved with the confidence and grace of a dancer. He smiled to himself. A little luck, a little ingenuity, and most people would follow the lead. He'd figured that after the tire changing she would be grateful enough and feel comfortable enough with him to invite him to her house. Here it would be easier to read her reactions to his questions. Maybe he would even have a chance to look around.

Still standing, he looked the room over. She seemed to have a penchant for antiques and had mixed them in with more modern pieces. There was a bit too much furniture in the room for his taste, but it was all artfully arranged and had a definite feminine flair.

He liked the cream walls and the way she'd repeated the color in the sofa and stuffed chairs. The accent pillows were a pale blue-green, like her eyes, and there were other pillows in a rose color that reminded him how soft and feminine Dr. Regina Lawton looked.

How would she feel locked willingly in his arms? Would her lips be cool or warm against his? The thought intrigued him. Would holding her be like capturing the gentle morning mists or trying to contain the fiery glow of sunset? He had a feeling he wouldn't rest until he knew the answer.

She was, he knew, a woman who'd seen the run of emotions in her patients. Had contending with the raw hurt and sorrow of death and contrasting it with the blissful joy of recovery made her lock her own feelings up? Or had it made her long to experience every precious human feeling first-hand?

Pierce picked up one of the rose-colored pillows and held it to his chest. He strolled to the rear of the room where a set of sliding glass doors opened onto the patio. A quick visual check of the lock assured him the door was secure. Turning, he made his way back toward the sofa. He gave the pillow a toss and it landed with a thump against the cushion. There was a large stuffed chair set back in one corner. He sat in it, settling into its comfortable contours, wondering if it had been selected with a man in mind, a particular man perhaps?

Pierce stiffened to attention. The noise he heard wasn't loud, but it was coming from beneath his chair. Oh hell, he thought, feeling a sudden tenseness string through his muscles. Slowly, he edged his foot aside as the growl deepened and took on the frantic sound of fear. Moving with slow caution Pierce got to his feet, then bent to his knees beside the chair.

"Come on, cat," he crooned to the white beast cowering behind the chair leg. "Give me a chance, won't you?"

Marley hissed and shot out of the room and into the kitchen like a balloon with the air let out.

"I see you've met Marley." She'd changed clothes and wore a pair of loose-fitting white cotton pants with a roomy white shirt and sandals. Her hair was still contained in the chignon, but she looked more relaxed. She carried a small round tray and two glasses of iced tea with a sprig of mint in each.

The cat followed her in, staying cautiously behind her legs and then bounding to the high back of an armchair to take up a watch post.

"I don't think he likes me," Pierce commented, accepting a frosty glass of tea from her. He stood beside the chair where he'd been seated a few moments earlier.

"Well, don't be offended. He's a bit spooked." As she placed a couple of straw coasters on the heavy, iron-banded sea chest, she gestured for him to sit on the sofa. He complied, wondering if she would sit beside him. She took a seat in a chair opposite the sofa. The cat sat like a sentinel in the other. The tea glass was poised at her lips but she spoke again before she drank. "We had a prowler last night and Marley got the worst of it."

Pierce's brows lifted abruptly. Her casual tone surprised him. He would have thought she would be terror-ridden from such an experience. But of course keeping a calm exterior would be another trait of the profession. She was accustomed to handling emergencies and adjusting to the unexpected, and doing it without alarming her patients.

"You weren't hurt?" he asked, the line of his mouth tightening fractionally. He took a swallow of tea as she shook her head. "Did he take anything?"

She exhaled a long slow breath as if she were dismissing the matter from her mind as something she couldn't allot the time to worry about. Her voice was lighter when she spoke again and he noticed that the weariness had left her eyes. It occurred to him that Regina Lawton was a woman who took control of her life and didn't let anything shake her loose for long.

"No, he just gave me and Marley the fright of our lives," she said, her eyes clouding momentarily as she felt something like a little pinprick nagging from back in her mind.

He smiled warmly, deliberately trying to bring a note of lightness into the conversation.

"That must have been a bad experience."

"It was." Her voice wavered and she cleared her throat. "The worst thing is knowing you aren't secure in your own house."

A brief quiver of her lips showed the first trace of the anguish she had undoubtedly buried under her professionalism and calm demeanor. The experience *had* shaken her and she wouldn't admit it to herself. Was that part of the reason she'd brought him here today, because she didn't want to go back in the house alone? He felt a brief flash of sympathy and wondered if he weren't way off base thinking a woman who looked, as she did at the moment, so fragile and gentle, could possibly be involved in a blackmail scheme.

He countered his feelings with a sidelong glance at the cat, who hadn't relaxed his vigil or taken his eyes off Pierce since returning to the room.

"You don't seem nearly as spooked as Marley."

"No." She laughed softly, seeing the ridge of fur standing up on Marley's back. "I'm more angry than spooked. I was careless. I left the sliding doors unlocked and that's how he got in." She paused to sip her tea. "I confronted the man and struggled with him, which is probably the most foolhardy thing I've ever done in my life. Fortunately for me, he didn't try to hurt me. He just wanted to get out of here as fast as possible."

"How do you know he didn't want to hurt you?"

"Because he didn't and he obviously could have."

Pierce drained the last of the tea from his glass. He was studying her face, though there wasn't a feature on it he hadn't memorized. His gaze locked with hers for a silent moment and then her pale eyes turned away.

He set the glass with its melted ice cubes and sprig of mint lost among them, back on the straw coaster. A look of concern flickered across his face. "I'm glad you weren't hurt."

He gave her an easy smile. "But I'm sure you'll be more careful in the future."

"Yes, of course." She rose. "Enough talk, Mr. Buchannan," she said briskly. "I want you to lie down here on the sofa."

"You do?" Pierce wasn't often caught off guard, but this time surprise registered in the dark depths of his eyes.

"I do," she responded and laughed. "Because as a doctor I'll feel guilty till the end of time if your knee swells and gets worse from your having stressed it changing my tire. About thirty minutes with a compress should help."

While she walked back to the kitchen Pierce slipped off his shoes and stretched out on the sofa. Why argue with good luck? he rationalized. A moment later she returned with a towel and one of those packs that could be heated or cooled. She wrapped it in the towel and placed it across his knee, using a pillow to keep it in place.

"Feels good." It did. And he meant having her care for him, as much as he did the soothing feel of the pack on his knee.

She smiled. He decided that smile probably cured as many ills as the prescriptions she wrote. "You stay right here. I'm going out to turn on the sprinklers."

"I won't move a muscle." He closed his eyes but her face was still there in his mind. He pictured her in yards of silk, white and flowing, her hair loose and tumbling to her shoulders. She hadn't touched him when she put the compress in place. Had she been afraid of experiencing again what he'd seen in her eyes that moment in the examining room when his hand touched hers?

He could hear her crossing the room. She left through the sliding doors. The moment the sound of her sandals clacking on the patio died out, Pierce slid the compress from his knee and went to her desk. In under five minutes he'd rifled through the drawers. He felt like a heel—she'd just told him how disturbing last night's burglary had been for her—but after all, Monica's welfare was at stake here.

He found medical journals, a stack of receipts and paid bills, an assortment of greeting cards and a roll of stamps. He found nothing to pinpoint her connection to Blake Andrews. Disappointed, he was pushing the last drawer shut when he saw the corner of a book beneath the cards. Quickly he lifted out a small leather address book and thumbed the pages. There was only one name that interested him.

Blake Andrews. The address was a postal box in a little village in Switzerland. So the elusive Mr. Andrews *did* have a permanent address. He knew the place. It was near a ski resort he'd visited last winter. The information should help his friends in France, too. He hastily copied the address onto a piece of pink notepaper on the desk.

He heard her footsteps before he finished and dropped the address book in the drawer and shut it. He was back on the sofa when she returned, compress in place, eyes closed and his head propped comfortably against a stack of pillows.

Regina stopped in the doorway. He looked incredibly appealing resting there, his chest rising and falling in slow even breaths. She sighed softly. Sleep was probably the only condition in which a man like Pierce Buchannan looked vulnerable. She liked the way sunlight from the window burnished his hair to a coppery color and lit the tips of his eyelashes with red highlights. What she didn't like was the little lurch she felt in the pit of her stomach or the warmth she felt spreading over her skin at the sight.

She couldn't imagine why she'd first thought him perplexing. He was downright chivalrous. She reminded herself he was here because she felt professional concern and because he'd done her a favor she felt obligated to repay. So what was she doing wondering if those lips would be gentle on hers or if the feel of his hands on her skin would turn her blood to fire?

Across the room Marley slept at his watch post. "Mr. Buchannan," Regina said lightly, lifting the compress from his knee. She'd let him rest another few minutes while she took the tea glasses to the kitchen, rinsed them and placed them in the dishwasher. As he stirred, her vision drifted casually over him noting details, the silk socks, the gold belt buckle, the scrap of paper protruding from his pocket. "How's the knee?"

"Better." He stared up at her. "Guess I fell asleep." The smile on his lips was as intimate as a kiss, and it drew a disturbing current of excitement through her. "I suppose I ought to be going."

She moved back to give him room to stand. "Perhaps we can see each other again sometime," she said.

What was going on here? she wondered. If her face was any reflection of his it was a magnetism that had exerted its pull too quickly. Something too strong was tugging at her, finding feelings she hadn't known she possessed and kindling them to a slow burn. None of it made sense—not without thought and logic and time to understand the implications.

Pierce got to his feet. He knew exactly what she was feeling, because he was experiencing the same thing. He didn't know why he'd looked at her that way. It hadn't been intentional. She wasn't a woman to be rushed. He knew that, too. He was feeling things he'd sworn never to succumb to again. It would be too easy in the darkness and heat of a summer night to forget she was a woman he didn't trust. And what of the danger of forgetting his purpose?

"I'll call you when I'm back in town," he said calmly. "I'm flying to Switzerland tomorrow." He knew he was being abrupt, but he had to slice through what was building between them and jolt his attention back to why he was here.

"Oh." She willed herself to relax, her heartbeat to slow its pace. So go, she thought, and spare me.

He saw no chilling in her features, no uneasiness at his mention of Switzerland. That brought more questions to his mind. But none he expected to get answers to tonight.

Regina took a long, restorative breath when he was gone. She felt as if a whirlwind had spun her around and then tossed her out. She would see Mr. Buchannan again, but not without fortifying her caution—and her control.

She *did* need a change of scene. And time to reflect and revitalize. A doctor's life never ran perfectly smoothly, but it was the life she had chosen. There were always the night calls and emergencies. Fortunately, the system she had with the other doctors in the clinic alleviated much of the uncertainty of that part of the work. Such things as answering services and alternating weeks on call gave her a degree of freedom that made the pressure bearable and helped her keep the job in perspective.

Regina wandered through the den tidying up, checking for bits of glass that might have become embedded in the rug. The cleaning woman had vacuumed, but sometimes glass was difficult to get up. Passing the sofa, she spotted a cushion that had fallen to the floor. She bent to retrieve it and, as she did, saw jammed beside the sea chest a narrow, metal cylinder. The flashlight. She had forgotten that the man dropped it.

Harboring an uncomfortable restlessness, she picked it up. There wouldn't be fingerprints. The prowler had worn gloves. She doubted it would be of any use to the police. She stood quietly for a moment looking at the penlight in her hand. The burglar had invaded her peaceful existence. But at least he only threatened her possessions, that which could easily be replaced. Pierce Buchannan was an invader as well, but he, on the other hand, had taken a rampant path through her emotions.

She dropped the penlight to the table and shook her head as if a physical gesture would shake out her thoughts. It didn't, so she turned to things that needed to be done, such as arranging for a friend to keep Marley while she was gone. She used the phone at her desk where she'd tossed her purse when she came in. As she chatted briefly with her friend she pulled out the airline ticket that had been delivered to the clinic.

A tidy person by nature, she unconsciously opened the drawer to drop in the ticket and a pencil that was lying on top of the desk. She was surprised to see her address book lying open inside. Last night she'd checked and rearranged everything in that drawer. The address book had been moved since and opened to Blake's Swiss address.

Who, when and why? The cleaning woman? Or Pierce? She remembered the bit of paper she'd seen in his pocket, pink like her notepad. She recalled the edginess he'd made her feel in the examining room. He was about the size of the burglar. And the paper could have been a receipt from somewhere and she could be getting paranoid.

The door chimes broke her thoughts. Marley came awake at the sound of them. A low growl started in his throat and the fur spiked up on his back. She closed the drawer without having put the ticket inside and, rising quickly, picked up Marley. He really was spooked, she thought, and not likely to be friendly. It was almost funny. She'd never seen him bristle that way except at another tomcat. Hurriedly she shut him in the kitchen and went to answer the door.

Two men stood there, both strangers, both well-dressed. One was tall, approaching six-three, with dark hair, dark eyes and handsome features. She noticed that he began appraising her instantly, making mental notes on her appearance, and knew instinctively he would be the one to speak first. The other man was much shorter with a wiry build. He had a ring of light brown hair around a balding dome and gray-blue eyes that also assessed but with far less aggressiveness than those of his companion.

"Dr. Lawton," the tall man addressed her. As he spoke he withdrew a leather case from his coat pocket. She saw that his companion held a duplicate case.

Her first thought was that the police had come back to get more information about the burglary.

"Yes," she answered, giving back an equally assessing stare.

"I am Inspector Jacques Marot, and this is my partner, Armand Larousse. We are French police officers on a special assignment." He offered his identification to Regina. "You may check with your local authorities. Your Lieutenant Langley would have accompanied us but was called away at the last moment. You may call this number to verify what we are telling you." He handed her a card.

"French?" Regina took the identification and the card from Marot and examined them carefully. She knew the card was Langley's. Last night he'd left one like it with her. She shook her head and returned the credentials to Marot. "I don't understand. Why are you here?"

Marot pocketed the leather case. "We would like to talk to you about a gentleman you know. Monsieur Blake Andrews."

Stunned, she couldn't keep the surprise from her voice. "Uncle Blake? Whatever for?"

"May we come in?" Marot asked in his smooth but official-sounding voice. He noted she was surprised and off balance. He always preferred to deal with people on those terms. It made it much easier to read the truth in their faces.

"Certainly," Regina said, her voice rising slightly. She led them inside, gesturing for them to sit on the sofa. Larousse sneezed repeatedly.

"My apologies," he said. "Allergies." He pointed to the vase of zinnias. "I wonder if I could trouble you for a glass of water."

"Certainly," she told him, removing the flowers and hurrying to the kitchen. Marley had hidden himself under the kitchen table and didn't come out. Regina was back in a minute.

Larousse took the water and pulled a prescription bottle from his pocket. "Allergy capsules," he remarked, popping one in his mouth and swallowing water behind it.

Regina seated herself in one of the armchairs. "What is it you want to know about my uncle?" she asked.

Larousse smiled. "We do not wish to alarm you, *mademoiselle*—forgive me—Doctor," he said gently, the French accent heavy. She realized then that Marot, in contrast, sounded as American as she did. "Your uncle is in no trouble himself, but we believe he has information that might help the French government prosecute an important case." His expression grew serious. "Have you heard from your uncle recently?"

"I spoke with him on the phone a few days ago." She pasted a demure smile on her lips, aware they were more interested in her reactions than her answers.

Marot dipped his head slightly. The corners of his mouth curved into a semblance of a smile. He looked as if he were concentrating on her, but his clever eyes were sweeping the room, obviously recognizing the Worldways insignia on the ticket folder on the desk.

"Can you tell us where he was when he called?"

"No. He didn't say." What was this really about? It seemed preposterous to her that Blake could ever have become involved in anything of significance to the French government. To him life was an adventure never to be taken seriously. She doubted he even knew the name of the president of France. She wanted more information before she offered more herself. "I wonder," she went on, "what could be important enough to make you travel so far just to ask me where my uncle is? And for that matter I wonder how you knew about me at all."

Marot exhaled a slow breath.

"No, no," he said. "We're investigating other matters as well while we're here. Your government and mine sometimes exchange information. Things like that become necessary as the world grows smaller. As for knowing about you, it isn't difficult these days to locate family members— a few keys on a computer and..."

"I see," Regina responded. "Still I wonder why—"

"Has your uncle sent anything to you recently?" Marot interrupted. "A letter? Anything?"

Marot had skillfully sidestepped and cut short her questions. Regina decided if he could be evasive, she could, too. It occurred to her that Pierce might have had the same reason—whatever it might be—for breaking into her house last night. Or was her imagination going wild again? Either way she wanted to know what was going on before she told anybody anything.

"No. Nothing. Uncle Blake doesn't write, he calls. And that rarely. We seldom see each other. Before he called this week, I hadn't spoken to him in more than six months."

"If you will forgive the intrusion, Dr. Lawton, what did your uncle talk about when he called?"

She was aware of the scrutiny in Marot's eyes. Something about his look stirred an uneasiness she couldn't ignore. Her own eyes were wide and guileless.

"Only family things. He said he missed me, which probably isn't true. Nothing significant. It was a short call." She shrugged her shoulders. "I wish I could help you more."

"That is the way of things," Marot said consolingly. "Families are not so close as they should be." He put his card in her hand. "If you see or hear from your uncle will you call this number and let us know?"

She stared at the card.

"In France?" As she looked up she caught a glimpse of Larousse's face. His eyes were on the penlight on the coffee table and his expression was one of puzzlement.

"The charges will be paid," Marot said quickly as he nodded to Larousse. "We are sorry to have troubled you, Dr. Lawton." Marot rose from the sofa and went to the door, pausing there until Larousse was out. His gaze slipped over Regina's face in a look that was strictly man to woman. It was a look she had experience with and knew how to respond to. A half smile crossed her lips.

"No trouble. I'm sorry I couldn't help." She shut the door, resting against it for a moment.

Dear God! She'd just lied to the French police. A dubious course of action but she was certain they hadn't been completely honest with her either. She would give Blake Marot's card. That was fair, wasn't it? What was happening to her life? All the smooth seams were coming unglued. And it had all started with the arrival of a little silver swan.

Chapter 4

Regina was practically the last passenger off the plane in Antigua. An elderly woman sitting next to her had dropped an arm load of bundles, and helping the poor woman retrieve them took several minutes. Consequently she found herself at the end of one of the snaking customs lines inside the terminal, being barked at by a less than friendly agent.

Regina shuffled her tote bag to the other shoulder and reached into her purse for her passport. Thankfully her larger suitcase had wheels, and she could just nudge it along with her foot as the line moved forward. She could tell this was going to take a while, so she turned her attention to looking over the airport. Through the glass of a partition she could see the fortunate travelers who'd already cleared customs, a horde of porters and a number of persons who were either waiting for planes or meeting arriving passengers. The terminal building was hardly large enough to accommodate the crowd. Spotting Blake in the mob would be difficult.

"How long will you be staying?" a uniformed agent asked as he assaulted her passport and travel forms with a stamp pad.

Just as he spoke her gaze swept over a familiar face in the outer room. A man in gray. Pierce Buchannan? Could it possibly be he? Or just wishful thinking?

"How long, miss?" the agent repeated his question irritably.

"Three weeks," she answered, forced to avert her eyes before she could be certain the towering figure in the gray suit was Pierce.

"Step ahead," the agent snapped.

Regina obeyed, hoisting her luggage onto a table where a second agent made a perfunctory search. Thirty minutes into her vacation and already her imagination was in high gear. Once more she scanned the crowd but now there was no sign of anyone resembling Pierce—if there ever had been. Where was Blake anyway? He was the one she ought to be looking for. Pierce Buchannan had occupied enough of her thoughts since the day he'd walked out her front door—and never called. Besides she was in Antigua to visit with her uncle, not to conjure up romantic dreams.

Finally out of customs, she scurried ahead into the thick, noisy crowd and found herself immediately swamped with porters vying for her bags. She waved them all away and threaded her way to a spot near the wall where she could wait for Blake. The place was hot, the hour late, and if Blake didn't show within ten minutes she was taking a cab. Those were her thoughts when the French officer Larousse waved to her from across the room. Seeing him heading her way, she stood and waved back.

This was preposterous. First Pierce. Now Larousse. Nothing seemed to make any sense.

Larousse, looking agitated, reached her an instant later.

"Mademoiselle," he whispered, his voice nearly lost in the din of airport sounds. "Listen to me. There's only a moment. He's here. Do you see him? You cannot trust—"

"Hey!" Regina shouted, looking around instinctively at what Larousse said. Instead of seeing anyone familiar, she saw her luggage being carted out the door. "Wait a minute," she cried to the man disappearing with her bags.

She whirled back to Larousse only to see him, too, disappearing into the crowd. She'd only half heard what he said and hurried after him, but soon found herself swallowed up by people and unable to spot him. Stopping in the center of the room, Regina looked around anxiously. Larousse was warning her about someone, about not trusting someone. But who? Suddenly, she thought she caught a glimpse of him heading out the door and rushed toward it, but just as she reached it felt herself being grasped and swung around.

"Whoa! Regina! Has it been so long you've forgotten what I look like?" Laughing, Blake hugged her against him. "You ran right by me."

"Uncle Blake!" Regina protested. "Wait. There's…" She pulled away, hurriedly looking around. But Larousse was gone and so was the man with her bags. Outside on the curb she saw a tall man in a gray suit getting into a cab, but the hat he wore obscured his face. And yet again she thought of Pierce.

"Is something wrong?" Blake asked.

"I don't know," she answered with a frown, her palms turned upward. "It's something we'll have to talk about. Meanwhile, I think we'd better get out there—" she gestured toward the cabstands in front of the airport "—and see if we can find the porter who took my bags."

A moment later Blake was pointing to a battered, blue vehicle down the line of taxis. "This fellow has them," he said, giving the hovering porter a tip and signaling for the cabbie to load Regina's luggage into the trunk.

Regina felt the humidity, still holding the heat of the day, closing in on her. She pushed her hair off her neck and took the opportunity to give her uncle the first close look since he'd met her inside. She smiled for the first time, too, as Blake expertly negotiated the fare for the driver to take them to their hotel. He could charm a cobra, she thought, and he positively exuded class. How debonair he looked in his white suit. And how cool. She couldn't believe he had anything more serious on his mind than tomorrow's dinner reservations.

A moment later they were inside the surprisingly clean though dilapidated car. The original floor carpet had been replaced by blue vinyl tile more appropriate for a kitchen floor. Regina smiled again at Blake and tried to relax, but found her body taken over by nervous energy. The questions were still coming to her mind nonstop, but she thought it prudent to wait until they were alone to talk.

"I could have rented a car," Blake started, "but the cabs are more fun and I wanted you to get a real feel of the place. Antigua is an old British sugar colony and there's still a lot of British custom here—like driving on the left side of the road," he explained as Regina was startled by the glare of headlights looming strangely to her right.

"I forgot," she said, falling back against the seat and realizing suddenly how tired she was. She'd gone to the clinic early to be sure she was leaving everything in order, then had dropped off Marley at a friend's. Then there'd been things to take care of at the house, along with some last-minute packing. The flight had taken several hours and now she longed for a good night's sleep.

The moonless night made the drive across the island a tour of darkness. But the hotel, the Paradise Inn, was well lit and gave her the first glimpse of Antigua's beauty. Bou-

gainvillea climbed a trellised entrance. In the courtyard banana trees, ferns and poinsettias grew in lush abundance.
The perfume of blooming flowers was mesmerizing and she
breathed it in, beginning to relax despite her anxiety.
Whatever Blake had to explain, whatever Larousse had
meant, couldn't possibly be as bad as she'd feared. It wasn't
possible for anything to be too wrong in a place as beautiful as this.

Blake called for a bellman to take her bags and led her
through the courtyard to her room. "This is yours," he said.
"Mine is next door. It's not the largest or most luxurious
hotel on the island, but sometimes charm is more important. Besides, this one has the best beach," he added.

The bellman placed her bag on a bamboo luggage rack at
the foot of the bed. The walls and furniture of the room
were startlingly white, and a multicolored floral bedspread
enhanced the light, airy look. A bouquet of flowers sat on
the dresser. Through the open closet doors she saw a white
terry robe, compliments of the hotel, and a large tiled bath
in tones of blue and green opened off the opposite wall.
Regina dropped into a white wicker chair as Blake dismissed the bellman with a tip.

"So how do you like it?" he asked.

"It's pretty, cozy," she answered, noticing a tempting
basket of exotic fruit on the table and a chilled bottle of
champagne in an ice bucket. "And you're sweet."

"And you've got something on your mind," he said as he
twisted the cork from the champagne bottle. A whoosh followed, along with a spray of foam Blake tempered with a
towel. "I haven't forgotten that look," he added.

"What look?"

"The one that has your mouth turning up on one side and
down on the other." Blake poured a glass of champagne for
each of them. "It's the same look you had on your six-
teenth birthday when you told me you'd dented a fender on

the car I'd just given you. I hope this doesn't mean you've smashed the Ferrari."

"The Ferrari's fine," she said, accepting the glass from him. "I take good care of your car."

"So what's the problem?" Blake sipped his champagne.

"I hope you can tell me." Regina took a small sip from her glass. "A while back I had a visit from two French policemen. They were looking for you."

"For me?" Blake's brows lifted. "Why?"

"They wanted to talk with you about testifying in some legal case. I didn't know where you were at the time so I just told them I'd relay the message next time I saw you." She opened her purse and pulled out the card Marot had given her. Blake took it. "He asked me to call this number in France if I saw you. Or to have you call."

"Marot." Blake turned the card in his fingers. "Never heard of him. Anyway, it doesn't sound too serious," he said smoothly. "Did you tell him you'd be seeing me here."

"No," Regina said. "But they're here. At least one of them is. He spoke to me at the airport. I think he was giving me a warning."

"A warning." Blake's voice sounded strained. "About what?"

"I don't know." Regina put her glass down. She really wasn't in the mood for champagne. "I'm not even sure what he said. He has a strong accent and then he ran off before he finished. What I've been wondering is if somehow they found out you were here and came looking for you. Uncle Blake—" Regina paused and drew in a deep breath "—are you in trouble?"

"No. Of course not," he said quickly. "I've no idea what this is all about." He slipped the card into his jacket. "But tomorrow will be time enough to find out." He smiled warmly. "Don't let it worry you. If this man Marot is on the island and wants to talk, I'm sure he'll find me."

"I suppose you're right," she said.

"I am right and I think you must be very tired." He glanced at his watch. "It's past midnight. Get some sleep. Tomorrow we'll talk, walk on the beach and just be very lazy." He kissed her cheeks.

"I'll enjoy that," she said softly, feeling as if a weight had fallen away from her. Blake wasn't worried. She wouldn't let herself be, either. She'd been waiting a long time for this vacation and small reunion. It would be a shame to let anything spoil it.

Blake started for the door. "You'll probably want to sleep late. When you're up come out to the beach and turn right. You'll see a cabana. We'll have breakfast there. Good night."

He left a moment later, having reminded Regina he was in the room next to hers. Hurriedly she unpacked her bags. A quick shower prepared her fatigue-flooded body to slip between the soft cotton sheets. Sleep descended easily.

A worried Blake Andrews walked quickly to the hotel bar, making one brief stop along the way to buy a Paris newspaper. Seated at a corner table he flipped through the pages, scanning the articles until he came to one that caught his attention and turned his skin pasty-white.

Singer Found Drowned in Swimming Pool

Singing sensation Nellie Thanet's bright career has been brought to a tragic end. Miss Thanet's body was found floating in the pool at a rented chalet outside of Paris. An inquest has been scheduled to determine if the drowning was accidental. Rumors are that Mademoiselle Thanet might have been dead as long as a week before her body was found. Police . . .

Beads of perspiration formed on Blake's brow as fast as he could wipe them away with his handkerchief. Closing the paper slowly, he called for a waiter to bring him a whiskey and soda. Hand clenched tightly around the glass, he gulped it down fast and ordered another before the waiter had left his table.

From the bar, busy with late-night revelers and casino goers, a dark-eyed man watched as Blake nervously opened the newspaper again and finished reading the article about Nellie Thanet. When Blake refolded the paper and left for a stroll on the beach, the dark-eyed man shoved a few bills on the bar and quickly followed.

From his table at the far end of the room, Pierce Buchannan watched both men leave. Blake was unaware he was being followed, but he would have to manage on his own, Pierce decided. He was much more interested in finding out what in that newspaper had taken the color out of the man's face. Pushing his chair back, he rose and walked slowly to the table Blake had occupied.

Bad luck! The paper was closed but Pierce was sure the section on top was the one Blake had been reading. Cautiously turning the pages he looked for anything that might give him a clue. About halfway through he found it, a wet ring made by Blake's glass when he'd set it down on the paper as he read.

A pair of stone-hard eyes moved over the page. It wasn't long before he guessed which article had been the cause of alarm. A suspicious death near Paris. It wouldn't take much checking to find out if Blake had flown in from France. Did he know something about the woman's death? Perhaps too much? Pierce would stake his fortune that the man shadowing Blake was a Frenchman. One of the things you learned in intelligence work was how to read the nuances of gestures and movements of various nationalities. The way the man at the bar used his hands and tilted his head as he talked said he was French. The only question was what he wanted with Blake.

Pierce moved silently through the courtyard and stood unnoticed as he watched Blake come up the steps from the beach and return to his room. He spotted the Frenchman beneath a coconut palm a few yards away. The man was good, Pierce granted him that. But he wasn't so good he was aware he, too, was being watched.

When the lights went on in Andrews's room, the Frenchman left his position and returned to the bar. Pierce, however, had a feeling Blake Andrews wasn't about to crawl into bed. Moving soundlessly, Pierce eased around to a window on the backside of the building and shielded himself behind the foliage of a banana tree. He heard Blake's agitated voice from inside.

"Every flight can't be booked. Check again. Please."

There was a pause as the reservations agent on the other end of the line apparently responded.

"So when is the next flight available?... To anywhere!... Two days! I need to leave here first thing in the morning." Blake's voice crackled. "There must be something...

"All right! All right! Put me on standby and notify me as soon as you have something." Blake gave his name and number then slammed the receiver down. A moment later the light was extinguished but Pierce could hear the sound of pacing steps on the terrazzo floor and see the tiny red glow of a cigarette. Blake and Regina were expected in Dominica in a week. Blake's hotel reservation was for seven days, but whatever had given him the jitters had him ready to change plans and leave Antigua immediately.

Pierce moved along to the next window. What he liked about these island hotels was that many of the windows had nothing more substantial than straw shades covering them. Very convenient for hot-blooded lovers or burglars or spies.

But Regina was asleep. He could hear the soft sound of her breathing and just make out those elegant features beneath the halo of blond hair. He resisted the urge to climb inside and take a closer look. That time would come later. For a while neither she nor Blake were going anywhere.

Rays of sunshine streamed through the straw shade of the window and over Regina's face. She awoke to the sound of waves slapping gently on the nearby beach. Refreshed from long hours of sleep, she stirred from her bed, hurried along by a growing appetite. She took only a moment to dress in a pair of white cotton shorts and a loosely woven, deep blue sweater that accented the paler color of her eyes. Brushing back her long straight hair, she shook it into place, then added a touch of gloss to her lips, hurriedly tucked her feet into a pair of canvas shoes and set off toward the beach.

By the light of day, the tropical courtyard, a captured paradise, teemed with chirping birds and people leisurely enjoying the beautiful morning. The area was rich with lush green foliage and the myriad colors and sweet perfume of tropical flowers. She strolled by the pool and had to jump to avoid being splashed by lively, unclothed children swimming and diving. Their towels draped, oil-rubbed parents lounged in chairs beside the sparkling water.

Laughing at the children's antics, Regina rounded the corner of the building only to be stopped in her tracks by the dazzling view of the ocean. The sky and the water loomed magnificent, blue, serene, with picturesque sailboats dotted here and there. The sand glistened white. She pulled off her sunglasses, wanting to see what was before her with the naked eye, then paused simply to absorb the splendor of the scene. The smell of the ocean, the rhythm of the waves, the brilliance of the sun all combined into an almost reverent peacefulness. But it was quickly broken by the sound of a distant shout.

"Hello!" a man called, his head rising from behind the briny crystal waves of the Caribbean. He waved to her then started to swim toward shore, the powerful strokes of his arms easily propelling him through the water.

Regina gaped. So she hadn't been wrong about seeing Pierce Buchannan at the airport. He'd been there, all right. What a peculiar coincidence he should show up here. She watched thoughtfully as he swam in, patently aware of the precision movements of rippling muscles challenging the motion of the waves. Evidently the injured knee was much improved.

Pierce swam into the waist-deep water nearer shore, then stood, a veritable Neptune surging out of the ocean. A gust of wind off the water doused Regina with salt spray and gave credence to the image he portrayed.

"Good morning!" He gave a vital smile, striding against the water to join her on the beach. The forceful movements of muscled legs drew him quickly out of the shallows. Rivulets of water streamed through the dark patch of hair on his chest and through the crinkling curls that trailed over a flat, hard abdomen.

As he splashed out of the ankle-deep water Regina's face went rigid. Just for a moment she thought he was as bare as the children in the pool, but then realized he wore a slim, European-style bronze swimsuit the same shade as his suncolored body. He also wore a somewhat challenging half grin. Neither did much to disguise the male factor.

"Good morning," she responded stiffly. "You *do* get around, don't you?"

He laughed. "All over. I suppose you're wondering how I just happened to turn up here."

Drops of water slid from the contours of his legs to leave a trail in the sand as he retrieved a towel from the barrier of rocks that marked the edge of the beach. He dried his hair and his body.

"I was, in fact," she said. "I thought you were making a trip to Switzerland."

Dropping the towel to the rocks, Pierce ceremoniously stepped into a pair of khaki shorts. He took a watch from his pocket and fastened it around his wrist, then gave her a teasing wink as he pulled a polo shirt over his head and combed the thick chestnut hair back from his face with his fingers.

"It was a short trip."

"And you just happen to be passing through Antigua on your way to—where is it you're from, Mr. Buchannan?"

Her loose blond hair shimmered in the breeze like spun glass. He knew it would feel like silk in his fingers. "Miami," he said. "And, other places. To be honest, my being here isn't a coincidence. I came to see you."

"Oh?" She inclined her head. "I don't remember telling you I'd be here." She doubted him, but nevertheless a small tingle of excitement started inside.

"You didn't. Your receptionist did. I said I'd call. Remember?"

"So you just flew down? To see me?" Their eyes met. Touched was a better word, she thought reflectively. The possibilities intrigued her.

"Something like that. Look, I'm starving. Have you had breakfast?"

"Well no, but..." She'd forgotten all about meeting Blake. "I'm on my way to the cabana to meet—"

"I'll go with you." His broad hand touched the center of her back, making it feel as if she had an instant sunburn in that spot.

She'd been surprised to see Pierce, but the look on Blake's face as the two of them approached was much stronger than surprise.

"Did you think I'd never get up?" Regina kissed her uncle. "Blake, I want you to meet—"

He half rose and offered a hand. "Pierce. You know my niece?"

"I know Regina. I didn't know she was your niece." Eyes twinkling, he shook his head and turned to Regina. "Now this is the damnedest coincidence. Your uncle and my aunt are friends. I met Blake at Aunt Monica's last year."

It took Regina a moment to absorb what she heard, another moment to wonder about it. But feeling no tension between the men, she dismissed the matter from her mind.

"How is Monica?" Blake asked.

"Feisty as ever last time I saw her. We talked about you." He gauged Blake's reaction but saw nothing to indicate any nervousness this morning.

Through a breakfast of fresh melon, scrambled eggs and just-baked bread, the conversation rambled through an explanation of how both Regina and Blake happened to know Pierce.

"Monica Whitechurch is a remarkable woman, Regina," Blake said. "You'll like her."

"Am I going to meet her?"

"That's my surprise," Blake said smoothly. "Instead of staying here the whole time, I planned for us to fly down to Dominica at the end of the week. Monica has a big house party at her plantation this time every summer. She's invited us."

"Dominica?"

Blake wiped a trickle of perspiration from his neck with his handkerchief. "You've probably never heard of the place. Most people haven't except for botanists and travelers who like out of the way places. It's near Martinique. Monica's plantation is probably one of the largest businesses on the island."

"And that's where you met Pierce?"

"Right. At last year's party," Blake said. "He was there a couple of days."

During the conversation Regina learned that Dominica was too mountainous to be very populous and definitely small enough to still have missed out on the tourist trail. Sometimes confused with the Dominican Republic, the commonwealth of Dominica was actually hundreds of miles south of the larger island. Exports of limes, coconuts and bananas were the main sources of income for the islanders. Pierce told her that Monica Whitechurch, widowed twenty years, operated a plantation that her husband had established fifty years ago.

"Your aunt must be elderly," Regina remarked.

"She is. But don't let her hear you say so." He smiled. "I've been trying to get her to retire and let me put in a manager to run the plantation. So far she refuses to let go." Again Pierce's eyes assessed Blake's face, but the chance of seeing any reaction to his words was spoiled by the arrival of the waitress who came to clear the dishes.

Regina glanced up at the palm top of the cabana as she sipped from a glass of passion fruit juice. The table sat beneath the thatched overhang with the tropical view serving as walls. In the horizon she saw the lofty lines of an imposing black sailboat and imagined it lent a reminiscence of piracy to the scene.

The island mystique of those bygone days hung heavy and completely permeated her thoughts. She imagined Pierce swathed in black, cutlass in hand, abducting her to the rolling deck of a pirate ship. She smiled inwardly at the thought of how well he would fit the part.

"I have a business appointment in an hour," Pierce said suddenly, glancing at his watch.

The announcement was a sharp point pricking her bubbly daydreams. "That's too bad," she said.

"I'm free for dinner, though," he went on quickly. "I'd like for the two of you to join me at the Buccaneer. They have the best island food. How about it?"

The Buccaneer fit right into her train of thoughts. She glanced at Blake and thought he showed just a moment's hesitation before accepting the invitation.

"Sounds good." Blake turned to Regina. "All right with you?"

"Fine with me."

"At eight then," Pierce said. "I'll meet you in the lounge."

Pierce left, striding down the beach with a swinging gait Regina's eyes followed. She noted the flexing movement of each tendon in his firm calves and buttocks, the broad shoulders and surging muscles defined through the knit fabric of his shirt. A businessman? Weren't they the modern-day pirates, after all?

"An impressive man," Blake commented. "Do you like him?"

Her face colored a little as she turned back to her uncle, but her smile was easy and free. "I hardly know him."

"He seems anxious to know you better."

Regina laughed heartily, enjoying the carefree feel of it. "More fatherly advice?"

Blake grimaced. "Damn! Am I sounding fatherly again?"

"Almost."

"I'm slipping. I'll have to watch that or my image will be shot." He laughed, drawing lines in his tanned face. "I believe I promised you a lazy day. My recommendation is that we spend it right here on the beach. You get your swimsuit while I get us a beach umbrella. That and a few piña coladas ought to make it a great afternoon."

Regina did as Blake requested, returning a few minutes later covered with lotion and wearing a yellow bikini. Blake had already planted himself in a chair and was sipping a frothy concoction topped by slices of pineapples.

"I'm going for a walk," she called to him as she tossed a towel and paperback novel into the other chair.

He mumbled something incomprehensible without opening his eyes. Regina trudged off down the beach, her thoughts impetuously straying to Pierce Buchannan. Each time she looked out at the billowing blue ocean she remembered him rising out of the water like a bronzed god of the deep.

She walked a long while, dragging her toes in the sand, wading, drifting in thought, losing the stiffness from the hours of sitting the day before. Had Pierce really followed her to the island? Or did he just happen to be passing through on his way to Dominica? She liked him, more than any man she'd met in a long time.

For a while she stopped to watch the playful antics of gulls dipping to the ocean and hopping along the shoreline. She joined their energetic and humorous play, laughing joyfully at her dancing shadow on the sand. After a time she turned back the way she'd come, splashing knee-deep in the gentle blue-green waters of the Caribbean.

She was enjoying watching the gulls dive so much she almost collided with a young boy splashing along in the opposite direction and just as distracted by a Walkman radio and a pair of binoculars.

"Careful," she cried, catching the boy by the shoulder and preventing him from falling over backward in the water. "We might both be in trouble if you got those glasses wet."

"Thanks," the boy said, sliding the earphones down around his neck. "Mom'd take away all my tapes if I ruined these. Wanta look? I can see ships way out there." He pointed to the ocean. "And all the people up on the roof of the hotel. Here, take them."

Regina took the glasses for a moment and peered out to sea. Several yachts were anchored offshore and beyond them were fishing vessels. She swung the binoculars toward the hotel and to the rooftop bar. People in resort clothes sat beneath thatched umbrellas having drinks and looking almost as relaxed as Blake in his beach chair.

Her view of those nearest the rail were clear enough that she could make out their faces. She let her gaze sweep past two men leaning against the rail, then abruptly pulled the glasses back to them. She felt a prickle of uneasiness on the back of her neck. Pierce and Marot. Did they know each other?

Hastily she pulled the glasses from her eyes and returned them to the boy.

"Thanks for the look," she said.

"You're welcome. You gotta go?"

"I'm afraid so. Someone's waiting for me."

"My name's Tommy," he said, looping the cord of the binoculars around his neck. "What's yours?"

"Regina."

"Um—maybe I'll see you tomorrow," he said, grinning and blushing at the same time.

"Maybe so," she said sweetly, realizing there weren't any other children on the beach, and Tommy was probably lonely for someone to play with. "If we run into each other we'll go for a walk or play volleyball. Okay?"

"Okay. Bye," he said, replacing the headset and switching on the music. "See you."

Blake was still in his chair and it didn't look as if he'd raised his eyelids since she'd left.

"I'm back," she announced, settling into the vacant chair beside him. She took a few minutes to smooth more lotion on her skin while Blake ordered the promised piña colada. She was grateful for the time to think. Something wasn't fitting together here. It was too strange, Marot, Larousse and Pierce showing up in Antigua at the same time she did.

All of them seemed to have a link to Blake, as well. She had an uncomfortable feeling she'd been used to lead them all to her uncle. "What do you know about Pierce?" she asked casually.

Blake's eyes opened slowly. "Not much other than that he's a resort developer and Monica's nephew. She only sees him a couple of times a year. He travels all over. Very successful, I understand."

"Then you really don't know him well at all?"

"No. I suppose not. Why the quiz? Are you interested in the man?"

"Interested? Let's say curious." Or disappointed. Or hurt. Or frightened. She was remembering that everything had begun the day after the burglary at her house. She'd met Pierce and the Frenchmen that same day. And now they were all here on one small Caribbean island. Coincidence? She was beginning to think that ought to be a four-letter word. "I've just seen Mr. Buchannan talking to one of the French officers who was looking for you."

Blake's face remained calm, but on the wooden arms of the chair his fingers clenched bloodlessly tight. "You know," he said, his voice as falsely calm as his face, "I think I've had enough sun for one day. Let's go in."

"You go ahead," she answered quickly. "I'm going for a swim."

She swam, cutting through the water in lap after lap. It didn't seem right having all this anxiety in this beautiful place. And she didn't know what worried her most, that Blake might not be telling the truth about being in trouble or that Pierce might not be telling the truth about why he was in Antigua.

Back in her room a few hours later she showered, letting the warm water cascade over her shoulders and limbs to wash away the salt and sand. A couple of things were very clear. Her vacation wasn't turning out at all the way she'd expected. And tonight at the Buccaneer ought to prove extremely interesting.

Chapter 5

The Buccaneer lounge looked as if someone had sliced out a piece of the jungle and brought it indoors. Ferns grew as large as trees beneath the skylights. Ceramic planters of bird of paradise completely encircled a small dance floor, lending their tropical beauty to the exotic atmosphere. Cushions on the lounge's wicker furniture picked up the bright oranges and greens of the flowers. At one end the lounge expanded to a bar. It was there she saw Pierce sitting on a wicker stool drinking a rum punch. Their eyes met in simultaneous recognition.

He was dressed informally in a white knit polo shirt, and a pair of navy trousers and deck shoes, a combination that heightened his masculine vitality. His hair was still damp from either a swim or a shower. He left the bar as she and Blake came in, directing them to a table. A few minutes later the three of them were drinking rum punch and exchanging small talk.

"Did you have a busy afternoon?" Regina asked Pierce, a trace of suspicion returning and growing. In what she thought a reasonable length of time since she and Blake had joined him, he hadn't said anything about talking with Marot. Perhaps a little prodding would get him to mention the meeting.

"Not terribly," he said, shaking his head. "I met with a friend who owns property on St. Kitts. He's interested in developing it through my company."

A smile covered her disappointment. He volunteered nothing and she couldn't very well ask outright why he'd talked to Marot or if he'd known him before. She fell quiet as he and Blake chatted about the desirability of further tourist development on St. Kitts. When Pierce glanced her way again her eyes were on the sugary depths of her rum punch and she was completely lost in thought. His deep, compelling voice brought her head up quickly.

"I believe our table's ready in the dining room," he said, getting to his feet and helping her with her chair.

His hand touched her back briefly. It was only another guiding touch but she felt a sudden steamy warmth in the room. For Pierce the action brought an unexpected mingling of emotions, wild and gentle emotions he had no idea could be stirred so quickly. He wondered as he watched her glide past him if he could make her feel them as quickly, too.

The dining room, like the lounge, was thick with plants, but quieter and more open. Their table was near a window that looked out over a balcony and the beach below, allowing a cool breeze to float softly through the screens. The conversation covered those things people usually talk about when they don't know one another well. She learned Pierce had grown up in Miami, that he was Monica White-church's only blood relative and that his mother lived in Arizona.

He learned she'd been raised by her aunt, Blake's sister, that she'd known since childhood she wanted to be a doctor and that over the years she'd generally seen Blake only on holidays.

Beyond that Blake entertained them with insider gossip about European jet-setters. Regina had the feeling none of them had actually scratched the surface about why they were together. What was worse was that she kept getting distracted by the way Pierce's white knit shirt set off his tan and the way the candlelight played on and off the planes of his face and reflected fire from his dark eyes.

The food was divine. He'd been right in recommending the Buccaneer's island cuisine and Regina told him so. While they had coffee, the band in the lounge started a slow tune and Pierce asked her to dance. As they got up, Blake excused himself to smoke a cigarette on the balcony.

Pierce led Regina by the hand to the dance floor. He was a superb dancer, light on his feet, confident, powerful. In spite of herself, she liked being in his arms. All evening, through the pumpkin soup, the curry, the lobster thermidor, the coconut custard pudding and the superficial talk, she'd been resisting the feelings that now had her body responding with a soft surge of warmth as Pierce whirled her across the floor.

She didn't want him to affect her that way, not when she had serious things on her mind, things she needed all her faculties to deal with. She wanted her head clear and her body under control. But at some point during the dance she crossed an invisible threshold, crossed it and conceded to the physical presence of the man who held her in rhythmic embrace.

He felt her moves, her grace. She looked as delectable as a luscious, ripe peach, all golden and pink from a day in the sun. In just that short time she'd taken on a cool, casual island look. He liked it. Her straight blond hair made him

think of captured sunshine. It had a softly natural wind-
blown look falling back from the stunning lines of her face.
Her darker lashes were long and thick and swept her cheeks
when she closed her eyes. But he liked them open. Looking
into them was like looking into the deep, clear, soothing
waters of the Caribbean. She wore no mascara, no makeup
at all tonight. Pierce liked that, too.

Her backless pink sundress was a wraparound design that
tied at the waist in a puffy bow. She wore low-heeled white
sandals and a shell bracelet she must have bought on the
beach. The dress was a cloudlike cotton and he was certain
she was wearing nothing but panties underneath.

Damn it! How the hell was he supposed to find out how
much she knew about her uncle if his mind was on what she
did or didn't have on under her dress? He'd expected this to
be a lot easier, but his body wasn't cooperating. The quickening in his blood, the tightening in his muscles, the heat in
his loins made it impossible to concentrate on anything beyond a desire to whisk her from the dance floor and take her
to bed.

Blake Andrews, he'd learned, made his money in dubious ways. In Switzerland Pierce had found nothing but a
closed-up chalet. But once they had that address, his friends
in France had been able to put that information together
with other clues to reveal a lot about Blake. One way he
supported himself was by selling art objects, paintings and
jewelry for people who wanted to raise money quietly and
discreetly. How the art items and jewelry were acquired was
open to question. He was also involved in other schemes
that were harder to pin down. Pierce's friends were still
checking out those leads.

Blake was believed to be currently in possession of a certain diamond necklace that several different parties were
anxious to recover. His friends wanted him to verify that
information and recover the necklace if possible. He still

didn't know what Blake's hold on Monica was. But he was getting closer. The important thing was to find out as much as possible without Blake catching on that he suspected anything. He had no idea how much Regina knew about her uncle, but before the night was over he intended to find that out too. He stifled the warm compulsion to forget that intent.

"You dance well," he said.

She thanked him. "I took lessons. As a child. Dance lessons, voice lessons, piano. Blake was an indulgent uncle. He always saw to it I had everything I needed or wanted."

He gave here a speculative look. "You don't strike me as having been a spoiled child."

She laughed. "I'm sure I would have been if Blake had been around more. However, Aunt Sada's theory of child rearing ran to responsibilities first and rewards second. She taught me self-discipline, and for that I'm thankful—it helped get me through medical school."

He pulled her a little closer. It wasn't wise to dwell too long on that face. He could easily forget anything else. "Ever been interested in getting into any other kind of business? I've heard doctors sometimes get bored with their work after years of practice."

"Not this one. I'm content with what I do and I don't see that changing." Regina lost herself in the dimple created by his half grin—a very distracting dimple she didn't need to be thinking about. "What about your business interests?" she asked. "Ever get bored?"

"No." He bent his head closer to her ear as the volume of the music swelled, finding the delectable spicy fragrance of her perfume lightly scenting her flaxen hair, finding one more thing he liked about her. "The next job's always a challenge. I can be negotiating with a foreign government one day and laying out a building foundation the next. I spent the past six months in Spain building a hotel. Before that it was Argentina. Right now I'm taking a few months off and then it's on to the biggest project I've done, a resort in the wine country in France.''

"I'd like to hear more about that one," she said, drawing back slightly to lock her eyes with his. "Let's go out for a few minutes. The music's a little loud for me."

"Hadn't you better tell Blake?" He nodded toward the bar, where Blake sat in spirited conversation with an attractive and attentive woman.

"No," she said, smiling and heading toward the balcony doors. "I think he'll be occupied for a while."

The coolness of the tropical night welcomed them beneath a vine-covered trellis and Regina leaned her back against the wooden rail. Streamers of moonlight slipped through the bougainvillea, lighting Pierce's face, illuminating his smile. He had a sensuous mouth. She wondered what it would be like to kiss him, wondered if the mustache would be soft or crisp against her skin.

She tilted her head back, reminding herself there were things she wanted to know about Pierce Buchannan and they weren't that he had the ability to start tiny tremors inside her like those that warn of underground stirrings. Briefly she shut her eyes to clear her head. She wanted to know if he'd really come to her office because of a chance comment by an old colleague. How he knew Marot. If he was in Antigua for the reason he'd said. Or if, like Marot, he'd only been in a hurry to find Blake. That matter had her in a quandary, too. Marot knew Blake was on Antigua. Why hadn't he gotten in touch?

She had a long list of questions. She'd brought them out here because it was a quiet place to ask them, not because she wanted to be alone with Pierce.

Pierce watched her silently for a moment, wondering where this might lead. "How about a short walk on the beach instead?" he said.

She glanced toward the ocean. The star-sprinkled blue-black sky, the moonlight-bathed water and sand were inviting.

"All right," she agreed.

He slipped his arm through hers, the warmth of his touch flowing suddenly through her. A small shiver of anxiety came with it, and she took a long deep breath. Careful, she warned herself. Stick to the plan. Don't allow yourself to be swayed by a handsome face and a charming smile. Think.

Regina paused at the foot of the stairs and stepped out of her sandals, carrying them in one hand as she walked through the sand.

He led her to the water's scalloped edge. They walked side by side, Regina wading in the foamy splash of the incoming tide, Pierce keeping to the dry sand. They didn't touch. They didn't talk for a while. She was considering where to begin. He took care of that for her a few yards down the beach, when he stopped to let a crab scurry by in front of him. Regina stopped several feet ahead of him and waited.

"You're very fond of your uncle, aren't you?" He caught up with her again.

"Of course I am." She smiled and kicked at the water. "He's all the family I have left. And I'm all he has. I'm hoping we can start spending more time together."

There couldn't be any duplicity in a woman who looked as she did with a soft smile on her face and the moonlight spilling into her hair. Still, he had to be certain, but he intended to probe carefully for what he wanted to know.

"I feel the same way about my Aunt Monica." He started to walk again and Regina paced herself alongside him. "I've been so busy the past few years I'm afraid I've neglected her. I was at the plantation a few weeks ago for the first time since last summer. She'd changed. She seemed older. Worried."

She dodged an especially aggressive wave as it almost drenched the hem of her skirt. "I imagine running a plantation would be a demanding job for anyone."

His smile flickered. He'd always found a kind of bait and hook technique effective in getting someone to open up about problems. Tell a person one of your worries and almost automatically that person follows up with something similar on their mind. Maybe it would work with her.

"It is," he said, sounding distressed. "But she's done it by herself for a long time. And I always thought she'd call me if she needed any help, or if she had a problem. It's strange. You can find out you don't really know people, even family, as well as you thought."

Her brows drew downward in a frown. "You're worried about her, aren't you."

She sounded genuinely concerned about a person she'd never met. He sure wasn't getting the reaction he'd expected. Maybe another tactic would be more effective, like hinting at what he thought was happening.

"Yes," he said, following his words with a heavy sigh. "I think she may have gotten into a business deal that isn't on the up-and-up or that she's being fleeced some way and is afraid to tell me."

"That's terrible." Regina stopped in her tracks. "What can you do about it?"

She saw a tensing of his shoulders, a tightening of his jaw and from somewhere far inside a hint of flinty hardness that didn't quite make it into his face.

"I'm doing what I can," he said. "Reviewing her business records. Investigating whoever's been at the plantation in the past year."

"Do you think that'll turn up something?"

Her question had a ring of innocence. He didn't think she had any idea Blake was the person he suspected.

"I think I'm getting very close," he said with deliberate slowness. He saw it then, the quick flash in the eyes, the little shudder in the lids, the slight twitch of the lips—suspicion. The obvious had occurred to her. He felt an ounce of regret at having brought it about.

"Oh?" she murmured. Oh. So that was it. He had an elderly aunt who'd probably gone a little senile and he was ready to accuse a friend of leading her astray. In a way it was a relief, because it was so ridiculous to imagine Blake involved in anything as despicable as fleecing an old woman. Did he think her uncle a disreputable con man? How absurd. Well, at least this had nothing to do with the other matter, the one involving the French police.

"Yes," he ground out his reply. He really didn't like what he'd done to her face. It had looked soft and gentle a few minutes ago. Now the lips that had been so pliant and inviting were tight and angry. He'd wanted to kiss her. He wished he'd followed that impulse instead. If he had they might now be falling to the sand . . .

Regina planted her feet in the wet sand and crossed her arms over her chest. She didn't like what he was implying about Blake, but then her uncle was his own man and could take care of himself. He didn't really need her rushing to his defense and she had no intention of taking up the gauntlet on his behalf. But another thing bothered her as much or more.

"May I ask you something?"

Her voice challenged, her pale eyes were almost cold, but he didn't think they could ever be completely—not even when she was much angrier than she was right now. She had too much compassion in her for that. He guessed what her next question would be and prepared for it.

"Ask," he said.

"Did you really stop over in Antigua because you knew I was here?"

He gave away nothing with his slow smile. "Yes," he said. That was truer than he wanted to admit, although it wasn't the only reason. He would have seen her again, somewhere, sometime. That it happened to be here and now only allowed him to kill two birds with one stone.

Her eyes flashed, warming a little. She considered his answer. He looked as if he meant it. There was an ease about his smile, maybe even honesty. She couldn't read anything in his eyes. They were incredibly dark brown, like fertile earth, and kept their secrets in the moonlight. But she didn't let that stop her from trying.

"I have another question." Her face showed outward calm, but her words came statically. "After you left the cabana today I saw you at the rooftop bar talking to a man who looked familiar."

He came a step closer, his brows lifting in surprise. "You have good eyes."

He did, too, and they were roaming her face, showering her with a look of—humor—of all things. It annoyed her. "I happened to be looking through a pair of binoculars," she snapped.

The one-sided grin came and remained. A heightened awareness of her came, too, the spicy scent of her perfume fired up by anger and the warm air. The essence of it poured over him, and he knew she would taste as sweet.

"I'm flattered."

Her chin shot up. He'd gone from backhanded accusations to outright teasing. Perhaps he hadn't meant Blake at all. Perhaps she was too skeptical of him. She needed to know.

"Don't be," she said curtly. "I wasn't looking for you in particular, but since you were there I couldn't help seeing you. Did the man you were talking to ask about Blake?"

He shrugged but she noted he knew precisely whom she meant.

"The Frenchman? No. We talked about sailing."

"I see." Regina moved restlessly, turning the gold ring on her finger. Perhaps that was true, perhaps it wasn't. How could she know? How could she know anything but the helpless twist of emotions inside? He was standing so close his breath fluttered a few wispy strands of the bangs on her forehead. Her heartbeat quickened but she willed it back to normal.

"No more questions?" His admiration for her had grown—no, been born and grown—in the past few minutes. Before, his feeling had been no more than the highest form of lust. He supposed there were degrees of it. Some women inspired a man to want no more than to toss her over his shoulder and cart her to the nearest horizontal spot. Others compelled a man to do noble things. He didn't quite know where she fit in with him on that score. He suspected she could mold him like putty if he let her—and he had no intention of doing so. This would have to progress on his terms.

Still, he hadn't shaken her into giving any revelations, if there were any. There was a tough, savvy lady underneath that satin skin and silky hair, behind those clouded blue-green eyes. He was beginning to like what a little anger did to her face, after all. It made him want to try some devious means of chasing it away.

She took a step back into the swirling waters. Sea foam clung to her calves as the next wave washed past her legs. She needed the distance if her head was to remain clear.

"Actually I have two more," she said, letting her voice cut through the webs of confusion in her brain. "One concerning your knee and one concerning my tire."

The half grin became a full-blown smile. How astute of her. He was liking her better and better every minute, the

sharp mind as well as the goddess's body. She affected him
deeply, shot bolts of longing through his flesh, but he was a
man accustomed to giving what he wanted to give and
keeping what he wanted to keep, and he wasn't due for a
change. Not tonight. He reviewed his choices then moved in
closer, letting the water lap over his feet, giving her no-
where to retreat except into the sea.

"Hmmm," he said, placing his hands on her shoulders,
gripping her firmly when a touch would have held her just
as well. "Pointed questions, aren't they? Tell you what. I'll
make a bargain with you. Give me a rain check on those two
answers and I'll level with you about something else."

"What's that?" She shivered beneath his touch, indig-
nant at it but unwilling to pull away, finding she was at odds
both with herself and with him.

He watched her mouth. It had softened some and her eyes
had gone from cool to hot. He dug his fingers into her
shoulders, drawing her even closer. Beneath their feet the
tide was pulling loose the sand and shell and trying to sweep
them away as surely as the unnamed emotion between them
was.

His voice went hot in his throat. "At the moment I'm not
thinking about your uncle, or my aunt or the Frenchman."

She let the silence hang between them for a moment.
"What are you thinking about?" A foolish question. It was
the same thing she was thinking about—his lips on hers, a
burning need with no basis she could find, but there none-
theless.

"This," he said, proving her right by looping his fingers
in her hair and finding it as he anticipated, soft and fine as
silk thread. She didn't resist as he brought her up against
him or when he pulled her head back, lifting her face to the
onslaught of his mouth.

He whispered something before he kissed her. It didn't
matter what, she knew the meaning. She wound her arms

around his back; he released her hair and dropped his hands to her waist, tightening her against him. The right answers to everything would have to come later. There was no market here for the truth. The commodity of the moment was passion, pure and pleasurable, hot and burning, deep and demanding.

"Pierce." She whispered his name only to confirm what she was feeling, half acceptance, half denial that it could be. His body pressed hard against her, his mouth savagely explored her own.

Her taste was sweet and drugging. He would want more and more of her. He knew it the moment they came together. The feeling stirred deep, down into banked emotions he thought he'd put away for good. His need for her was strong. His heart thundered. His loins ached. She could definitely be habit-forming, and long ago he'd learned that habits equaled weakness.

She sighed. This was what she wanted, at least for this moment—to taste him, to feel his tongue curling against hers, to feel the faint rasp of his beard on her cheeks and chin. Electricity seemed to curl and arc from his body to hers and the response was overpowering. His hands played on her bared back, leaving a tingling trail on her skin, then fell to caress the curve of her hip. She looked up into a pair of eyes dark as umber, dark and alive with longing.

"What are we doing?" she whispered, catching a moment of sanity as she pulled away from his mouth.

"Ahh, Regina." Her name rolled caressingly from his lips, a sound like the wind rustling on a spring morning. "No more questions." His voice turned dark, rich and mellow. Now it made her think of fine brandy, soothing and fiery at the same time.

His hands, ever active, rounded over the curves of her buttocks, jolting her against him. She caught her breath. A combination of apprehension and reckless excitement coursed through her veins. He smelled faintly of sandal-wood, strongly of maleness and strength; his heat seeped through her clothes, a hot liquid fire, burning away what little reserve she had left.

Those brown eyes possessed her, moving over her body in a visual touch before he brought his lips back to her mouth. The urgency and hunger of his kiss spun into her. Wild thoughts raced through her head, thoughts that had nothing to do with who they were or why they were together. What she was thinking went to the very core of passion, as man does to woman. But even as she thought it, felt it, she knew this was more than pleasure, and once they'd come together neither would ever be quite the same again.

With a groan, he tore loose the sash that fastened her dress, thrusting the layers of pink cotton aside, thrusting his hands to her breasts, running them over the softness, the taut tips. He brought his mouth hungrily to the curve of her throat, then to her breasts. He could taste her sweetness there as he had on her lips, honeyed wine, potent, intoxicating.

He stripped off his shirt and dropped it to the water. The tide carried it away in an instant, but it had been a barrier to flesh against flesh. He lifted her from the water, crushing her soft nakedness to his chest, carrying her from the sea into the dark shadows of the beach.

She was startled, disappointed, when he set her down and pulled her dress together. But then she heard the ringing laughter of a trio of nighttime beachcombers. Turning, she saw them only a few yards away, nets and buckets in hand, lingering on the beach, showing no intention of leaving the pair of lovers alone.

"Come to my room," he whispered unsteadily, almost painfully. "Stay with me tonight." His hands grasped her arms tightly.

Yes leaped into her mind, unable to placate that innermost trembling in her body even now. "No," she said, pushing away and regaining something. It wasn't control; that wouldn't come back quickly or easily. What had made it possible for her to refuse was only a small unstable piece of resolve. "It's better if I don't."

"Better for what?" he challenged, dark eyes blazing. He closed her in his arms, making her fight the feelings again. "Better to deny what we both feel and want here? If those three hadn't come along you'd be making love with me now here in the sand and the moonlight."

He was right. "I don't deny that," she said, surprising him with her honesty. "I just don't know how I'd feel about it later. Somehow it's important for me to know that." She retied the sash and shook the tangles from her hair; he noted with satisfaction that the glow in her eyes remained. "I'm sure Blake's missed us by now. I'm going in. Are you coming with me?"

He laughed brittlely as he let her go. "It'd be difficult to explain if I did."

She saw what he meant. His shirt was somewhere in the Caribbean. He'd given his shoes to the tide, as well. His trousers were drenched to the knees, and there was a look on his face that would have been clear to anyone.

She crossed her arms over her chest, both to block him out and to hold her own tattered emotions in. "Perhaps we'll see you tomorrow."

He gave her a penetrating look that caused a strange shiver on the back of her neck. "I think it's inevitable."

She found her sandals not far away and quickly put them on. Leaving Pierce on the beach, she hurried back to the Buccaneer where she found Blake giving the bartender tips on concocting a new island drink. He had the man make one up for her, then took her to a table. The drink had a kick but she sipped it eagerly. She needed it.

"We went for a walk by the water," she said, combing a tangle from her hair with her fingers.

He cast her a strong look. "*In* the water sounds more accurate."

She glanced down at her skirt, seeing that at least four inches of it had been soaked by the ocean. She could only guess how the rest of her looked. Her lips still throbbed, her cheeks were probably flushed. At least he couldn't see the dull ache of suppressed passion she held inside.

"We did wade," she said, smiling, hoping her face wasn't as readable as Pierce's had been.

Blake patted her hand gingerly. "Not too deep, I hope."

Regina sighed. "We were talking."

"I see," he returned. "It must have been an animated conversation."

"In a way. We talked about you and his Aunt Monica. Tell me, have you been involved in any business deals with Monica Whitechurch?"

He stiffened. "Business deals? No, not really. Why do you ask?"

"Pierce seems to think his aunt has gotten into a bad one. He thinks she's worried but she refuses to talk about it. I got the impression he thinks you might know what it is."

"Does he?" Blake sat back in his chair. "That's interesting. But I'm afraid he's wrong. My relationship with Monica is only social. We met at a house party in London years ago and hit it off. She invited me to her annual summer fling and I've been going back ever since. We share an interest in art objects, so if I come across a piece I think would fit into her collections I send it to her. That's really the extent of our business."

"But you've never been involved in any investments together?"

"No. No. Nothing like that." He shook his silver head vigorously.

Regina laughed. "I knew it was preposterous."

"What?"

"You selling gilt-edged bogus stocks or bonds to little old ladies. I think that's what Pierce pictured."

"Humph," Blake mumbled. "He can't know Monica too well if he thinks she'd ever be hornswoggled by anyone."

"Then you don't think maybe she's getting senile."

He laughed. "Monica? Not a chance."

It was as Blake was ordering another tidal wave, the name he'd given to the drink he invented, that a message arrived from the Paradise Inn. He read it while Regina took a few more sips of the lethal liquid in her glass. She ought to ask him what was in this tidal wave, she thought, for it seemed to be delivering a few soggy punches to her brain. But not so many she couldn't see the instant flood of worry on Blake's face.

"What's wrong?" she asked.

"Nothing." His smile didn't clear all the worry off his face. "I asked the desk clerk at our hotel to relay any messages over here. Will you excuse me for just a minute? I have to make a call."

He left and Regina decided to try her luck with what remained of her drink. She could taste coconut and pineapple juice and detect a few other exotic elements. She decided it was aptly named, after feeling what a few more sips did to her head. Any more and she would be trying to swim back to the Paradise Inn. But at least the drink was helping her forget what had happened on the beach.

Blake had to go all the way to the front lobby to find a phone. It took several more minutes to get his call through.

"Surely you've had a cancellation by now. It's urgent I leave here immediately. Make one more check. Please. I don't care if it's a cargo plane." He drummed his fingers on the wall of the phone cubicle while he waited.

"Nothing."

"Yes, I've tried that." His face grim, he hung up and slowly made his way back to the lounge.

"You're worried about something," she said thickly as he took his seat at the table.

"I'm worried about you. You're half-sloshed."

"Your fault," she mumbled. "I was hit by a tidal wave."

He took a swallow from his drink. "The proportions may need a little adjustment."

Regina turned her hazy vision on him. "They need a big adjustment if the bar wants to sell more than one drink per customer."

Smiling, Blake pushed back his chair and got to his feet. "I think maybe it's time for us to turn in."

Regina yawned. "I think maybe you're right. Because if I'm not off my feet soon I'm going to fall asleep right here, which wouldn't be a very dignified thing for a doctor to do."

"It's amazing how spent you can be after a lazy day," Blake said, helping her get woozily to her feet.

"Not to mention after drinking a tidal wave," she added.

Pierce spent a miserable hour jogging on the beach. It took all the reserves of determination he had not to burst into the Buccaneer lounge and drag her out. Drenched with sweat, he cursed all women in general and one in particular. After racing himself to near exhaustion, he returned to his room to douse his heated body under the cold spray of the shower. But the hot flow of desire didn't stop even with that.

Damn her! He would make her pay for dragging him too far inside himself and opening a hunger he wasn't sure could be satisfied by a simple physical act.

Chapter 6

I've ordered coffee in my room. Come on, I think you can do with a cup," Blake said, guiding Regina past the door to her room, around a hibiscus bush and on to the next door.

She laughed, snapping off a fuchsia blossom as she went by and tucked it behind one ear. She wasn't sure which one.

"Anything to dilute this poison you've fed me."

Blake, keeping one eye on her unsteady progress, pulled the key from his pocket and slid it into the keyhole, only to find the door wasn't locked.

"Guess I'm getting careless," he mumbled. Stepping in ahead of Regina he swept his hand over the light switch, getting nothing but a dull click. "Watch your step," he called over his shoulder. "The bulb must have blown. I'll turn on the bedside lamp."

Regina eased inside not terribly certain she had the balance to navigate in the dark. Knowing there were steps just past the closet, as there were in her room, she slid one hand along the wall until it made contact with the short rail beside the steps.

"Damn! What's all this?" she heard Blake grumble before she tested the floor with her foot for the first step down. At the same moment a sinewy arm shot out of the closet, clamping around her chest and slamming her backward into a rock-hard body.

"Blake!" She managed to get out only his name before a second arm appeared wielding a wicked-looking knife directly in front of her face, the deadly tip of it only inches away from her eye. She tasted fear before she felt the numbing fury of it.

"Stay where you are, Regina," Blake called out from the bedroom. "The lamp's broken and this place has been ransacked. We need to get out of here quickly."

The man holding her tightened his grip, jerking his arm up so that the steel bands of his forearm pressed against her throat, half closing her windpipe. The icy blade of the knife now lay against her cheek. She knew he meant for her to keep quiet and gave him no cause to think she wouldn't cooperate.

Blake, cursing in both French and English, stumbled back in their direction. "We're leaving here in the morning if we have to use a rowboat to get off this island. Get your things packed..." He paused midsentence, realizing she'd been silent a long time. "Regina!" His voice registered alarm. "Where are you?"

Blake's shadowy form moved in the darkness, slowly, cautiously. She wanted to warn him back but couldn't. There was only pain in her throat, no words would form. Her eyes, wide with terror, hadn't even blinked since the knife blade touched her. For the first few seconds she'd turned to stone and felt nothing, but now the fear gushed through her like a raging river let loose.

Other elements of awareness came back, too. The man holding her was tall and he knew his business. Something was familiar about the solid threatening power of the body jammed against her, but she was too frightened for that thought to be more than a twitter in her mind.

"Stay where you are, Andrews. I have the girl." The voice rumbled from the chest of her captor, rough, muffled, or maybe it was the pounding fear in her ears that made it impossible to place.

"Regina! Are you all right?" Desperation shook Blake's voice.

The man shoved her forward so Blake could see her helplessness. "She has nothing to say," her captor taunted. "Talk to me."

"Who are you? What do you want?" Blake demanded.

His voice grated. "You don't need to know who I am. You already know what I want. I didn't find it here. Where is it? Does the woman have it?"

"No!" Blake burst forward one step, then realized he was making a mistake and fell back. "She knows nothing about it. Let her go. We'll talk."

The laughter chilled her blood. She felt the arm stiffen across her waist as she gulped for breath. "I had in mind a trade."

"Regina?"

More cold laughter spilled out of him. "Think fast, Mr. Andrews, I haven't got all night. Where is it?"

"Not here." Blake's voice broke. He could see the glittering blade and the ruthless grip of her captor.

"How long will it take you to get it?" She felt angry impatience building in the man.

"A few minutes." Blake's eyes stayed fixed on the knife. He dared not move without permission.

"We'll wait."

"And then?"

"You'll have to take your chances. They'll be better than they are now."

Regina felt faint. He wasn't letting much air get through, maybe not much blood, either. Her mind wasn't working right. What could Blake have that was worth this desperate act? Why did she feel she knew this man? She couldn't know anyone so vicious, so cold, so deadly.

He must have sensed her fading out. He released the pressure on her neck a little. She choked on a gasp of air, and felt the frantic rush of blood to her brain. She was going to have a killer headache tomorrow—if she was alive.

The call from the doorway jolted them all, and her captor tightened his arm on her neck again. He dragged her down the steps and toward the French doors.

"Mr. Andrews!" It came again with a loud knock that shattered the brittle air. "Coming in, Mr. Andrews."

The man, swearing like a demon, shoved Regina into Blake's arms, the momentum throwing both of them to the floor. Before either could get up, he'd fled through the French doors and disappeared into the heavy foliage of the courtyard.

"Are you hurt?" Blake cried, a spasm of panic in his voice as he helped her to her feet. She leaned heavily on him to avoid crumpling again; her legs had lost the ability to hold her. "I'm sorry, very sorry to have caused this for you," he said.

She couldn't answer. Her throat was tight and dry and locked. But when she could talk, Blake had plenty of explaining to do.

The corridor door swung open, but it showed the bellman nothing more than a room that looked as if the wildest party in the Caribbean had been held in it. Regina huddled in a fan-backed chair, face in her hands, and Blake leaned over her. The bellman, though young, was trained well enough to know not to linger when people and a place looked like that. He set the coffee tray on the floor just inside the door and retreated without even waiting for a tip.

Blake poured two cups of black, strong coffee. Regina held one in trembling hands and gulped a few swallows.

"We have to call the police," she told him.

He shook his head. "We can't. This isn't like home. The laws are different, the police are different. If we report this they'll hold us here for days while they conduct an investigation. We can't even tell them anything was stolen. The safest thing for us to do is get out of here as quickly as possible."

She gave him a dubious look. What was it Pierce had said about finding out you don't really know people as well as you think, even relatives?

Regina imposed a stalwart control on herself. "Is that really the reason you don't want the police?"

"We have to leave here." He moved around while he talked, picking up clothes, pushing in drawers. After a few minutes he stopped and gave her a pleading look, his face chalky white. He'd been as frightened as she had.

"Did you know the man?" Did she? Why couldn't she stop thinking he was familiar? It seemed like paranoia, but she couldn't erase the thought that the burglar in Atlanta and this man were one and the same.

"No." Blake shook his head as he hoisted the mattress back onto the bed frame.

Regina gulped down more coffee as a frightening thought came to mind. "Do you think he'll try again?" she asked grimly, hoping Blake would tell her it must have been a terrible mistake.

Blake gave an empty sigh and stopped throwing things back in place. He came to the chair beside her and sat down. "Not if I can make the right moves first."

"You do know what he wanted?"

He rubbed his temples, then slid his nervous fingers through his hair. "Yes."

Her shadowed face implored. "Are you going to tell me what it is?"

"Regina." He was battling with himself. She could see that in the pained gray eyes. "It's better if you don't know."

She forced a stiff smile. "That sounds like a line from a B-movie."

"It's true."

"All right," she said. "I won't pursue it now, but only because I'm too shaken tonight to think I could handle anything else. But later I'll want an explanation. You owe me an explanation, if you expect me to come this close to being murdered and not report it."

"What I want," he said, taking her hands and squeezing them anxiously, "is to get you away from here as fast as possible so you'll be safe and nothing like this can happen again. Believe me."

"I do believe you," she said, finding her voice small and childlike. "Why else would I agree to this craziness?"

He got up, paced around, picked up a few more of his things, then turned back to her. "I'll sleep in your room tonight."

She nodded. "I won't argue with you. I'm not feeling particularly brave."

That was the understatement of the decade. She didn't know if she would ever feel safe again. The trembling had stopped but the fear lingered like a bitter aftertaste. She'd been through this twice in less than a month. It didn't exactly reassure her that the world was a safe place.

Twice. She returned to that thought. Two break-ins. It was difficult to believe there could be a connection when they'd occurred thousands of miles apart. Anyway, this one had involved Blake, she'd only been involved because she happened to be with him. She remembered Lieutenant

Langley's warnings to be more cautious. Somehow those stinging admonishments had a ring of comfort.

Regina awoke early the next morning, the sharp cries of gulls fishing for breakfast near the beach serving as her alarm. Blake was asleep in a chair as she crawled out of bed. She tiptoed to the window and raised the straw shade halfway to peer out at another gorgeous Caribbean day. The early sunlight scattered diamonds on the ocean's surface. Sugar-white sand, washed free of footprints by the tide, gleamed behind the receding water. The water was so blue, so pure, it competed with the sky for perfection. Eden had been like this, she thought.

She smelled the fresh perfume of newly opened blossoms, heard the songs of tree frogs and birds welcoming the day. Something in her welcomed it, too. It was impossible to be surrounded by peace and beauty and be unmoved by it, almost impossible to believe what had happened last night could have happened here. If Blake hadn't been there to remind her it had been real she could have convinced herself the incident had been a nightmare.

She lifted her hand slowly to her cheek. Last night she'd had to look in the mirror to be sure the print of the blade wasn't still there. She did so again. Blake stirred and moaned. She looked at him. He must feel as if he'd been tied in knots having been cramped in that chair all night.

"How are you?" he asked, stretching his arms, wincing with the effort.

"Not bad." She smiled wanly. "I slept."

His eyes sped to his watch. "Seven," he said to himself and her. "I'm going back to my room to pack. I'll call and get us transportation to the airport. You call room service and order some breakfast. Make mine light."

She headed for the bathroom when Blake was gone, showered quickly and packed her toiletries in her makeup bag. She decided on white linen slacks and a green silk blouse for traveling, realizing as she hustled around the room gathering her clothes from the closet and drawers that she didn't even know where Blake planned to go. She really didn't like the idea of running away; it offended her, particularly since she didn't know just who and what they were trying to get away from.

When all her things were in her bag, she made the call to room service, ordering a light breakfast for both of them. Her appetite was suffering, too, but she didn't think it would be wise to eat nothing at all.

Blake returned shortly after the breakfast tray was delivered. He'd showered and changed, but fresh clothes and a shave hadn't removed the worry from his eyes or taken away the grim set of his mouth. Frowning, he pulled a second chair up to the little table by the French doors in her room and sat down.

"The only flight open is to Martinique. I booked us on it. We can take a launch from there."

Regina considered what he was saying as she poured coffee for each of them. "Just where is it we're trying to get to?" she asked.

He speared a piece of papaya with his fork and held it in midair for a moment. "I called Monica," he said. "We'll go on to Dominica early. No one's likely to look for me there."

Regina added milk to her coffee. She intended to remain calm about this no matter what Blake said. "Who is looking for you?"

He frowned. "I can't be completely sure. That French agent is watching me. There must be someone else, as well." Blake put down his cup and reached across the table to take her hands. "Regina, I'm sorry." His voice broke. "The last thing I ever wanted was to get you involved in anything dangerous."

It was the last thing she wanted, too, for either of them. But here they were the morning after a horrifying attack, and she had no idea why it had happened. Now she wanted answers.

"I could be less upset about that if I knew just what's going on," she insisted. "It's time you told me."

He sat back and lit a cigarette. "I suppose it is," he said reluctantly. "It's just that it all started so innocently. If I'd known the complications I'd never have gotten involved myself. Certainly I wouldn't have let it get so far that you were involved." He made a helpless gesture with his hands. "Even now I can only guess at the facts." He stopped to blow out a cloud of smoke.

"So tell me your guesses," Regina said impatiently.

He hesitated a moment longer, then went on. "In France," he said, "I met a young woman. She reminded me of you a little, I think. We became friends—just friends. She had a lover, a married man. He was extravagant with her, gave her money, clothes, jewelry, helped her move along in her career. In France it isn't so unusual to have a mistress," he added. "But something happened between them. They had a fight, she broke off with him. She was upset and wanted to dispose of the jewelry he'd given her—quietly. She asked me to help." He drew heavily on his cigarette.

"Why you?" Regina pushed aside her toast. Her appetite had dwindled to nothing.

Blake shrugged as if it should be obvious. "Because I was her friend and she knew she could trust me."

Regina tried her coffee but found she'd lost her taste for that, as well. "Go on," she said.

"Most of the jewelry was unexceptional," he said, crushing out his cigarette in an ashtray. "I was able to sell it in Paris. However, there was one prize piece, an exquisite diamond necklace, very old and very valuable—an heirloom. I was surprised. It was from his wife's family. I asked my friend if she was sure about selling that one. But she was certain." Blake lit a second cigarette.

"You sold it?"

"No. This piece required a special buyer. Special arrangements had to be made, which takes time. You must understand this particular necklace had a history—like Josephine's tiara, or the crown jewels. It couldn't pop up just anywhere."

Her brows lifted quickly. If what she knew about such things was true, not just anyone could sell a piece of jewelry like that. It took someone with the right connections, someone with experience. Was Blake telling her this was one of his . . . talents?

"Then you still have it?"

She didn't like what she was seeing in his eyes as he shook his head. "No, but I know where it is."

"Then why don't you just get rid of it?"

He was halfway through another cigarette and blowing smoke with every word. "It isn't that simple," he said. "Not anymore. You see, the young woman who gave it to me has since been murdered."

"Murdered," she repeated, then deliberately attempting to stay calm, went on. "Let me guess. By someone wanting to get the necklace."

The frown that had been on his face since the conversation began, deepened. "That's what I think."

This was getting worse, much, much worse. "And you think that's what the man in your room last night wanted?"

"I'm sure of it."

The tone of her voice went flat. "You could have given it to him, and all this would be over."

"No," he said sadly. "If he'd gotten his hands on the necklace, neither of us would be alive this morning."

She could feel her heart thumping louder as the color drained from her face. "I think you'd better tell me everything."

"I wish I knew everything. I wish I'd never seen that necklace." He swore. "What I *do* know is this. The girl's married lover is a man high in the government. His position, his money, everything he has, came to him because of his wife, and the necklace belongs to her. She won't be pleased to learn it's missing. A wife may turn her head at a mistress, but at the loss of diamonds such as these..." He threw up his hands.

"Then why did the man give it away? Surely he knew."

"Who knows what happened? Perhaps in a fit of passion, he gave the necklace to his mistress. But if his wife finds it's gone he could be finished, professionally and personally."

"I don't quite understand this." She touched the back of his hand. "Why can't you just send the necklace back to him?"

"Because I don't know who's trying so hard to find it. If it's the official himself and he's already had his mistress killed, he won't want anyone else left alive who could talk about it. If it's someone who wants to see this man toppled from office, I'd never get near him with it. The only chance I have is to get the necklace to someone I know I can trust." He smiled ineffectively. "Right now I don't know who that is."

She thought of Marot. This was surely why he sought Blake. "The French police," she said. "They're here. You can talk to them. They can help you."

He shook his head. "How can I be sure they aren't corrupt? This thing goes very deep in the government. Important people are involved."

"Then let's go back to the States. We can get help there."

"No," he said. "Not yet. I've started making some arrangements. I need to get to Dominica to carry them through. I think you ought to go with me. But Regina, believe me, I had no idea when I arranged this trip anything like this could happen. At the time putting the necklace in the hands of a buyer seemed a simple transaction."

"I'm glad to hear that."

"When you told me that the French police were here, I still wasn't too worried. It wasn't until I learned the girl had been murdered that I knew there was serious trouble. I made some calls to France and found out what I could. The rest of it is just my guess. But . . ."

"You don't have to convince me that we're both in danger," she said flatly. "I was the one the man held the knife to."

"I'll never forgive myself for getting you involved." The agony in his voice struck her sympathy.

"We'll worry about that later. Right now let's just take care of—"

The ringing of the phone startled them both. Regina listened to it for two more rings, then picked up the receiver.

"Hello," she said.

"Regina."

"Pierce." Surprised, she covered the mouthpiece with her hand and whispered to Blake. "It's Pierce."

Blake nodded and rose from his chair. He strolled around the room as she talked, pausing at the bed beside her open suitcase. He looked methodically inside, then seeing she was apparently finished with her packing, closed the lid and snapped it shut.

"I'm glad I caught you before you went out," Pierce said. "Listen, it's just a thought, but I'm flying my plane on to Dominica later this morning. I wondered if you and Blake might like to hitch a ride and go down a few days early. What do you think?"

Coincidence again? Her brows furrowed in a frown. "Blake's here," she said hurriedly. "Let me check with him." Covering the mouthpiece with her hand again, she relayed the message to Blake.

"Tell him yes," Blake whispered. "It'll be difficult to trace us out of here on a private plane."

"He says that'll be nice," Regina went on calmly. "How soon are you leaving? In three hours. We'll meet you at the airport. Tell me where." She made a note of the information and hung up.

"That's a stroke of luck," Blake said, lighting still another cigarette.

"Yes it is," Regina agreed. A very convenient one.

Two hours later a cab whisked them back across the island to the airport. Regina felt as if her stay on Antigua had been little more than a layover. Certainly it had been a poor start for a vacation. And one last time before they boarded Pierce's plane, she asked Blake if he was sure they shouldn't contact the local police.

"You're certain this is the right decision?"

"I'm certain it's the *only* decision," he responded, warning her by cutting his eyes toward the front not to say anything the cab driver might misinterpret.

Frowning, she slumped back against the seat. She had other worries, too, some very clear, others she couldn't quite get a handle on. Last night she'd almost allowed herself to be completely swept away by a man she knew only casually, a man she had reason to believe had contrived, for not particularly admirable reasons, to meet her in the first place. Now she couldn't get it out of her mind that his reason for approaching her somehow tied in with this other business concerning Blake. Everything was just too well-timed not to be connected.

She didn't want to believe Pierce had deliberately arranged the details of their acquaintance, even down to that moonlight walk on the beach, simply as a means of investigating her uncle. Considering the way she'd felt, and the ease with which she could have found herself making love with the man, she didn't like the way it looked. Could he possibly have anything to do with that situation in France? He'd mentioned starting a project in the wine country, but somehow the conversation had never gotten back to what was involved. Suppose Pierce was dealing with the same official who wanted to recover the necklace. Suppose he was doing a favor for a favor.

If that were the case he would try again.

She wondered if Blake had the necklace with him. Odd she hadn't thought to ask him that before. She would. Soon. Well, maybe not soon. They might not have a private moment again before arriving in Dominica. As for Mr. Buchannan, he wouldn't be the only one doing a little investigating.

The cab pulled up to the airport drop-off zone. Regina could see why Blake had had trouble getting reservations anywhere. The terminal was swamped with members of an international travel club arriving for and departing from an ongoing convention. Fortunately she and Blake wouldn't have to fight the crowd since they were traveling by private plane. Within minutes the two of them had passed through the building and were being shown to the twin-engine Cessna where Pierce waited.

"Right on time," he called, climbing down out of the cockpit and directing the placement of their bags. "Sorry the plane's a little crowded. I'm taking in some supplies for Monica, things she has trouble getting. Dominica's off the main shipping routes so we utilize my trips in and out by plane. I haven't been much good to her this year so I'm making up for it today." He stuffed a few bills into the hand of the man who'd loaded the luggage. "One of you can sit back there." He indicated the passenger area filled by cargo except for one seat. "The other will have to take the co-pilot's seat up front."

"You take the seat up front if you don't mind, Regina," Blake said. "Maybe I can get a little sleep back here."

"Thanks heaps," she whispered under her breath as she climbed on board.

Blake climbed in after her and strapped himself into the passenger seat. Pierce gave Regina a hand with a troublesome seat belt and she found herself shrinking away from his touch. Fortunately, he didn't seem to notice that she felt any awkwardness at finding herself in the tiny cabin with him. But then he didn't know her skepticism about him and his motives.

"All set?" he asked, adjusting his headset.

She nodded yes, but not without reservations. She did have a few uneasy moments, thinking it might not be wise to go up in a plane with a man she didn't trust. But then she reasoned that he couldn't very well do them any harm while he was piloting the plane.

For the next few minutes Pierce was occupied testing the engine and getting clearance to take off. Once they were airborne, Regina was too absorbed by the beautiful aquamarine sweep of the ocean and the jewel-like dots of the islands beneath them to worry. She said a silent goodbye to paradise, wishing her stay hadn't been so brief or so ill-fated.

A glance back through the cabin door confirmed that Blake indeed intended to sleep. Already his eyes were closed, and his chest rose and fell with deep, steady breaths.

Alone with the wolves, she thought as the plane continued to climb. Pierce motioned for her to look out the window. She did and was soon lost in watching the ever changing, ever more beautiful cloudscapes. As far as she could see the horizons of heaven were marked only by the billowing masses of white floating freely in the azure sky.

Reflected rays of golden sunlight revealed the radiance of fluffy contours and curves of white meadows and hills suspended high above earthly reality. To look through the double-glassed portal of the plane made her want to leap, to run, to roll through the feathery mists. Only the silver tip of the wing stretching out to mar the illusion, checked the mind from believing it had defied the laws of nature.

Soon the serenity of the slumbering puffs soothed her frazzled emotions. As the tenseness left her muscles and nerves she shifted her attention to Pierce, who was still busy checking gauges and readouts. He fit into his pilot's seat as one might into a well-worn glove, handling the plane with expertise and evident enjoyment. Regina watched him, put at ease by his competence, telling herself there wasn't much else to look at in the plane, discounting the fact that she found him particularly eye-pleasing in his khaki trousers and shirt.

"Do you like it?" he asked, swinging around to look at her and wearing his characteristic half grin.

"Like what?" she shot back. Unless he'd gone into mind reading she didn't know what he meant.

"Flying."

It occurred to her flying was something he probably did as much for pleasure as for necessity. "I guess I've never given it much thought. On a commercial flight you're hardly aware you're off the ground. But this is different. It's . . ."

"Special." He supplied the word she was looking for. "I was a Navy pilot. Used to fly jets. Actually, those fighter planes almost fly themselves. I like this better. The plane needs me. Without me it doesn't stay up here. In the fighters I always felt secondary to the computer systems."

"Is that your way of saying you're an uncomplicated man?"

He laughed. "I don't know if I'd put it quite like that. Maybe it's just that getting up here is my way of getting away from it all."

"So you feel the need to get away from everything sometimes?" He was making it easy for her to lead the conversation in the direction she wanted to go. "I'm surprised.

Last night I got the impression you found your work totally satisfying.''

He raised a brow as if amused. "Is that what you remember about last night?"

She felt heat in her cheeks but there was no help for it. "I remember everything about last night," she said bluntly. "Even that you never got around to telling me about your new project in France."

"My apologies." His grin widened. "I got sidetracked."

She refused to snap at the bait and plunged ahead toward what she wanted to know. "I find it interesting that you plan to put a resort in the wine country. It seems a rather out-of-the-way place for anything on such a large scale."

"That's what I'm counting on to make it a success. It would be either on or near the grounds of an operational winery, a place geared completely for relaxation. Not quite a spa but with those features for those who want it."

"It sounds good. Do you ever have trouble getting governments to approve foreign investment and development?"

"Sometimes. We have to show we're going to benefit the local economy and that we aren't putting in something that will adversely affect the area's ecology. The third-world countries surprisingly offer the most resistance. Sometimes we have to do everything short of bribery to get the officials to agree."

"That doesn't bother you?" she asked, narrowing her eyes. "Coming just short of bribery."

"No." There was a nearly imperceptible change in his expression. "Bribery's a subjective term. Maybe sometimes we go just a little past it. It doesn't bother me if I know in the end we'll be putting a whole village to work and doubling or tripling the local standard of living."

Along with your own profits, she thought, almost glad the plane had run into some minor turbulence and Pierce was occupied with guiding it through. Had she hit on the truth? That Pierce wasn't above padding someone's pocket or perhaps taking care of a piece of untidy business to get what he wanted. He was persuasive. She could attest to that. Was he ruthless as well?

Dark clouds built overhead as the plane approached the thick mountain jungles of Dominica. Even as an inexperienced flier she knew they had only a few minutes to get down before the storm moved in from the sea and struck the island. There was no airport in view as they crossed overland, just an unbelievable number of hills and trees and whispers of mists wrapped around the mountaintops.

"That highest peak is Morne Diablotin, almost five thousand feet," Pierce commented as the plane dropped below the mountain.

He drew quiet as he steered the aircraft in, decreasing altitude until it appeared they would crash into the tops of palm trees close by. Regina held her breath, wondering where he was putting them down. Momentarily she saw the small landing strip beside a broad river. Beyond the river a solid wall of green vegetation trailed long, looping vines into the flowing water. The runway stopped where the ocean began. Only an expert pilot could land a plane here.

It occurred to her as the wheels touched down with the smoothness of a gliding bird, that she no longer had qualms about trusting her safety to Pierce Buchannan.

Chapter 7

The air was rich and thick beneath a sky rapidly changing from bright blue to the gray of rain clouds. Dominica made Regina think of being in a terrarium. She could feel the misty air touching her skin as she climbed out of the plane onto the cracked concrete of the runway. Heavy green plant life threatened to reclaim the very airstrip on which she and Pierce and Blake stood waiting for a cart to be rolled out to take the baggage and cargo to customs. To intensify her impressions, the heavy tropical downpour that had been threatening for the past half hour started before they could reach the Mellville Hall terminal. Soaked to the skin they dashed inside the small building.

She saw at once the terminal was nothing like Antigua's busy, tourist-packed airport. No more than a dozen people were inside, and half of them were either customs or operations staff. Besides private aircraft, only a few flights a day landed at Mellville Hall. Two or three Americans were there waiting for afternoon departures, and Pierce identified them as students from a small medical college located on the island. Regina tucked that bit of information away thinking that later she might like to make a visit to the school. It should be interesting to compare the program here to her own days studying medicine.

Once through customs, Pierce found Thomas, who'd been sent from Whitechurch in a silver minivan to pick them up. She'd thought landing on the tiny airstrip a hair-raising adventure until they made the twenty-five-mile drive across the island with Thomas at the wheel. The road was hardly more than a trail carved from steep cliffs that continued to slough off mud and rubble during heavy rain. On the other side, perhaps twenty or thirty feet below, the ocean roared and crashed against the rocks.

The narrow road wound along the side of the mountain like a corkscrew, at points having washouts large enough to swallow a car. For part of the journey, while Pierce, up front with Thomas, was busy catching up on things, Regina could do nothing but grip the edge of her seat and close her eyes.

"You'll get used to it," Blake reassured her. "This is the main road."

Regina braved a look out the window only to confirm what she feared, that the car tires were running within inches of the edge. "I'll never get used to this," she insisted. "If you recall I never liked roller coasters."

Blake laughed. In spite of her nervousness, she noted that he was putting on a very good front for a man in rather desperate trouble. She wondered if it was for her or for Pierce.

The rain continued to fall in torrents, but Thomas kept up a relentless pace on the road. When he turned into a narrow lane beneath a sign reading Whitechurch Plantation, Regina breathed a gratified sigh of relief.

"Monica will be annoyed," Pierce told her as he helped her out of the van and led the way into the house. "She likes impressing her guests, even with the weather. It's certainly been uncooperative today. Usually this afternoon rain is only a light twenty-minute shower."

Shielding her eyes, she hunched her shoulders against the rain. "I hope your aunt has a propensity for bedraggled cats. I'm sure that's what we all look like."

The three of them hurried up the paved walk. It wasn't possible to tell much about the house, except that it was white and rambling and low to the ground. Only two steps led up to a sort of sweeping veranda where at last they were out of the downpour. Regina shook and squeezed the excess water from her hair, but her silk shirt and linen trousers clung to her more like wet paint than clothes. She saw, with satisfaction, that Blake and Pierce didn't look any better.

There wasn't, in fact, much of Pierce's well-muscled body that wasn't revealed through his rain-soaked clothes. His shirt was papered against him showing every contour, even the shadow of the patch of hair on his chest. Swinging her eyes toward the painted white door, she forced back a memory less than twenty-four hours old and resisted the sudden stir.

The door was flung open by a small elderly woman in a pale green and yellow voile dress. One hand rested on a cane. With a fluttering sleeve and a motion that immediately made Regina think of butterflies, she waved them inside.

"Please come in," she said softly, first beaming a smile to Regina, then giving her nephew a recriminating look. "For goodness sakes, Pierce, haven't you heard of umbrellas? They were in the car."

"Sorry, didn't think about them, love," he told her. "We were already soaked anyway." He pretended he was about to give her a hug, then laughed as she frowned and motioned him away.

"Don't be a nuisance. You'll spoil my dress," she chided, though her dark eyes revealed affection for her nephew. Turning, she took Blake's hand. "I'm so glad you could come early. It'll give us some time together before the crowd arrives." Even as she finished her sentence her attention flew to Regina. "And you're lovely, my dear. I can tell that even when you're soaking wet. Edie—" she whirled around calling to the maid "—take Dr. Lawton and Mr. Andrews to their rooms. I'm sure they want to get into dry clothes." She brought her eyes back to the two of them. "Thomas will have your bags here in a moment."

"Thank you," Regina said, feeling an immediate liking for Monica Whitechurch. She apologized for all of them having made puddles on the stone floor, then hurried off after Edie and Blake while Pierce lingered for a few more words with Monica.

He watched Regina walk away, enjoying the sudden rise of desire in his body. She was the farthest thing imaginable from a bedraggled cat. There was something feline about her all right, the smooth, easy walk, the graceful moves, the way her eyes came suddenly alive with excitement, the way they glowed with pleasure in the dark. The need for her still lingered inside him, banked but insistent. He had unfinished business with Dr. Regina Lawton, which he intended to take care of soon, and somewhere there would be no chance of an interruption.

Under other circumstances he might have been tempted to be honest with her. She knew things weren't quite what they seemed. He had the feeling she was both smart and straight, involved in this mess only by chance. Maybe she could understand that he'd been put in a position of having to do things he really didn't want to do. Maybe she could accept that. And maybe she couldn't. What he needed was caution. He couldn't afford to give in to that yearning to bare his soul to her. Blake was her uncle and she was obviously devoted to him. It was hard to predict just how far off course even an honest person would go to protect a loved one.

Still dripping, Regina followed Edie through a series of corridors. One large wing of the house, she discovered, was entirely guest rooms. It was there Edie led them. Regina's spacious room was pink and white, the floor covered with handmade grass rugs. She imagined every bedroom in the Caribbean had a set of doors leading out onto a patio or into a garden. This one was no exception, although because of the rain the doors were shut and the blinds closed over them. The room had a private bath of pink ceramic tile, not large but certainly adequate.

Monica had said she would have tea ready in an hour. That gave Regina time for a leisurely shower and for unpacking. Refreshed from the warm water and a vigorous rub with a bath sheet, she began to empty her bags. As she carefully placed her belongings in the dresser drawers she came across the small gift box containing the silver swan. It was no wonder, but Blake had forgotten all about having the inscription done in Antigua. To her regret there hadn't been time or opportunity to do any of the things they'd planned.

All she could hope for now was that soon things would be back to normal, that Blake could quickly bring this unpleasant affair to an end. While her mind ran over the recent chain of events, she absently took the music box out of the packing and wound the key underneath. Since it was here she might as well enjoy it.

Later, dressed in beige trousers and a yellow sweater and with her damp hair pulled back and tied with a ribbon, Regina felt much better. She was about to leave her room when something shook the straw shade over the window. A cat.

She'd heard there was black magic in the islands. Had thinking about cats conjured up one?

"Here, kitty," she called. The white Persian, larger than Marley but very much like him, jumped to the floor, and purring, walked over to her. "You don't like getting wet, either, do you?" she asked, on the way to the bathroom. She got a towel and rubbed the animal's fur dry while he stretched out and enjoyed the attention. Realizing it was time for tea, she opened the door and left. The cat followed.

"So you've gotten acquainted with Winston," Monica said, greeting her in the den. "Don't let him annoy you."

"We're old friends," Regina assured her, giving Winston one last stroke before he ambled out of the room.

Monica Whitechurch, Regina determined, was very British. Tea was an event of the day, complete with biscuits, scones, jam and clotted cream. Everything was delicious and she didn't have any trouble taking seconds.

The house proved to be something of an oddity. The main structure was old and had been added to over the years, which gave it its rambling appearance. Walls inside and out were of white stucco, and the furnishings were eclectic, some antique English pieces interspersed with those locally made of rattan and bamboo. Everywhere were the collections Blake had mentioned. Monica had diverse tastes. There were numerous paintings, heavy silver bowls and pitchers, small boxes, Chinese vases and European figurines. The figurines apparently were her real weakness. She didn't seem to give as much thought to value as to style. Ceramic, silver, bronze, porcelain. Some were worth only a few dollars, others must have ranged into the thousands.

Regina paused beside a table holding an assortment of boxes.

"Blake recently sent me the onyx and ivory one," Monica said, smiling sweetly at Blake.

Regina picked up the cup-size onyx box and turned it over in her hands. The hinged lid had been carved and inlaid with a geometric design of ivory bars. "It's lovely."

"I rather thought you'd like it," Monica said without lifting her eyes from her tea.

Regina rubbed her fingers on the smooth polished stone. "I've always had a fondness for onyx," she said, replacing the box on the tabletop. "Blake once sent me an onyx cat from Mexico."

"He's always thoughtful. It's the thing I like most about him," Monica insisted, patting the sofa seat beside her and inviting Regina to sit there.

Regina quickly learned that Monica was as shrewd as she was charming. She ran her large plantation with hardly a hitch. At Regina's insistence she told of how she'd had to step in after her husband's death and take over.

"It wasn't long after the war," she said, waving in Edie to take the tea things. "The banana trade with England was booming. John, my late husband, planted double the number of trees we'd had before. He hired more workers. When he died everything was invested in the plantation. I had to keep it running. Women weren't supposed to do such things. I had to learn fast, but it was either that or lose all he'd worked for. Somehow I've managed to stay afloat since."

"She's modest," Pierce interjected. "In the seventies, when the bottom fell out of the banana market, other plantations folded, some older than Whitechurch. Monica switched to other commodities and managed to stay solvent."

"I was lucky," Monica said with a sweep of her hand.

"You were smart," Pierce insisted, then turning to Regina added, "Whitechurch is the best plantation on Dominica. You'll be amazed."

"I'm anxious to see more of it," Regina said. She was accustomed to Georgia's fields of soybeans and peanuts and cotton. But to see bananas, breadfruit, coconuts and vanilla vines growing and harvested would be a new experience.

"Pierce can show you," Monica said, making it a gentle command. "He's a very good guide. His specialty is making property appear attractive."

Pierce flashed a quick grin at his aunt. "I plan to take Regina on a tour of the entire island."

Regina gave Pierce an assessing look. That definitely sounded as much like a threat as an invitation, but it brought a little whir of excitement to her blood. Odd. From a man she had doubts about, it didn't sound like such a bad idea.

"Monica, I'm getting old," Blake said on a note of despair. It was late, an hour after everyone had gone to bed that he'd made his way to Monica's sitting room.

"I find that remark in especially bad taste, considering that you're twenty years younger than I." Monica poured Scotch into a glass and handed it to Blake. "Here, take this. It should make you feel better. It's older than both of us."

"How can you joke?" he said sternly. "After what I've gotten us into."

"Maybe because I don't know enough of the details to be as worried as you are, and because I'm enough older to realize every problem eventually has a solution." She poured a generous amount of Scotch into her own glass. "You'd better tell me what else has happened."

Blake began an account of what had occurred on Antigua. Monica listened through it all without interrupting until he mentioned the necklace.

She put her glass aside. "Have you gotten any information about who wants it so badly?"

"No. It's hard to do that and try to keep my location a secret. I don't want to lead anyone here," he said apologetically. "And that's it to date," he added. "Other than what you already know."

Monica tapped her cane on the floor, waking Winston, the white Persian cat under her chair. "What did you tell Regina?"

Blake exhaled heavily. "As little as I could to satisfy her. I had to tell her something after that attack. By the way, thanks for helping get us off Antigua so quickly."

Monica's narrow white brows rose. "What do you mean?"

"I mean Pierce, the plane. After I called you this morning and told you we were flying out, didn't you arrange for him to invite us down early?"

"No." She shook her head, looking worried for the first time since Blake had come to her room. "He called me first and suggested doing that."

The frown on Blake's face deepened. "Do you think he knew we were in trouble?"

She sniffed. "I know he's had his nose where it shouldn't have been."

"Now that you mention it." Blake considered. "It's strange he should have met Regina by chance in Atlanta and then show up in Antigua while we were there." He reached for his cigarettes. "Doesn't that seem strange to you?"

She nodded.

"What do you think he's after?" Blake blew out a puff of smoke, which Monica fanned away.

"Whitechurch Plantation, I suppose. And seeing that his old aunt doesn't lose it before she dies. Property value on this island is going to skyrocket in a few years. It's one of the few remaining Caribbean islands not filled with luxury hotels, casinos and duty-free shops. Imagine what a resort developer would do with it."

Blake moaned and put aside the cigarette to take a sip of his drink. "Aside from this, is everything arranged?"

Monica smiled. "Completely. Everything's done."

"You don't think Pierce will cause trouble?" Blake frowned. "All we need is one more thing to worry about."

Monica chuckled and took a swallow from her glass. "I'm not worried about Pierce Buchannan in the least."

The previous day of sight-seeing had been delightful. In that short time Regina had come to feel safe. Blake had assured her it would be extremely difficult for anyone to learn of their departure from Antigua—he hadn't canceled the reservations to Martinique so anyone attempting to follow would have a false lead. His friendship with Monica wasn't widely known, and at the very worst, he'd continued, the plantation was isolated, therefore making it nearly impossible to locate them.

"I'm making progress," he said now, offering her a false smile. "My calls to Paris are getting results. Any day now I expect to be able to settle this thing. I'll get the necklace off my hands and the danger will be done with."

"I'm glad and I hope it's soon," she told him, kissing his cheek before she left her room to meet Pierce in the foyer. Blake had declined going with them this time, saying he preferred remaining at the plantation to help Monica with preparations for the house party.

Today Pierce had scheduled a trip to Trafalgar Twin Falls, about a thirty-minute drive from the plantation. Yesterday he'd been a perfect gentleman, never more than brushing her arm or tapping her shoulder to point out a sight she was about to miss. He'd taken her through a couple of small settlements, then on to Roseau, no more than a colorful village, although it was Dominica's capital city.

On the way the road had led over one of the many rivers on Dominica. She saw villagers pounding and washing clothes on the rocks and drying them in the sun.

"That's the local laundromat," Pierce told her. "There aren't many of the luxuries of life here. Whitechurch has one of the few washing machines on the island. When it's in need of repair even Monica resorts to having clothes washed in the river."

She laughed. "The name Roseau, it's French, I suppose?"

He flashed her a smile. "Maybe, I'm not sure. I understand it's actually the name of a weed that grows along the river, one the Indians used to make poison-tipped arrows. The Indians," he went on, "are believed to have been here two thousand years. They were fierce fighters who resisted European occupation for nearly two hundred years, which is one reason Dominica wasn't settled as early as some of the other nearby islands. When the British finally defeated the Caribs they banished them to a reservation near the windward coast. They're still there living pretty much as they always have. I'll take you to the village another day."

"Sounds intriguing. I look forward to it." She had enjoyed his company more than she expected. He was a charming guide, and it was easy to push skepticism out of her mind.

On foot they had toured the lively streets, visited a few shops, watched industrious women weave baskets and rugs of vetiver grass and wild banana strands. Groups of children in colorful uniforms marched down the narrow streets on the way to school. Pigs, goats and chickens freely roamed the streets of the capital city. Yet the inconveniences of the undeveloped country were astoundingly offset by the primitive unspoiled beauty.

Later in the morning they had strolled through the botanical gardens and then lunched on sandwiches and soda on the second-floor porch of the Guiyave Restaurant. That vantage point gave them a view of several city streets. The structures lining them were mostly wooden, a few stucco, a hodgepodge of architectural styles showing the influence of various nationalities.

Trafalgar Twin Falls was an entirely different environment. Surrounded by jungle Regina found herself climbing a slippery trail to the falls.

"Local legend says the falls are male and female," Pierce remarked as they reached a small plateau on the trail gained by climbing over a mound of rocks then fording a shallow river. "You can see why."

Regina pushed aside some of the heavy foliage. She could indeed, gazing up at the silver flow of water spewing from the high crest of the mountain in all its phallic power. Beside it flowed a fall of equal size but issuing from a deeply etched V-shaped notch. She could imagine the native Indians performing fertility rites beneath the falls long before the French and English found Dominica and drove them deep into the rain forests.

There was something provocative about the place. It was luxuriant with wildlife and with trees filled with ripening fruit. The twin falls made pulsing, rhythmic music splashing into the river. The scene definitely made one think of the primitive reaction of male to female. Something flowed through Regina, too—memories, desires, hungers, all unwarranted, all unwanted, all there. She'd completely forgotten that part of the reason for these outings with Pierce was to glean information.

He caught her hand, leading her forward where the trail proved hazardous. The impersonal touch of yesterday was gone. This one had currents that rippled through her flesh. She thought she felt the same shudder in him, too, but soon he'd let go of her hand and she couldn't be sure it hadn't all been fanciful thinking.

While Pierce waited quietly she risked taking a few snapshots in the dampness, then tucked her camera back into her tote bag. She was soaked, again, this time from the spray of the falls and wading through the river making the climb.

"This must be the wettest place in the world," she commented on the way down the trail.

"You're on the edge of the rain forest," he explained. "There's always a mist here besides the heavy spray. You'll dry out down below where we're having lunch."

Papillotte was an unusual place, but Regina was learning Dominica was made up of the unique. The dining room was in the open air beneath a thatched shelter, the kitchen mysteriously out of sight. Not far from their table was the mineral bath where guests, if they wished, might have a therapeutic soak as they dined. Pierce chose a few native dishes—flying fish, fried breadfruit—and after lunch a house specialty, coconut milk and rum sprinkled with freshly ground nutmeg.

Regina had seen little of Pierce in the evenings since arriving in Dominica. He had friends on the island and went out after dinner each night, leaving her alone with Monica and Blake. Not that she complained of the company. The other two were entertaining whether at a game of cards or as she watched them battle over the chess board. She was also happy to see some of the strain leave Blake's face.

Her third day on Dominica brought about the promised trip to the Carib village. Pierce was unusually quiet on the long drive, letting her absorb the scenery on her own. She found she missed his colorful descriptions and explanations of what she saw. At times she was tempted to ask him the name of an unusual tree or of the plants being cultivated in the fields, but sensing he was in deep thought, let it go.

At the village he left her to wander at will while he went off into the forest with several native guides he knew. She bought baskets and a hat and talked with the children, noting that even though they lived a simple, and by American standards primitive, life, the majority of them looked healthy and happy.

The Indians spoke an unusual French patois mixed with English, and she felt fortunate to find a few village leaders with whom she could communicate. From them she learned that the children received medical care from a clinic team that visited regularly. In addition, they told her, the village had a witch doctor, who took care of everyone between visits from the medical team. She would have liked an opportunity to talk with the local witch doctor, but knew that she and Pierce were due back at the plantation for dinner and that Pierce, by now, would be waiting for her at the van.

Wearing her new hat and carrying her load of baskets, she was bubbling over with comments about the Caribs but noticed that Pierce's mood hadn't changed. Sensing his feelings, she repressed her own desire to talk. But after an hour on the road winding down the mountain she could stand the silence no longer. If he hadn't wanted to go today he could have said so. She could have hired a taxi—at the least the driver would have talked to her.

"I'm beginning to feel these sight-seeing trips are an imposition."

"No. Not at all." He gave her a puzzled smile. "I volunteered. Remember."

"I know. I just thought maybe you were beginning to regret having done so."

He had a few regrets, and they weren't about the time he was spending with her. That was all pleasure even when he was keeping his distance. The regrets were about what he would soon have to do that would spoil their relationship for good.

"Aren't you having a good time?"

"I'm having a very good time. It's just that you've been so...quiet today. I wondered if you wouldn't rather be doing something else."

He shook his head. "There isn't anything else I'd rather be doing." That was a lie. What he'd like to do was stop the car and drag her off into the rain forest and make love with her until neither of them had the strength to crawl away—or wanted to. The only thing that kept him from doing just that was knowing it wasn't the right moment. She was softening toward him again, warming up, but she wasn't quite ready, not for the way he wanted it to be with them.

There he went again, thinking he had a plan for it. He didn't. Maybe that was the real reason he'd put a barrier between them today. She stoked fires in him he thought had been put out for good. He'd watched her in the village when she hadn't known he was there. The way she touched the children, the way she looked them over wasn't as a curious tourist but was with concern and interest in their health and welfare. He knew she'd asked the leaders about their medical care, told them she might come back with the clinic team if they would let her.

He kept telling himself that all he wanted from her was to make love—pleasure, passion, the kind you enjoy and walk away from. So why was he holding back? Why wasn't he trying to seduce her here where even the countryside had a sensuous power? Was it because he knew with her it could never be as simple as that?

There he went again, she thought, lapsing silent, looking as if his mind were far, far away. It made her uncomfortable to be ignored. She forced herself to be honest—it was disappointing, considering the way he'd roused her so easily, that now he could sit there and give her the same regard he might a sack of coconuts he carried in the car.

She tried telling herself it was only the seductive setting, the plush beauty of the rain forest that touched her. But that wasn't true. She wouldn't feel—if she gave a name to it— desire, for just any man. It was a feeling she had reserved for him since that first time she'd seen him and felt her professional reaction go haywire. This was crazy. She still didn't know what it was he wanted from Blake, or how she fit into his scheme. What was worse—she almost didn't care.

"Maybe you just have things on your mind," she said coolly, her eyes resting starkly on him. "You were worried about Monica, I remember. She does seem a little nervous."

He turned toward her, his face no long inattentive. "Yes, she does. More than before. I wonder why."

His mood had gone from distant to intent so quickly she missed the hint of anger in his voice. "Do you think something else has happened?"

"I think something has amplified her problem—" Now she heard it, a hard edge pulled quickly in place. "And it seems to have coincided with the arrival of your uncle."

She listened as carefully to his tone as to his words. He wasn't just insinuating, he was accusing. "Which means?"

"Which means Blake is mixed up in whatever is bothering Monica." The small muscles around his mouth tightened. He hadn't intended to strike out at her.

He was pushing at something, and Regina wondered what it was. "I think you're wrong," she told him.

"Do you?" His eyes narrowed. "I've noticed your uncle isn't his usual cool, debonair self. He's nervous as a caged cat."

"Blake hasn't been feeling well," she said, annoyed at how easily he had her on the defensive. She didn't bother to add it wasn't Blake's physical health she referred to.

"Since when? Since someone broke into his room in Antigua." He knew he wasn't being fair. If he wanted to throw punches he ought to be confronting Blake with this, not her. It was obvious to Pierce that he was doing it to fight the weakness she made him feel, and he didn't like himself any better for that.

Her face froze in surprise. "How do you know about that? We didn't tell anyone. How *could* you know, unless..." Unless he'd been the man in the shadows. The man who had come only inches away from slashing her throat.

He cursed himself silently, cut by the look she gave him. "There are no secrets on an island, Regina," he said, easing the sharpness in his voice. "You'll learn that when you've been here a while. They're like small towns. People talk about everything."

Her eyes condemned him. "I don't know how that could have become the subject of the idle gossip." What was he doing? The look on his face belied everything he was saying.

"You're forgetting the bellboy," he went on smoothly. "The same one who served your room served mine, as well. He just happened to mention the disarray."

Relief surged in her as she heard his explanation. Somehow it had been terribly important to know what her heart already believed, that the man who'd threatened her hadn't been Pierce. Her voice faltered. "Which is why you conveniently called the next morning and invited us to fly down with you."

"I knew you'd be going somewhere. It seemed like a good idea."

"So you wouldn't lose Blake? You were looking for him all along, weren't you? Following him? That's why we met in the first place."

His answer tore at a truth he'd kept even from himself. "Maybe it started out that way. But I didn't have to see him in Antigua. He was coming here in a few more days." His need for her went far deeper than his understanding of it. He wanted to offer her something to make up for the hurtful things he'd said. "Look." He smiled outwardly. "Let's try to see this rationally. Blake is in trouble. Monica is worried. I think there's a connection, more than just a friend upset about a friend. They're people we care about. Why don't we try to work this out together? You tell me what you know and I'll tell you what I know."

"I really don't think I can do that." She couldn't forget there might be more at stake here than Monica's state of mind.

"Why not?" he demanded.

"Because I don't know where you stand in all this."

"Meaning you don't trust me."

"Why should I trust you?" Why should she trust a man who could turn her inside out for his own purposes? "You've deceived me. Maybe everything that's happened between us has been a deception."

His voice lowered and a slight smile appeared on his lips. "Not everything."

"Would you like to point out which small segment of our relationship has been on the up-and-up."

"Do I need to point it out?"

"I think you should."

"Okay then. That night on the beach. That was real. What I felt—what I think you felt, was real."

"Thinking back on that I have the distinct impression you used that episode to feel me out about Blake."

"That's true." His smile intensified. She didn't miss much. He gave her that. "I needed to know if you were part of the problem. I didn't have to get that close to find out."

"I'll accept that for now," she told him, eyes glued to his face for any indication he didn't mean what he was saying.

"I'm glad," he said, reaching across the seat to take hold of her hand. "I *did* offer to fly you down because I wanted to keep an eye on Blake, but I also wanted you out of danger."

If believing him made her a fool, then there was no help for it. He gripped her hand gently but firmly, holding it steadfastly as the miles rolled away. It was effective, she realized, a gesture so simple, so sincere, so powerful, that it reached inside her and reawakened all the feelings that had first been brought alive by much more intimate touches.

Now she was content with his silence. A curious, if fragile, bond laced them together. Her pulse fluttered. His had a steady drumming beat. Whatever else might come between them, whether or not they found themselves on opposing sides of an issue, this would remain, and it would have to be dealt with. It was an entity of its own, demanding recognition, acknowledgment, satisfaction. Regina knew the satisfaction would be sweet—what would come after it was beyond her.

Pierce knew it, too, and it didn't set any better with him than it did with her. The longing for her was beginning to claw at him, tearing away the walls he'd built to keep him from ever caring again. Once in a lifetime was enough to have someone you love and believe in let go of what you thought could never be broken. He realized what he felt was fear, and it almost brought a bitter laugh from his lips. Pierce Buchannan, the competent, persuasive international businessman who'd never yet lost his footing when negotiating a deal, was afraid of falling in love.

Why did he keep thinking it could work with her? He didn't know if he could ever give himself completely to a woman, no matter how softly beautiful, how compelling, how caring she was. And even if he did, one day she would learn the whole truth about him and she wouldn't like it. Not where it concerned her uncle.

He rolled his shoulders, loosening the kinks in his back and neck. Maybe it wasn't as complex as all that, after all. Maybe once he'd had her it would all be over. She would be just another woman who'd shared his bed. Maybe it was just all the other complications—Monica, Blake, the connection in France—which made it seem as if his whole world were suddenly tied to Regina Lawton.

Abruptly conscious he'd been silent for a long time, he squeezed the delicate hand he'd been holding. A moment later he released it and wrapped his fingers tightly around the leather-covered steering wheel.

"Guess I'm doing it again," he said apologetically.

"What's that?" She turned in the seat, putting her back against the door and pulling one leg up under her so that he was the only thing in her view. It wasn't a bad one. He had a profile one of the master sculptors could have used as a model.

His eyes were clouded, his brow lined with a frown. "Driving along like a robot. I'm sorry. I don't mean to be..."

She laughed gently, and briefly closed her hand over his on the wheel. Her pale eyes flickered. She didn't know all he'd been thinking but some of it had definitely seeped through. "You've been quiet," she said softly. "But you've been communicating."

Chapter 8

Dusk in the tropics was a time for mist-draped trees, the slow, hypnotic song of birds, muted reds and golds in the evening sky as the sun slipped into the ocean. The water swallowed the light quickly, leaving the sky with a deep blue glow and the early brilliance of stars. It was a sight worth seeing. Pierce stopped the car on an old iron bridge over a river that emptied into the Caribbean and showed Regina the best spot for taking pictures.

"There's hardly any traffic here," he said. "So take your time."

She readied her camera and snapped shot after shot, catching the sun first when it was a full, brilliant shield, then a half round and last only a fiery sliver over the sea.

"Thanks," she told him, knowing the photographs would be magnificent if the camera had captured only half of nature's daily miracle.

"You're welcome. It's my compensation for being a lousy guide today."

She smiled, replacing the lens cover on her camera. "It's more than enough. If they come out I'm going to have these enlarged and hung in my office. Then when the pace gets too fast or the pressure too heavy, I can look at them and remember there's a spot in the world where time takes its natural course." She drew in a deep breath of the fresh clean air. "I could get used to going native. I know it's been only a few days, but I find I haven't missed driving a car or watching television or reading a newspaper less than a week old. It's rather refreshing not to worry about what you're wearing or how your hair looks or if your makeup is on right."

He laughed. "It's like that for a while. After another week you'll start getting restless, and actually miss all those annoying things."

"Withdrawal symptoms?" Regina lifted her brows lazily.

"Maybe."

"We'll see," she said.

Neither of them had made a step toward getting in the car. For the moment both were content to prop themselves against the rusting iron rail and watch more stars blink on in the sky.

"You like your work, don't you?" A thought had come to him that halfway eased his troubled mind. She was the kind of woman whose first loyalties would always be professional ones. Not the kind to get caught up in love and commitment or personal entanglements.

Sighing, she pondered his question as a thousand exotic smells and sounds drifted in from the riverbanks and seashore. She breathed them in, placing the scents, trying to sort out the sounds just because they were new. This is the life, she was thinking, but for interludes only. Pierce has a point. Too much of it and anyone would grow fat and lazy and enjoy every impotent moment. Life, progress, would slow to a crawl.

Paradise was wonderful, but give it to her in small doses. Maybe she would want to come back here to retire after a long, full, busy life. Did she like her work? Not only did she like it, she needed it, as muscles need exercise and flowers need rain.

She shifted her weight to one arm on the rail so that she was facing him. "I love my work," she answered cheerfully.

"You've never married."

That was a twist of topic she hadn't expected. She wondered if it was a statement or a question. "No. I never have. You?"

His tone altered slightly; she tried to pinpoint the change. "A long time ago when I was very young. It was short, only a few years. I was in service stationed in Europe, and I took my bride along. I was away a lot, and during one of those absences she met a German count. His title and a crumbling castle impressed her more than my military rank and base housing. She's Countess Ranke now."

"Bitter?"

"No. Not now. I was for a while. I felt like the poor man whose lamb made dinner for the rich guy with the flocks. But no. She did me a favor. I left the service a few years later and went into business. I've been successful. If she hadn't shaken me up then I'd probably be pushing paper behind a desk in the Pentagon."

"Would that be so bad?"

"No," he admitted. "Just not as satisfying."

She could understand that. There was something about being master of your own fate that was eminently satisfying. She liked the feeling, and couldn't fault it in anyone else. But she had a suspicion he still held a hidden trace of the bitterness that had first fired him on. Still, she knew the ending of any relationship left marks—a person was better or worse for having loved, but never, never untouched.

"I know what you mean. It's exhilarating knowing your successes and your failures are your own. I wouldn't want my life to be any other way."

The conversation was serious. It didn't belong to this night, under a pale gold moon made for another turn of mind altogether. The same thought must have come to Pierce at the same time. He stretched an arm around her shoulders and brought her to his chest.

"I wouldn't either." His voice melted into a smooth dark whisper. "I wouldn't want you to be any different than you are."

He brought his lips to hers in a single soft stroke, lingering a moment then pulled away.

"Pierce," she whispered, letting him know it wasn't enough. She slid her arms around his back, tightening her fingers into his shirt. He crushed his mouth back to hers, letting her know he'd never meant one taste to be all.

She was sweet, honeycomb sweet. The taste drew him on beyond her lips into the receptive warmth of her mouth for a dueling delight with a tongue as eager as his own. He knew he was bruising her lips, but he couldn't ease the pressure. That taste was maddening. His hands roamed her body then ended up tangled in her hair; hers had slipped beneath his shirt to rake his back. Somehow he'd turned her so that her back braced against the rail. His arousal pressed as hard against her belly as he felt her bare, silken legs entwine with his.

A vibration started in her body as it seemed every cell tingled with the feel of him. The skin under her hands was smooth and hard as glass, and yet she could feel a small quiver wherever her fingers probed. She realized this passion had been smoldering in both of them for days while they'd acted civilized and distant from each other. Now that it was again blazing hot and wild, she didn't stop to think how easy it was to overlook all the things that should have come first, the talk, the courting. Nothing mattered but that this fire be allowed to rage and burn in all its sweet fury.

The soft sounds from deep in her throat, the cadence of her hurried breathing were maddening. Hadn't he known it would be like this again? Passion hot and fiery drove every other thought out of his mind. Need bolted through him, desire ripped at every fiber. By all of hell he was going to take her here on a public bridge. There was no helping it, no stopping it. Not by wit or will. He had neither left.

Her shorts fastened with a drawstring, a convenient device, he thought. He slid his hands beneath the waist, moving forward to find the tie even as he continued to press his weight against her. A moment later he was grateful he had a good grip on the fabric. The rusty old rail holding them hadn't the strength to endure their ardor. It groaned and gave way and would have taken Regina with it into the river if he hadn't kept his balance and held on tightly. Swearing, he whirled her away from the opening.

A splash sounded from a few feet below. It wasn't a long fall into the shallow water, but it wasn't one either of them would have enjoyed.

Regina let out a shuddering sigh. "That would have been one to tell the grandchildren about."

"I'm . . . Hell! I don't know what to say. You aren't hurt, are you?"

"No." She breathed in deeply, thirsty for the oxygen that would cool her fevered blood. "I think I'm fine."

"Come on," he said, managing a laugh and urging her into the car. "I don't even want to try to explain to Monica why we're late for dinner."

It turned out it wasn't necessary, as Blake told them Monica had gone to bed early with a headache.

"I want to look in on her," Regina said, concern coloring her voice. "I'll just be a few minutes, then I'll be back to join you for dinner."

She found Monica on a daybed in her sitting room, Winston lying beside her. The lights were out and she asked Regina to leave them that way.

"Migraine," she said softly. "I get them once in a while. Nothing to worry about."

Regina knew Monica wouldn't want to talk long but took time to learn if the treatment she used was up-to-date and adequate. Finding that it was she said good-night, deciding to go to her own room to freshen up before going back to the dining room.

While they waited Pierce poured a drink for himself and one for Blake. He was in a bad temper after learning Monica was sick with a headache. Just the other day she'd told him it had been months since she'd had one of those attacks, and he was sure this one was brought on by a bad case of nerves. He was just as sure Blake had something to do with bringing it about.

"Regina doesn't know, does she?" Pierce asked abruptly, opening a subject he'd kept bottled up a long time.

The corners of Blake's mouth twitched. "I don't know what you mean."

"You know what I mean." He swirled the liquid in his glass carelessly but his eyes were hard and dark. "The business you're in. The way you make your money."

"My investments?" Blake laughed nervously.

"Don't try to con me, Blake. I've seen through better players." The steel in his voice grazed the air. "Maybe things would be clearer to you if I called you André."

Blake's head snapped up. "André?"

"Yes, André. André Binot. Your French name. Or would I be more correct to say your French alias?" Blake started to open his mouth to deny it but saw there was no use. Pierce went on. "I know about the name, the two passports, everything."

"Everything?" Blake's worried eyes widened.

"Even an ex-naval intelligence officer has a few contacts left. You're slick, I grant you that. Using the dark hair color is very effective. I suppose it washes right out when you want to change?" Blake nodded. "The authorities have never really put your two identities together. I guess that's one reason you've been successful. If they were looking for an American, you were French. If they were looking for a Frenchman, you were American. Clever."

"Thanks," Blake said solemnly.

"But your luck's run out." His eyes were as cold as his voice. "Oh, maybe they won't actually be able to charge you with anything. It would be difficult to prove you knew the valuables you were selling were—stolen."

"Not stolen," Blake corrected. "Just out of sight."

"A nice way of putting it. It's been very lucrative, hasn't it? Acting as middleman—"

"Art and jewelry dealer," Blake corrected again.

"Pardon me." The term brought a humorless smile to Pierce's lips. "I hope you've got most of your profits in a Swiss account. International lawyers can be expensive."

"I took precautions," Blake said smugly.

"The only thing I don't know is how you got Monica into this. It's the only reason you're still operating. She's stubborn. She won't tell me a thing. But as soon as I know what your hold on her is, you're finished. God help you if you've been blackmailing her."

"The last thing I'd do is hurt Monica." Blake eyed his adversary levelly. "She's a friend. A very old and very good friend."

Pierce's expression darkened. "Don't misunderstand all of this, Blake. I know about all of it. I let you come here because I wanted to keep an eye on you. Monica's sentimental enough to help you because she cares about you. But I won't let you drag her deeper in this thing. You're in serious trouble. I know about that, too. As I said, I still have friends in France. Right now it suits them and me for you to stay here. But, Blake, don't push your luck with me." His voice had a chill that made Blake shudder.

Regina's return cut off whatever Blake might have said in response. She paused in the doorway of the dining room, puzzled to see the hard look on Pierce's face and the grim one on Blake's.

"Something wrong?"

"No," Pierce said quickly as Blake drained a long swallow from his glass. "We were just worrying about Monica. How is she?"

Regina smiled easily, feeling much refreshed after a change of clothes and a splash of cool water on her face.

"She has a migraine. I think it's easing and she should be fine by morning. There really wasn't anything for me to do."

"That's good," Pierce said and Blake echoed the same sentiment. "Would you like a drink?" His gaze was warm and direct. She looked like a girl in her denim sundress and ponytail. The thought brought a quick light to his eyes. Back on that bridge they'd acted like a couple of teens who just discovered sex.

Regina saw the flicker in his eye and recognized it for what it was. She acknowledged it without embarrassment, meeting the intimate look with a slight smile.

"You two have fun today?" Blake, having put aside his empty glass, led the way to the mahogany table in the dining area.

Regina's smile went full-blown as Pierce answered before she could think of a suitable reply.

"I think Regina found it a really moving experience."

"That I did," she joined in. "The Caribs are fascinating. Those on the reservation don't seem to have felt the influence of all the different cultures elsewhere on the island. I think I'm intrigued enough to turn into something of a history buff. I want to look into the origins of these native Caribbeans."

"Check with Monica about her library," Pierce advised, helping her into her chair. "She's collected almost everything written on the topic. Some of the books are quite old and rare."

"Sounds like a good way to spend tomorrow," she said, accepting a seafood salad from a servant. "I'm sure you need an unencumbered day," she told Pierce.

He made no answer other than to lift his brows over a mouthful of salad.

After dinner she asked for the drink Pierce had offered her earlier. While he was getting it, Blake let her know he wanted to talk with her privately. Blake was upset, she could tell; he'd fidgeted all through the meal, hardly eating anything. It had almost made her feel guilty about having such a huge appetite. Something unexpected must have happened during the day. She felt a little guilty, too, about having been away from him so much since arriving on Dominica. But he'd insisted emphatically that she make the excursions into the countryside.

Although anxious about Blake she took her time with the drink and kept up her part of the conversation. But when her glass was dry and Pierce offered a refill, she told him she was tired and wanted to get to bed. He didn't mask his disappointment but didn't try to change her mind. Blake quickly said he was ready to turn in as well and left the room with Regina.

"What's happened today?" she whispered as they reached the corridor.

"Wait," he said quietly, then hurriedly opened the door to her room. He stayed on his feet, pacing around as she took a seat in a cushioned chair. He passed the dresser, pausing when he saw the silver music box, looking at it in silence for a moment, then at her. Eventually he picked it up, resting the weight of it in one hand as he wound it with the other. "I didn't get the inscription done for you."

The delicate ring of the music filled the room. "It wasn't necessary," she said, hoping her smile would relieve the frown on his face. "I won't forget you gave it to me."

"No. I suppose not." Suddenly he didn't seem to be thinking about the music box any longer. His eyes clouded and she saw that beads of sweat had formed on his temples. "Regina." He breathed out a troubled sigh. "I got word today that the people looking for me know where I am. I'd hoped for more time. Now it looks like I may have to leave here in a hurry." He stopped as he saw the quick anxiety in her face.

"Your contact in Paris," she said. "Has he found someone you can safely turn the necklace over to?"

"Maybe. But I may need to arrange to meet him elsewhere. I wanted you to know why I might leave unexpectedly."

"All right," she said, though still somewhat skeptical. "If you're sure you'll be safe." It would be dangerous for Blake to return to France carrying the necklace and he'd hoped to have the right person come to Dominica for it. Now that plan had been compromised.

"I'm not worried about my safety," Blake shot back. "It's you and Monica I'm worried about. I've handled this whole thing badly and put everyone's life in danger. I want to get it over fast."

"I know," she insisted. "But don't worry about me. Do whatever is necessary. I'll be fine."

"I wish I could be sure of that." Shoulders drooping, he plunged his hands into his pockets.

"Will you leave soon?" It was strange to see him worried and frightened. In her mind's eye she'd never been able to picture Blake with a care in the world. This all seemed so wrong, so out of character. Maybe that was why she had the impression he was keeping something from her.

"I hope I have a few days. The guests for the house party begin arriving day after tomorrow. I want to slip out quietly. Monica has a friend keeping tabs on the airports. It shouldn't be hard to spot..."

"Monica? What does she know about this?" She'd been extremely careful during their stay at Whitechurch not to drop a hint of any trouble. To learn Blake had taken Monica into his confidence stunned her.

Blake snatched a linen handkerchief from his pocket and mopped his brow. "She knows I'm in trouble. She's trying to help."

Another worrisome thought crept into her mind. "Monica doesn't have any connection with this business about the necklace, does she?"

Blake hedged. "She's concerned, Queenie. She's trying to help."

"That's all?" she asked, aware that he only lapsed into calling her Queenie if he was very upset.

Blake looked away. "Yes."

Regina squeezed her hands so tightly her nails cut at her palms. "It really bothers me knowing a sweet old lady like Monica is tangled up in this."

"It doesn't make me feel good, either," Blake said glumly.

"Maybe that's what is bothering Pierce."

"What's bothering Pierce?" Blake asked, his gaze jumping to hers.

Regina took a deep breath before she continued. "He's suspicious of your relationship with Monica. She's been upset and he's decided you're the cause. I believe he still thinks you're a con man, as ridiculous as that is. I'm certain his acquaintance with me started out as a means of investigating you."

"That's possible." He rubbed his eyes, then continued slowly. "Monica isn't the only one with a headache. I think I'll get a couple of aspirin and go to bed."

"You do that." She rose and went to him, kissing him gently on the cheek. "I'll talk with you in the morning."

An hour later she'd changed to a short silk gown and sat on her bed thinking—hard work with all the loose puzzle pieces floating in her head. Nothing fit together well enough to get even a start. It was as if there was more than one puzzle here and the two sets of pieces weren't sorted out.

Another hour later she'd slumped to her pillow deep in sleep. A gentle breeze floated in the open windows, stirring the soft silk folds of her gown. Regina stirred, too, as the soft gusts of air touched her, slipping deeper into the dimness of her dream.

A man stood in an arrow of light, a dim ray breaking the heavy floating mists. Stepping nearer, he whispered her name. She shuddered and shifted lazily, reaching out, beckoning. The voice came again, like a caress touching her cheek, bringing a sigh that parted her lips in pleasure. She reached out to the phantom man.

"Regina," the silver voice whispered.

The fog faded slowly from her mind. "Pierce," she murmured, not sure which side of the dream she spoke from.

Warm, rough fingertips trailed over her shoulders. She preened to the touch, lifting to it, whimpering for it to continue, as the last hazy vestige of sleep drifted away. She saw him clearly then, not a shadow, not a dream. Pierce. One tantalizing finger touched her lips. He shook his head.

"I tried to stay away," he whispered. "I tried to think myself out of coming." The finger on her lips edged over her chin, over her throat and continued downward. His husky voice lowered. "I don't know if I can leave if you tell me to."

Her heart leapt as he sat beside her on the bed, a hand curving around each of her shoulders. His chest was bare. In the moonlight she could see the gleam of his dark eyes, see the stark line of his chin, feel the insistent heat of his desire—and her own.

"I won't tell you to leave," she whispered, acknowledging her need without question. "I'll ask you to stay."

His mouth came down fast, brutally. She met it the same way, arms twined around his neck, pulling him closer, letting herself go completely. With him it was easy. He filled her heart, her head, her arms with more than flesh and wanting. She had no name for it, not now, no thought for putting one to it while the wildness raged. He was here. She wanted him. That was enough to know for the moment.

The silk gown tore beneath his urgent hands. He tossed it away and took another moment to strip off his trousers. His body above hers, he reclaimed her lips. A sense of urgency drove him. He found his breathing as difficult to control as the mad yearning to possess the woman captured beneath him. Hunger burned in his lungs, burned in his blood. He wanted her without a thought for what it might mean or how it might change them.

His hands trembled on her soft skin. How he'd longed to feel every satin inch of her. Now he fulfilled that longing, beginning at her breasts and not stopping until his hands had caressed every smooth warm part of her.

Her hands were as rampant, touching, exploring. Strange, she'd never seen, never felt the beauty in a man's form as she did in his. Heat rushed through her body, starting at the core, surging out, surging back hotter than it had begun. Velvet over steel. That was the feel of his skin over tight, corded muscles. His hair was silky, sensuous, a tingly caress against her skin.

His mouth followed the trail of his hands, touching, loving, reveling in the taste and feel of her. She moaned as his tongue sought secret places, found hidden desires and gave fulfillment. He'd never wanted a woman the way he wanted her, never thought he could burn and burn and burn this way and not be consumed. Her pleasure was his pleasure. He felt it in his flesh as he brought it to life in hers. This excitement, this longing, was more than carnal, more than lustful sex, he knew it deep in his mind but let the thought go. It was much too sane for what he was feeling.

With a groan he coiled his legs around hers, rolled her on top of him then over again and rose to his knees dominantly above her. The small gasps coming from her lips heightened his fever. He nudged her thighs and eased himself down.

This was torture. She caught his hot, damp hips in her hands, pulling him down. He lowered his weight to his elbows, his lips just brushing hers. She closed her eyes for a moment, almost believing she was back in her dream, floating on a golden cloud of passion. Then she lifted lids over the glittering heat in her eyes; she saw it reflected in the dark burning ones above her. He whispered her name, other words too ragged to hear, and plunged into her.

She knew nothing for moments but white, raging heat, building even higher. Sounds came back first, night sounds, birds, the wind, a swaying vine; his scent and hers intermingled sweeping the room, sandalwood, violets, sweet tropic air; the heady taste of his mouth filled hers, nectar, love. She pleaded with him to take her beyond the madness, past the delirium, past the yearning. But he only drove her to a higher plane of wanting and held her there endlessly until she was sure she would die on the very edge of ecstasy.

"Now!" he cried, thundering over, taking her with him, finding a level of passion neither had reached before.

She drifted down slowly, lips whispering his name, her body quivering, her skin flushed and shimmering, knowing she had given more than she expected to give and no more than she'd gotten in return.

Pierce rolled to his side, cradling her in his arms, unwilling to let go, and wondering why. He'd expected satisfaction and finality after what happened. He'd expected to be clearheaded and ready to walk away. It wasn't what he got. A part of the hunger was still there, smoldering inside, harboring a flame that wouldn't die.

She awoke many hours later in a state of fuzzy astonishment. The first tenuous rays of dawn crept inside the windows. She found surprising gratification in learning he hadn't left her during the night. His hair was mussed and bronzed by the early light. The dark shadow of a beard covered his cheeks and chin. He slept sprawled but had kept a possessive hand on her all through the night, which pleased her as well.

This was all too crazy. She was a careful person. She led an orderly, planned life. She didn't fall into bed with a man unless she knew just where he fit into that organized life. To date that niche for any man hadn't included permanency. So it was crazy to be thinking how much she could like waking up every morning next to Pierce. She hardly knew him, and had no idea where she fit into his life, either. She just knew that looking at him made her heart lurch and butterflies take wing in her stomach. She wasn't sure she wanted to admit it, but it felt like love.

She watched him for a while, pushing back the sheet for a closer look at the muscular body, the bronze skin. It was much too tempting to touch what her eyes were enjoying. Her fingers splayed lightly over his chest combing through the silky curls, teasing over the small nipple buds, following the line of hair over a hard, rippled belly and then... She felt the radiant flow of warmth spread over her skin, the small stir of excitement, the quickening in her most feminine parts. Was it possible just touching him could twist a coil of heat inside her?

Last night he'd aroused her before waking her and she wondered if she could do the same. It was a sweet temptation. She touched the nest of dark curls where his manhood lay. His body trembled, the muscles in his thighs tightened convulsively. Made bolder by his response she touched him again, gently at first, then urgently, spurred on by the heat and the furious rush of blood beneath her fingers.

Pierce groaned and mumbled her name as he rolled his hips and responded to the rhythm of her hand with moves of his own. He was aroused to full fury, and she wondered why he wasn't awake. She wanted him awake, awake and wanting her as much as she wanted him.

"Pierce, you can't be asleep." She bent over him, ruffling his mustache, teasing his lips with her mouth. His breathing was slow, labored. She paused, frowning in disappointment as she started to move her face away.

"Witch," he growled, grabbing her waist and dragging her astride him. His eyes gleamed like dark, fiery crystals. "Don't think you won't have to finish what you've started."

"Devil! You were faking," she snapped back as muscular arms lifted her above him and held her there, letting his hardness tease at her. "I always finish what I start."

"You don't know how glad I am to hear that," he murmured as he positioned himself beneath her.

She wiggled herself down until she was almost on him. "Is that supposed to arouse my sympathy?"

He grinned wickedly and shook his head. "Sympathy isn't what I'm looking for." He eased her down, sliding into her satin sheath, filling her then holding them both still for a moment of awe. "Have I told you I'm crazy about your bedside manner?"

"I'm getting your message," she said softly, rocking her hips slowly.

"You're sweet," he groaned. "Sweeter than anything I've ever known or dreamed of. I don't think I'll ever have enough of you."

"I hope you never do," she whispered achingly. "Never." She moved her hips faster, lifting, falling, rocking, feeling him deep inside. His body tightened and strained beneath her. She quickened the pace, watching the room blur and disappear until she was aware of nothing but his face and the crashing fusion of their bodies.

He thrust himself deeply inside her, feeling the quaking and quivering of her soft flesh drain him of all control. Heaving beneath her, once, twice, again, he cried out in pleasure, struggling to hold on to the last vestige of his will and losing the battle.

When they awoke again the sun was throwing full light into the bedroom. Pierce got up and showered in her bathroom, then dressed in the rumpled trousers he'd so hastily thrown aside the night before. He waited in the room until she'd showered, too, and came out of the bathroom wearing a short silk robe.

She was unpretentious, leaving her hair towel-dried and uncombed as she came to sit beside him. He liked that ease about her. She was one of the most beautiful women he'd ever known, but she didn't seem to feel any compulsion to constantly dazzle others with her looks.

"I guess this is the part where we say what it all means and where we go next," she said matter-of-factly.

"I guess so," he agreed, playfully pulling her into his lap and kissing her radiant scrubbed face. "I don't think I've ever been drawn to a woman as I am to you. I've never even considered a permanent relationship with anyone since my marriage ended."

He banked the dark thoughts that came whenever he remembered April and how it had ended. The pain was always just as strong as when it had been new, and the loss...

Regina felt a tensing in his body. "Is something wrong?" she asked.

"No. Just thinking." He pulled her in closer and nibbled at her lower lip. "I guess it's lucky for me you've already got your life mapped out." Regina started to interrupt but then thought better of it and let him go on. "Otherwise I'd be tempted this time."

She felt as if a heavy weight had crashed against her chest. For her, giving her body to him had meant giving part of her heart. She hadn't known how different it was for Pierce. Awkwardly, she shifted her weight off him and got to her feet, the words she wanted to say catching in her throat.

"Just what is it you expect to happen now?"

"The same as you, I suppose." He shrugged, not liking what he saw flashing in her eyes but not yet understanding what it meant. "We'll see each other as often as possible. I understand your position. Your work is your first priority. That's true for me, too. You've got your career—I've got mine. There's no place in our lives for commitment, certainly not marriage. It's the best way."

Regina crossed her arms over her chest, her pale eyes blazing. "You're way off track, Mr. Buchannan. I'm not unmarried because I'm opposed to marriage or because I don't have room for commitment in my life." She felt the angry thud of her pulse. "I have every intention," she said icily, "of marrying the man I love."

Chapter 9

The guests began to arrive at Whitechurch. First came an old and wealthy British couple, the Cookes. After them a portly Italian man named Vasari, who seemed to despise the tropics and rarely left his room. Then a pair of Americans from Los Angeles, Linc Taylor and Jeff Kent, who were owners of a small but exclusive art gallery. They seemed an odd assortment and Regina puzzled over the diversity of Monica's friends.

Another half dozen guests arrived the morning of the following day. That evening the summer festival began with a colorful costume parade in Roseau. Some of the guests wanted to attend, and Monica and Blake were driving the car in. Pierce was scheduled to drive others in the van. Reluctantly and only because Monica asked her to go along, Regina planned to accompany Pierce and the guests in the van.

She'd seen little of him since the morning after she'd welcomed him into her bed. It had been a hard lesson, that one, a misjudgment on her part, but she couldn't fault him completely. He hadn't offered anything more than passion. The fact that she'd thought more was there was due to her own tunnel vision. Still, she couldn't shake the belief that he cared for her a little, and at that more than he would admit.

Regina knew it hadn't been just sex for him, not the way he'd held on to her afterward, the way he'd caressed her as they fell asleep. That unguarded tenderness came from something deeper. The thought gave her a little hope. He'd built a wall inside himself—but walls could crumble.

As street revelers cheered the parade, Pierce and Regina stood on the edge of the crowd the others from Whitechurch had disappeared into. After a few minutes Pierce placed a hand on her shoulder and pulled her back a few steps so that the music and noise didn't drown out his words.

"Regina," he said, his voice almost toneless. "I'm sorry."

"About what?" she came back quickly. If he was going to apologize she didn't want to make it easy for him.

"Not about making love with you." His eyes went sharply to her face. "I'm not sorry about that. It's just that I didn't know—"

"That I took making love seriously." She met his gaze steadily. "I do. I don't mean I didn't enjoy it with you. That was obvious. But it's not something I could ever be as casual about as you suggested."

He rolled out a sigh. "I know that now."

"Now?" She managed to keep her voice cool. "I think you had a very good idea how I felt about intimacy. If you put another interpretation on it, it was rather than take a risk with your own feelings." Her brows raised sharply. "Am I being too honest for you?"

"No," he said hotly. "I think that about covers it and settles it."

"Does it?" She started, not content to let it go at that, but trailed off as she saw someone standing on the steps of the Reef, a small hotel across the street. Her heart skidded. "Marot," she whispered under her breath. "And Larousse."

Pierce saw them, too, though it was doubtful he recognized Larousse. "The Frenchman," he said. "Interesting."

Regina had left his side and was threading through the milling crowd searching for Blake. It wouldn't do for him to come face-to-face with Marot, not without a warning. Frantically she searched for a quarter of an hour, up one side of the street, down the other. It was difficult moving through the pressing throng, but eventually she came to a familiar face among all the strange ones.

"Monica," she cried, rushing past the steps of a small house. Balanced with her cane, Monica stood on a low wall watching the festivities. "I'm looking for Blake."

"Oh my," Monica responded, her eyes cutting unintentionally toward the Reef. "I'm afraid you won't find him here. He had to leave suddenly." She looked curiously back at Regina. "He said you'd understand. He took the car."

She breathed easier as she left Monica. If Blake had seen Marot and Larousse, he would be on his way to the airport and leaving on the first plane in the morning. Or perhaps he would arrange a charter and be out tonight. In a few more days the necklace would be returned to wherever it belonged in France, taking Blake and everyone else out of harm's way. But that knowledge didn't prevent her skin from crawling when Marot approached unexpectedly and spoke to her.

"Doctor Lawton," he said. "How delightful to see you again. This is wonderful, is it not?" He spread his hands, indicating the activity all around them. "Are you enjoying the celebration?"

"It is . . . stimulating, isn't it?" she answered, feeling an odd tingling, one that told her she should be careful, one she could never explain away scientifically.

He nodded in agreement, then went straight to the point as she expected he would. "I wonder if you had a chance to relay my message to your uncle."

Nevertheless, her eyes flickered with astonishment at what he said. Did he think she didn't know he'd seen them in Antigua or was he simply being shrewd? "I believe he'll try to get in touch with the French authorities."

Marot's lips tightened fractionally but he spoke smoothly. "I'm glad to hear that."

"Are you here on vacation or on another case?" She gave him a wide, and she hoped, innocent smile.

Marot laughed, though it seemed to her, without humor. "Even a policeman needs a holiday."

"Then I hope you enjoy yours," she said, feeling her teeth grate against each other. She followed with a quick good-bye and slipped away quietly into the crowd. Marot intimidated even when he was polite. It wouldn't do for her to try to get away and go back to the plantation. In case Blake had gone there first, she didn't want to lead the Frenchmen to him. So she would stay, waiting out the festival with the plantation guests, hoping Blake had made his escape.

Late that night in her room, she sat quietly in the darkness listening to the tinkling melody of the music box, that sad-sweet melody that seemed to be the theme of her life recently. When the music was disrupted once again she picked up the music box and wound the key, but it refused to play. Even a doctor, she thought recklessly, knows that mechanical things sometimes need a bump or shake to get them going. She gently knocked the music box on the dresser top a few times but got nothing more than an irritating twang.

She tried shaking it, only to have it slip from her fingers and thump onto the straw mat at her feet. With the impact the silver swan separated from the base. She gasped, upset with herself for breaking Blake's gift. Hurriedly she picked up the pieces and laid them on the dresser, noticing something was there but didn't belong, something that glowed like a white-hot coal in the moonlight. Quickly she turned on a light. Falling out of the hollow body of the swan was a diamond necklace.

Her head flooded with confusion. Why was it there? When had Blake put it there? Why had he left without it? And worst of all—what was she going to do with it? Nervously she pulled the necklace free of the swan's body and examined the shimmering oval stone that was as large as a bird's egg. It was in an archaic gold setting with smaller matched stones, and it was by far the most beautiful piece of jewelry she'd ever seen. She held it up to her throat and gazed in the mirror. It was something one might expect to see around the neck of a queen. It was a piece men might kill for. And they did, she thought grimly, remembering the young Frenchwoman Blake had told her about.

Her surprise at finding the necklace was minimal compared to her worry about Blake. He'd known the silver swan was on her dresser, and surely he'd known the necklace was inside. She couldn't imagine anyone else having hidden it there. Perhaps Blake *did* intend coming back to the plantation tonight. Or perhaps he'd only wanted to leave it in a safe place until he was sure about the person he was to turn it over to. Regardless of the reason, the necklace needed to be hidden, and in a new place, because for all her efforts the swan wouldn't fit securely back on the base. Fastening the pieces together as best she could she tucked the music box away in a drawer and started to look around.

She could think only of the obvious places to hide a treasure—under the mattress, in the toilet tank, behind a picture—the places anyone would look. She needed something. It occurred to her she might have to outsmart people far more experienced at concealing things than she was. Finally, after rummaging nervously around the room she thought of a place that might be foolproof.

Hurrying back to the dresser she opened a drawer and took out a long black silk scarf. She folded the necklace inside, then twisted and knotted the scarf around it. That done, she tied the scarf safari style above the brim of the straw hat she'd purchased at the Carib reservation. Then she hung the hat back on the clothes rack just inside her door, in plan view of everyone, and hopefully in so obvious a place no one would notice it.

The discovery of the necklace had alarmed her, and she needed to talk with Monica. If Blake had left to meet his contact and return the necklace, something was very wrong. She needed to know what Monica knew about his sudden departure, or if he'd left a message Monica hadn't felt free to mention at the festival. It was hours past midnight and all the guests were asleep. Monica would likely be, too, but this couldn't wait until later in the morning.

Regina followed the corridor in the back of the house, past the office and on to a wing opposite the one where the guest rooms were, moving quietly without turning on lights. The servants were gone for the night, except for the few who lived in cottages out back. Because she knew the main part of the house should be empty, she was startled to hear a deep voice coming from the office door as she passed.

"I said the Frenchmen from the agency are on the island, both of them. Sorry, the phone service here isn't first-rate."

Stomach churning, Regina stopped outside the closed doors. He was shouting, otherwise she could hardly have heard him through the thick mahogany. There was no mistaking the voice. She knew it as well filtering through the door cracks as she did whispering sweet words in her ear.

Pierce. He was obviously speaking to someone long distance. But why was he reporting the arrival of Marot and Larousse?

She wore soft-soled shoes, nevertheless she moved like a shadow closer to the office, and holding her breath, leaned an ear against the door.

"He's dropped out of sight." A low, rough laugh followed. He had to mean Blake. "No, but I will. You can be sure of that. I've got a lot at stake here myself. I won't let you down." He fell silent and Regina wished she could hear who the other party was and what they were saying. "Let *me* worry about that." Anger echoed clearly in Pierce's loud words. "You just remember this cancels all our debts." Again there was a nerve-fraying silence. "I'll call you when I have it or have news. It shouldn't take long now."

She didn't know if she heard the phone click or imagined that small sound had been as loud as his voice. But as a precaution, she quickly concealed herself behind an immense fern a few doors away and waited. Just minutes later, Pierce came out, headed down the corridor and left through an outside door. He looked furious, his eyes deadly. It took only a glimpse of his face to learn that. She didn't waste a moment deciding if she should follow—within seconds she slipped out after him, dodging behind trees and shrubs as she followed him down a path.

He went into a thicket about a hundred yards from the main house and entered a cottage almost concealed by flamboyant trees. It was called the Sisserou cottage for a species of large, purple-winged parrots. Monica maintained the cottage for guests who wanted greater privacy, and Pierce always used it when he was on the island.

She wondered if the thought patterns she was getting came from instinct or shattered emotions. Either way, she'd proved herself something of a simpleton concerning Pierce. That was about to end. Thanking the heavens for the damp ground that absorbed the sound of her footsteps, she crept up to the cottage, telling herself there was a chance Blake was inside, either by choice or force.

He wasn't. Pierce was, stripped down to his briefs. Before she could turn away he shed those, as well, then disappeared to bathe. Her throat went dry as she flattened herself against the wall and damned her body for its betrayal. Shortly she heard water running and made a hasty decision to take a look inside while he was showering.

The door wasn't locked. She eased it open, hoping she wasn't making the mistake of the century. She had the sensation of blood siphoning from her face and brain, leaving her weak and queasy, but determined.

The room was fastidiously neat. The clothes he'd just taken off were carefully folded over the back of a chair. His wallet lay on the dresser top. She knew she had only a few minutes and thought the wallet might be the best place to start. Disappointingly, it offered nothing except the usual plastic cards and driver's licence. She put it down and opened the top dresser drawer, finding only clothing. Other drawers yielded no more.

Still unwilling to give up, she turned and spotted the one drawer in the night table and quietly moved to it. Sliding it open she got only a glimpse of a blue-black gun barrel, before hearing the water cut off in the bathroom. Panicking, she pushed the drawer shut and got out the door and into the cover of the shrubs only seconds before Pierce returned to the bedroom. She could see him distinctly, wearing a towel and a savage smile. There was no privacy behind those straw shades. She fell back deeper into the shadows, telling herself she would have to remember that. Because her heart was beating too wildly to leave, she simply edged herself around the trunk of a coconut palm and plopped her weight against it.

Why did he have a gun? Or need one? She choked on a bitter laugh. How naive could one woman be? She'd been berating herself about misunderstood intents and purposes of a very personal nature when there was something much more serious and deadly going on in Pierce Buchannan's mind. While she was thinking about love and romance, he'd been thinking about Blake and the missing necklace. He wasn't worried about Monica. That was just a ruse to cover his interest in Blake. She moaned out loud in spite of herself. If fools could be platinum-plated, she would be worth a fortune.

Numbly pushing herself away from the tree, she shuffled through the whispering shadows on the dark path. But only a few feet from where she'd started she collided with a hard and unyielding chest.

"Oh!" she gasped. "Pierce." Her face washed as white as the pale moonlight. He hadn't dressed, and the towel hung low on his hips. The fresh scent of soap still clung to damp flesh. He must have heard her outside and slipped out a window.

Scowling, he gripped her upper arms with bruising force. "I thought I heard someone out here, but I didn't think it would be you."

I'll bet you didn't, she returned silently. Aloud and calmly, she said, "I like walking in the moonlight."

His hands stayed on her arms. "That isn't something you ought to do alone." His voice fell, dark and seductive—dangerous.

She hated that the change affected her and told herself it was only caution and fear that sent the little shiver down her back. "Sometimes alone is best," she said with surprising control. "I like to meditate. A late-night walk is a good time to do it."

He felt a slight tremble beneath his hands and saw the telltale blink of her eyes. She was lying. He wanted to know why. "Well—" he drew out the word "—since you're in the neighborhood, why don't you come in? There's still a bottle of brandy left from the last guest."

She listened to the charm of his voice and fought it. His crushing grip became a caress, his thumbs massaging where moments ago they'd bruised. She shrugged away.

"I'm not making house calls while I'm on vacation."

His eyes darkened and filled with rage. "No?" He growled an oath. "Let's see."

She pushed at him, knowing what he would do and knowing she wouldn't resist if he took her in his arms. Whirling away she darted off, but he caught her in a step and dragged her against him, crushing her in his arms, devouring her mouth in his fury.

She struggled, wrenching her body within the viselike embrace, outraged at his high-handedness and at the passion that, against all reason, shot through her. She thought it wasn't fair to find an enemy in her own body, not when she needed all she possessed to keep her head.

"I despise you," she told him, giving up the struggle as the last of her will melted away.

"No, Regina. You want me," he returned triumphantly, quieting her with the pressure of his kiss. His lips were urgent, demanding, wild. She could feel her heart pounding against his, different beats, different needs, too different for love.

With his mouth on hers, he moaned. She was seeping through him, filling him with a warmth he didn't know a man could feel. It was the wrong way and the wrong time, but the feeling was too right for him to tear his arms away and let her go just yet. He needed her, needed to have what she could give. He needed to learn how to end the hollowness inside him. But not now and because of what he had to do, maybe never. He could taste the pain of need in her, and understanding it, pulled his mouth away.

"I'd want more than this." She trembled and her eyes misted sadly at his words, then she turned and ran up the dark path. She could understand that she wanted him; that she wanted his love was too much to comprehend. She needed love from a man who could give openly and freely and honestly, above all honestly.

He watched her go, though he wanted to hold her, endlessly, and to tell her he was willing to be all she might ask. He didn't call her back. Instead, again he cursed the forces that had brought them together at this time and in this way. She was finding his vulnerabilities and making him weak— and right now he could afford no weaknesses.

Regina slept late, awaking only because Winston came through the window demanding she open the door and let him into the corridor. The sun was high and hot. She hardly felt as if she'd slept at all because she'd been caught in a tempest of dreams. For once, though, she'd awakened clearheaded—sometimes nightmares had that power.

Music, fast moving and island style, pumped in the windows. She'd forgotten this was the day Monica invited villagers to the plantation for a day of celebrating. It was to be a continuation of last night's festival, with people in costumes, dancing, games, prizes. She moved listlessly to a window and pulled open a shade.

The front grounds of Whitechurch were decorated with paper streamers and gay balloons, and tables of food were set up close to the house where the small band played. Already a sparse crowd had collected on the lawn, among them most of the servants and plantation guests, and Monica, never forgetting her hostess duties, flitting among them.

Monica. A sweet-faced, mildly exuberant elderly woman. Could she have any part in this sinister business? There was, after all, no magic age people passed that suddenly filled them with integrity and principles. If people were unscrupulous at forty, wouldn't they still be so at seventy, unless they simply ran out of energy? Monica wasn't out of energy. Maybe this was a family affair and whatever Pierce's position, Monica supported it. Maybe Blake was the victim in this, all around. The wisest thing for her to do would be to act as if she knew nothing and try to find out everything.

She dressed, giving the act little time. That was easy to do on an island. All one needed was something light and loose, and a quick brush through the hair. It was ironic that she could think this life easy after what it had done to her. Blake missing. Danger hidden in strangers' faces—as well as friends'. Or had she any friends here? The thought chilled her as nothing else had. She was alone in paradise. But this paradise, this Eden had an evil charm.

By the time she reached the front grounds the crowd had built up until it resembled that in the streets of Roseau. She wove her way through it, slowly, speaking to everyone, looking behind masks, looking for something that would jell in her mind.

"You slept late," Monica said softly, stepping from behind a tub-sized punch bowl. "I thought you might need to, so I didn't have Edie wake you."

Regina listened, trying to read anything unusual in that smiling face, finding nothing misleading. "I couldn't sleep last night after the festival," she said. "Too much excitement. I took a walk."

Now the blue-shadowed lids lifted speculatively. "What do you think of our party?"

Regina captured a smile somewhere deep down and brought it to her face. "It's your way of saying thank-you, isn't it? To the villagers, those who work for you? I've noticed that everyone gets a prize."

Monica agreed. "They're generous to me. It's a small thing to do, and I have as much fun as any of them. Forgive me," she said, glancing at her watch. "It's time for a special game with the children. I have to be there."

Telling herself that the most logical explanation was that Monica knew nothing of Pierce's activities concerning Blake and the necklace, Regina left the front grounds. At an aimless pace she walked around to the back gardens where she might have a few quiet and private moments to think.

As she turned the corner of the house and entered the rose garden, she saw a man running in the distance. He wore a mask and a brightly colored festival costume. She called out, startling him, but he only stopped for a moment to look around before turning and bolting into the thick tropical growth. Almost at the same time she stumbled over an object on the ground. Not an object, she realized with horror as she looked down—a man! Larousse. Giving a quick cry for help, she bent over him and swiftly checked for vital signs. Detecting a weak but fading pulse she immediately set about trying to revive him.

"What's wrong?" Pierce asked, appearing almost immediately from one of the rear entrances.

"He's unconscious! Call for an ambulance!"

He didn't question her instructions. A quick glance was enough to send him into the office at a run. He was back in minutes reporting that the island's one ambulance was on the way. Regina continued to work on the man but feared there was little hope for him without medication. By then others began to gather around, watching, waiting. The ambulance was slow to arrive, but when it did Regina quickly told the doctor who'd accompanied the driver what she'd done. He hurriedly started an IV and medication and shortly had his patient on the way to the hospital.

Pierce and Monica ushered bystanders back toward the front grounds. Regina, shaken, desperately in need of someone to talk to, found a solitary bench across the garden. She'd been there only a moment when Inspector Marot made his appearance.

"I understand you found my partner." Solemn faced, he took a seat beside her on the bench.

"I hope in time. Was he taking medication for his heart?"

Marot shook his head slowly. "To my knowledge he was healthy. Only those annoying allergies. With a heart condition he couldn't have stayed in our line of work, so I don't believe he knew there was a problem." Marot gave a resigned sigh. "That is possible, isn't it? An attack without warning?"

"It happens," she said consolingly.

Marot nodded stiffly. "I wanted to ask if you noticed anything unusual when you found him."

"No. I saw a man across the garden but I don't know if he'd seen your partner or not. Though Larousse must have fallen there only minutes before I found him. Were you here to see my uncle?"

"Yes."

She considered telling Marot the entire story, but Blake's apprehension of the man surfaced in her mind. "He isn't here," she said.

"I know. Mrs. Whitechurch told us he left last night. She invited us to stay for the party. That's why I thought it a little odd that Armand was so far from the crowd."

Regina pursed her lips. Monica invited them to stay. Innocently or because she thought Blake might be back? Why had Larousse left the party?

"A heart attack sometimes starts with nausea," she said. "He may have been looking for a private spot if he felt sick. Or maybe he was trying to get to the house for help."

She glanced at Marot. The way he was looking at her she was certain his mind wasn't completely occupied with thoughts of Larousse or of Blake. His eyes, his words, lacked warmth and they made her uncomfortable. Perhaps it was only part of his training that made him seem so cold.

He stood, dismissing whatever glimpse inside had briefly appeared in his eyes. "He can tell us that when he's conscious, I suppose. Now I must go to the hospital and wait until Armand is better. I only wanted to talk with you a moment first."

"I hope he's going to recover," she told Marot. Professional experience told her his chances were slim. "He was weak."

He acknowledged her concern and started to walk away, then shook his head as if he'd had another thought. He ambled back. "Dr. Lawton," he said. "I think the time has come for us to be frank. I have learned that your uncle's life is in danger. Larousse and I came here to warn him. Tell him he can come to us for safety." His eyes dimmed as he remembered Larousse's condition. "To me. He can trust me. Tell him I will guarantee his safety. I'm staying at the Reef. He can reach me there or at the hospital. Tell him there isn't much time."

The tone of his voice, the words he used, jarred a memory that wouldn't quite take form. Only the word *trust* stalled in her thoughts. It had been part of Larousse's warning in the airport, but whom had he meant? It could have been anyone—Pierce, Blake, even his partner.

"I'll try," she mumbled, feeling her throat constricting, wondering if it was Marot and his shrewd look or just the circumstances that made her apprehensive. Until she knew, she couldn't quite trust him.

"Dr. Lawton," Marot said gravely. "If you care for your uncle, do more than try."

She answered with a nod. Marot's words still stuck in her mind like bits of glass as she returned to her room. It was one reason she didn't realize at first that a sixth sense was telling her someone had been in the room recently. Not until she noticed the closet door ajar and some of the drawers partially open did she understand the reason for her uneasiness. Her next observation was that the hat with the black scarf around it was just as she'd left it. She went immediately to the drawer where she'd put the music box *Gone*. But whoever took it didn't get what they wanted.

But who? Had Blake come back for the necklace? Had he been the man running from the garden? Or had someone persuaded him to tell where the necklace was hidden? Someone who could give a chilling laugh and say that Blake had dropped out of sight. And what of Larousse? Had he been giving chase to that person when he collapsed?

A call to the hospital confirmed what she feared about Larousse's condition. He hadn't regained consciousness and the outlook wasn't hopeful. Thanking the young Dominican doctor for his time, Regina hung up the phone.

Supper was late, a buffet out by the pool. Most of those present had only a nominal interest in the man who had suffered a heart attack earlier in the day. Polite questions were asked of Regina and then most went on with enjoying a feast of native dishes. Worry rimmed Monica's eyes as she tried to persuade Regina to eat.

"Even for a doctor a thing like that must be a shock. You're upset naturally. You ought to eat. I don't believe you've had a thing all day."

That was true. She'd slept through breakfast and hadn't wanted lunch. She wasn't hungry now, but to appease Monica she took a serving of broiled fish and seasoned rice and some fruit. Moving to a table farthest from the activity, she called Monica to her side again.

"Do you have any idea where Blake has gone?" she asked softly.

Monica hesitated, seeming to stumble over what she wanted to say. "I'm sorry I don't." Then recovering, she put her hand over one of Regina's on the table and patted it.

"I'm sure he'll be in touch with you soon. Try not to worry."

She felt something in Monica's touch, saw something in her eyes that encouraged another question. "Do you know why—"

Pierce interrupted. Nodding to Regina he called Monica away and held a short but intense conversation with her. Monica looked back guiltily at Regina but didn't return to her table. Shortly afterward Pierce slipped away and went into the house. Something clicked in Regina's mind and she followed. As she expected, he entered the office and made a call, probably a local one because this time his voice was a normal pitch and reached her as only a mumble through the tightly closed doors.

About an hour later while everyone else was still by the pool dancing and talking, he slipped out of the house the back way. The moonlight was sparse but lit the path well enough that she could hang back a safe distance and still follow. The path led past a field of banana trees, through a section of jungle and finally to a hill overlooking the black volcanic sand of the beach. They were a mile, maybe more from Whitechurch. Ahead she saw light glowing from the window of a palm-topped shack almost hidden in the underbrush. Reggae music blasted from a radio inside the shack.

Regina, shuddering with apprehension, slid into the cover of tall grass as for the first time Pierce stopped and looked back. His eyes ranged from the hillside to the beach and then back to the shack. Seeing nothing threatening to account for the noise he'd heard, he knocked on the door. It opened momentarily, revealing a dark-skinned man who invited Pierce inside.

She had no weapon but caution as she propelled her way through the waist-high grass, not daring to go back to the open path. From her vantage point crouched beneath a window she could see four men besides Pierce, none of whom looked very friendly, with their knives and guns. On the table there was a bundle of what she was sure would be termed an "illegal substance" in the States. All five of them were drinking and sounds of harsh laughter rattled above the music, but the talk was low and drowned out by the reggae beat.

Blake wasn't inside. She felt relief that he wasn't with these men, then fear that he might have been. She reasoned that if they had him he would still be safe. The necklace hadn't been found.

One of the men kicked back a chair and got angrily to his feet. He shoved one of his companions against the wall. Her blood froze as she saw the second man move his hand toward the knife at his belt. But instead of pulling out the knife he spit on the floor and turned away. Pierce spoke afterward, consoling the first man by the look on his face. She ached to hear the words that came next, but couldn't. Everything was effectively screened by the music.

When it looked as if the parley was about to break up she eased away from the window, back to where the grass was thick enough to conceal her. She hadn't learned much, except that Pierce was friendly with dangerous men who were most likely criminals. Creeping away from the shack, she wasn't at all prepared for the slash of a machete no more than an inch from her nose. Blades of grass shot into her face, stinging her skin and blinding her for a moment. Before she caught her breath again a burly arm looped her waist, snatching her from the grass.

"What do you have, Arthur?" The men in the shack had come outside at the sound of a shout from the fifth man, the one with the machete who held her as if she was a sack of rice.

"Woman!" He laughed. "What can I do with her?"

"Bring her here," one of the four at the shack commanded.

The one called Arthur half dragged, half carried her to the lighted door of the shack. There with the lamplight on his face she could see that he was Carib. His face was savage and cruel under long twisted tufts of hair. That machete swinging in his hand looked as ominous as a guillotine blade, and he obviously enjoyed using it.

The one who'd given orders caught her by the hair and lifted her head to see her face. "A woman," he said. "A nosey woman." He let her go and nodded to Arthur, who dropped her to the dirt.

She glared up at all of them defiantly but said nothing, intuitively knowing these men wouldn't appreciate any talk not asked for. Flakes of ice formed in her blood. Pierce made a threatening step toward her. His dark eyes held pure glaring fury. He looked as if he could snap her neck himself and would welcome the chance.

Chapter 10

She's mine, Bandy!" His stare as savage as the Carib's, Pierce's eyes bored holes in her thin shield of dignity, one more challenge to her slipping sanity. "I told you to stay at the house!" He jerked her brutally to her feet.

Hot color burned into her ashen face. She wanted to shout an obscenity at him but instead dropped her head, cowed. He was giving her an out and she would be a fool not to take it.

Arthur grunted his disappointment. "I could teach her manners," the one called Bandy growled, eyeing her hungrily. Looks from the other three were equally as lecherous. She guessed they were smugglers and would as soon slit a throat as say good-morning.

Pierce lassoed her with an arm and hauled her against his side. "You can't teach a jealous woman anything. Not when she thinks you've gone off to meet another lover."

Raucous laughter erupted from all the men but Bandy. "I don't like uninvited guests." His voice fell low and menacing. "Not good for my business."

"Don't worry about her." Pierce winked at Bandy, conveying a masculine intent, and gestured toward the beach. "I know how to make her forget everything." Bandy uttered a coarse acknowledgment and allowed them to leave.

Roughly, so she couldn't resist, Pierce gripped her arm and ushered her down a steep path leading to the beach. Branches slapped against her arms and face, and she nearly had to run to match his stride.

"Let me go now!" she demanded, trying to wretch her arm from him. He clutched her tighter.

"You little fool! Do you know how close you came to being fish food by morning?" Pierce snarled the question as anger ripped at him.

She stumbled, trying to stay up with him. He dragged her along until she got back on her feet. "They wouldn't have killed me?" Goose bumps rose up on her skin. "Would they?"

"In a heartbeat." He confirmed her fears, his eyes glittering fire. "Do you have any idea what you're dealing with here? Or is the dumb act part of your cover?"

Tread cautiously, an inner voice warned. He might be little better than those men. She flung her head back. "I don't know what you're talking about. I went for a walk and saw the lights. I was curious. How would I know you were dealing with drug smugglers or bandits or whatever they are."

"Damn stubborn woman! A walk! A mile from the house in the middle of the night?" He spat out an oath. "All right. Leave it at that for now. Just hope my act was more convincing than yours is." Stopping, he crushed her against him unexpectedly. "Put your arm around my waist and try to behave a little like a lover."

With a hiss she jerked back. "You've got to be kidding."
The anger almost choked her. "Don't start believing that
rubbish you told Bandy. I'm going straight back to the
plantation and you can't stop me!" She pushed at his chest,
marveling at her false bravado, knowing, of course, that he
could easily do whatever he wanted.

His hands were like grappling hooks jerking her nearer.
A shadow of amusement passed over his face. "Regina, my
dear, regardless of what you think of me, I'd hate to see that
lovely body washed up on the beach tomorrow. You don't
think those guys are stupid enough not to confirm my
story?"

"Meaning what?" Her pale eyes glowed hotly. He'd
managed to find and prod every ignition center her temper
had.

"Meaning we're being followed." Bending his head close,
he lowered his voice. "Watched. Bandy and his crew don't
take chances on anyone."

"But you're a friend, you do business—"

"They have no loyalties. If they even thought I'd crossed
them . . ." He gripped her shoulders tightly. "Believe me, if
we don't make love on the beach, neither of us will see day-
break. And I for one am not ready to depart this world,
whatever the cost."

In a swift move, he pulled her into a grove of coconut
palms where they were partially obscured from the bluff
above. Inside his anger burned like hot, smoldering coals.
He was furious at her for following him and at himself for
leading her into such a dangerous situation. The thought of
what Bandy and his cutthroats might have done made him
shudder.

Her thoughts ran a similar path. That deadly machete,
those degenerate men. Men like that were horrible magi-
cians who could make people disappear without a trace.

As soon as Pierce reached the shadows, he stopped. Regina collapsed against him, trembling, just beginning to realize the gravity of what had almost happened to her, of what Pierce had said. She was sure she abhorred Pierce Buchannan and yet she clung to him, guided by an unacknowledged inner belief that she was safe as long as she was in his arms.

"This is serious, isn't it?" she whispered.

Mumbling a curse, though softly this time, Pierce eased her against the trunk of a wind-bent palm and began removing his shirt.

"Any dealing with those men is serious." His voice shook, no longer with anger but with relief that she'd been discovered before he left the shack. A step forward brought him so close she could feel his hot breath rustling her hair. He brought his hands to her cotton shirt and tugged at the buttons. She stilled his hands.

"Don't," she pleaded, realizing what he was about to do. She shook her head as if to clear her mind. Part of her wanted him to do just what he was doing, knowing that in making love with him she could for a time forget all else. Part of her rebelled that it was Pierce who could grant her that sanctuary.

He caught her hands and pulled her tightly against his chest, sensing her conflict but in too much turmoil himself to deal with it gently. "Cooperate," he warned.

"I can't," she said unsteadily, remembering those vicious men and their cold eyes. "They're up there."

"Consider the consequences." Pierce glanced back at the bluff above the beach and saw two hulking shadows sink to the ground.

"I'd rather die."

"Exactly."

"Oh, no." Defeat was a whisper. Her fear of those men from the shack was horrendously greater than her reluctance to do as directed. Pierce felt, in fact, even more warm and reassuring. A ripple of surrender shook her shoulders even as she voiced another protest. "We can't," she whispered. "Not like this. Not with them watching."

His hands were gentle, his voice became so as well. "Relax," he told her. "I find this just as distasteful as you do. We're just going to pretend. Now do your part. Remember, your life depends on it."

"All right," she said weakly as he slipped the shirt from her shoulders and dropped it to the sand. She could pretend.

"That's better," he mumbled, resting his hands on the gentle slope of her shoulders and stepping back as the silver moonlight flooded the soft white curves of her breasts.

She saw longing in his eyes. She stiffened, not due to her growing doubts but remembering there were men looking down at her nakedness.

As if reading her thoughts, Pierce stepped in closer, shielding her body with his. From the corner of his eye he saw the two shadows rise and steal away toward the shack. The men were leaving. There was really no reason to go on, but having her close against him sent a heavy surge of desire rocketing through him. Combined with the smoldering heat of his anger, it made a volatile combination.

"Don't worry..." he started, moving his mouth close to hers and whispering above the ocean's gentle rap of waves on sand. The other words, telling Regina the men were gone were lost as his lips met hers. Her warmth and sweetness assailed him. Just a kiss, he promised himself. He would kiss her, cool his blood a little, then take her back to Whitechurch. He lost sight of that promise as he felt her respond.

"I'll try," she whispered back, trying to muster up some poise and dignity from her despair as she slid her arms easily around his waist. The warm vapor of his breath moistened her lips. She reminded herself it was all an act as his mouth came down harder on hers.

The fire leaped. Regina moaned softly. It was a kiss not an act, and Pierce felt himself dragged back into the furnace—despite his good intentions. No pretense existed in the hot flow of desire that ran on a channel from one to the other.

Pierce held her closer. He'd forgotten he meant to stop. He'd forgotten nothing she responded to, the slanted play of his mouth across her, the flick of his tongue on her lips. He remembered every slight move that had given her pleasure and now tormented her with them and her flesh responded and her mouth moved with his. He knew her well.

Pierce caressed the small of her back and upward, stroking along her ribs, finding her naked breasts, feeling the peaks tighten with a shudder of betrayal.

Regina struggled for desperately needed control and lost. Desire raged inside her, as she wanted him and lacked the will to question her wanting. For the moment it was enough that she felt safe in his arms. "Pierce, hold me," she cried, "hold me."

His need carried him beyond reason, still he made one last attempt to pull away and to tell her they were alone on the beach.

"Regina, listen," he said raggedly. "The men—"

"Don't talk. I don't want to hear. I don't want to understand. I just want you to hold me, make love with me."

"Oh God, Regina." Desire snapped away his last sane thought. His mouth found hers, his hands once again the warm, yielding flesh of her breasts. Moments later he kissed and nipped where his hands had been. She moaned slightly when he suckled the pink crests. When he reached for the button of her shorts, she helped him with the unfastening, then wriggled and squirmed until the garment fell to her feet.

Naked against him, the familiar, bittersweet yearning multiplied inside her. Feverishly, they worked at the snap of his shorts and within seconds he stepped out of them. Nothing separated them—not garments, not emotions. Pierce dragged her to the sand where the shadows concealed all but the sounds of love. She'd completely forgotten Bandy's men nearby.

Pierce swore silently. The feel of her inflamed him. He hoped she wouldn't regret this, nevertheless he knew he was powerless to turn back.

Regina sighed, reveling in the pleasure of his hands moving like molten fire over her skin. This was madness. True madness.

His mouth, a warm flame at her ear, traced a sensuous line around the inner rim, quickly dazing her mind, clouding her thoughts.

"I can't hate you," she mumbled, not truly conscious of her words.

Moments later she felt him probing her softness, felt him plunge hotly inside. All the world shattered and fell—the good, the evil. Nothing remained but the two of them on a black sand beach beneath a pale tropical moon.

Hot and damp with perspiration and sprinkled with sand, they lay locked together in the aftermath of pleasure. For a long time they remained that way, her head resting on his shoulder, his hand on her cheek.

"You give a great performance," Pierce said when the heat had cooled and the moon disappeared behind a ragged cloud.

Forced out of her blissful cocoon by his remark, she remembered the men on the hillside and felt shame wash over her. Suddenly it was impossible to reconcile what had happened with what she believed about Pierce. "Thanks," she said icily, rolling away from him and attempting to cover herself with the first thing she could find, his shirt.

Pierce sensed her emotional withdrawal and stiffened. "Regina, I didn't mean..."

"I'm not a fool," she snapped. "I know exactly what you meant." Something hard flashed in his eyes and made her shiver. Tears welled in her eyes and suddenly she was all anger and fury. "What kind of man are you?"

She swung at him, but Pierce broke the blow with his palm, capturing her hand tightly and holding on to it. His temper rose. "The kind you like," he growled.

An emptiness hung in her eyes as she shook her head. He had the feeling he'd just lost something, perhaps the one thing that might have been worth holding on to. He'd only meant to put on a show to satisfy Bandy's men. He'd never meant to really make love with her. But how could he explain that the thought of how close she'd come to being killed had made him a little crazy. He'd just wanted to hold her and protect her. He hadn't known that seeing her, touching her in a wash of moonlight would push through his control—and hers.

Her voice lashed at him. "Damn you! You made me do that while they stood there and watched. I don't know how I can ever face anyone again."

Angry at himself, and more hurt by her outburst than he cared to admit, he shrugged away her fury. "I don't think I made you do anything you didn't want to do."

The truth of that stung. "No, you didn't. But I was upset, not to mention, terrified. You shouldn't have listened to me."

"Hell!" Pierce got to his feet. "If it helps your sensitivities any, they didn't see a thing, Regina. They left before it all started."

"They left!" She got up, too, angrily tossing his shirt to the ground. Her eyes were blue ice. "Why didn't you tell me?"

Pierce shook his head and exhaled a heavy breath. All the repentance fled from his face. Still he scowled, seeing that hurt flood over her anger. He hated himself for doing that to her again. Where she was concerned he always seemed to do the opposite of what his heart told him. He shook his head again as frustration took over.

"Oh hell, Regina! I tried to tell you, but you have to admit that talking was the last thing you wanted to do. Go rinse in the surf and put these on," he ordered, tossing her clothes to her. "We have to talk, and now I have the presence of mind not to let you stop me."

Hurrying off, she did as he said. She wanted to wash the feel of him away. In the water, she ducked under the waves, staying as long as her breath would hold. The force of the surf tugged at her, the cold water chilled her limbs. But it was hopeless. Every touch, every word was imprinted in her brain, forever. Finally, wet and shaking but clothed, she came back to the grove. Down the beach he'd rinsed himself, too. He came back a few moments after her.

"What is there to say, Pierce?" She crossed her arms over her chest. "It's all very clear. You're a man who can share a drink with smugglers as easily as with members of a corporate board. You are whatever you have to be to get what you want. Success at any cost. Seduction must be one of the fringe benefits. Does that sum it up?" Regina realized she was lashing out at him unreasonably, but she wasn't ready to deal with the desire he inspired within her.

He glared with furious umber eyes, all his anger back in one leap. "For an intelligent woman you can be incredibly dense," he growled. "I'm trying to help Blake."

"How? By handing him over to cutthroats?"

"No. By getting that damned necklace back where it belongs."

She took a quick sharp breath. His reply caught her off guard but only for a moment. "And where is that?"

"To the vault where it should have stayed in the first place. Where it can't be used to topple a government or cause any more loss of life." Her brows lifted sharply at that statement. "I can't give you names," he added.

"I'm not asking for names." She felt as empty as her voice sounded. The truth was out. He wanted the necklace. But was the noble talk real or a clever guise? A spark of hope warmed her. She desperately needed to know. "I want to know how you learned about this."

His voice was smooth but strong. "And why I hobbled into your office a few weeks ago?"

"Especially that," she retorted.

He shoved his hands, now fists, into his pockets. "I didn't know about the necklace then. I thought Blake was black-mailing Monica."

"That's preposterous."

"Not really." A muscle twitched at his jaw. If she knew the truth she might be easier to handle. "I came across Monica's private records by chance. For years she's been regularly paying Blake large sums of money. Your uncle walks a fine line of legality with his little operation. I suppose you think he makes his money with investments, sound stock market plays. You're wrong. Blake Andrews specializes in connecting buyers with special merchandise. Well-known painting and art objects make their way into secret private collections through Blake's hands."

She backed away from him and what he said. "That isn't true."

"It's true." For the first time in years he wished he hadn't given up smoking. A cigarette could have helped right now—or a good stiff drink. "Who do you think this strange menagerie is at Monica's house party? They're buyers making bids on the merchandise. That's Monica's part, providing the cover and the place for the exchange. It's not hard moving items in and out of here. A yacht offshore, a rowboat. It's done.''

"Then Monica's involved, too." Some of the bite had gone out of her voice.

"So it seems." His eyes locked on hers. They were distant and cold. "Can you believe it?"

"No." She moved her gaze away not wanting to get caught again in those dark, depthless eyes, not wanting to be swept where they might take her. "I'm not sure I do. Though it *does* explain why Blake was given the necklace in the first place." It also hurt. She turned away. She wanted no link with him now, not even a look.

"An unwise choice of merchandise," he said.

"Which you're trying to recover."

"Yes."

"Why you?"

His face clouded with more frustration. Given a little she would want to know everything. They were reaching the point where he had to draw the line. "Because I have friends in France associated with the government who knew I had certain—capabilities. Because I was in the right place."

"How convenient for your friends. Tell me, do these friends have any connection to your resort project in France?"

"Some of them do. That's why they thought of me."

"I see."

His lips thinned. "No, you don't see." Why couldn't she make it simple? "Blake needs my help. That's what you have to see."

She gave him a blank stare.

He groaned. "Why do I have the feeling I'm not getting through to you?"

"Oh, you're getting through," she returned matter-of-factly. "You want the necklace. Marot wants the necklace. Everyone wants the necklace."

"Stay away from Marot," he warned, eyes darkening. "You can't trust him."

"And I can trust you?" Her voice had sharpened at his comment.

"I saved your life tonight. Believe that."

"I wonder if that wasn't part of the whole charade."

"Look. I was mad as hell at you for following me, for risking your life. Maybe I went a little too far." His voice softened. He didn't want her angry at him. He wanted her to know that what happened came about because he cared. "But you—"

"Maybe?" she cut him off. She lifted a brow, unable to admit the large part she herself had played in just how far he'd gone. It was the only soft line on her face. "You went a damn sight too far, Mr. Buchannan. If I had it to do over I'd have taken my chances with the smugglers." Frost hung heavy on every word. "Just why were you with those men, anyway?"

He clenched his jaw for a moment. "Those men carry passengers as well as merchandise on and off the island. I wanted to know if they've had recent customers."

"Have they? Did they take Blake?" she demanded.

"I can't tell you what they said. I gave them my word it would go no farther than my ears."

Her eyes bored into him. She could tell by his determined tone there was no use pleading for word on Blake. "I'm going back to the house," she said.

He caught her arm. "Regina, you have to trust me."

"You mean after you arranged to meet me—twice, and after I find you with cutthroats? I should trust you? I wish I could. I want to," she told him, shrugging away from his grasp. An instant later she took off in a trot down the beach toward Whitechurch.

"Regina!" Pierce shouted after her, then cursing, let her go. He'd done enough damage for one night. She was better off out of it. He'd found out what he needed to know from Bandy and his men, and he'd used precious time with her. There were still other things to do before he went back himself. Another twenty-four hours and it would all be over. Then he could make his peace with Regina. Or try to forget her.

Adding up the few facts she had, Regina decided Pierce might be lying. If Blake was still on Dominica that meeting she'd observed might have been to enlist those men to search Blake out. Maybe Pierce wouldn't harm Blake himself, but he might not be above hiring someone to do it for him.

She raced into Whitechurch, going by her room only long enough to make certain the necklace was still there and to change into fresh clothes. Afterward she made her way to Monica's room.

"Monica. Monica. Wake up," she called, keeping her voice deliberately calm.

"Regina?" Monica stirred from sleep and quickly turned on a bedside lamp. "What is it? Has Blake—"

"That's who I want to talk to you about," Regina interrupted, dragging a chair up beside the bed. "I'm guessing you know all about the diamond necklace."

Monica hung her head. "Yes."

"You and Blake are business partners—of a sort."

"Yes."

She cringed. That part of Pierce's story was true. "Do you know where Blake is? If he's safe?"

Monica pulled herself into a sitting position. She looked very small and old in the bed. "He's safe for the moment."

"Then why did he leave so quickly? So unprepared?"

Monica's decision to answer that question came with a deep sigh. "He made a call from Roseau the night of the festival. The news he received caused him to panic, and he didn't think it was safe to go back to the house."

Regina laced her fingers tightly together. "Then it wasn't because he saw Marot?"

"I don't see how it could have been," she said. "He knew someone was watching him but he never saw the Frenchman because he never actually went near the parade that night. I spoke to him in a café about half an hour after we arrived. He wouldn't tell me everything but he said he had his contact and he'd get in touch with me when the transaction was finished."

Regina shuddered. Had someone warned him about Pierce? It all made sense. Who but Pierce could have made Blake feel going back to the house was unsafe?

"He didn't have the necklace with him when he left."

"No." Monica pulled the covers to her throat though there was no chill in the warm air. "But who would know that? His plan was to slip back into the house during the party yesterday when nobody would notice him and get it."

Regina *had* seen him. Why hadn't he come back when she'd called out? "Do you know where it was hidden?"

"In the silver swan," Monica said sadly. "I'm sorry, my dear. That was a mistake. Blake was supposed to mail the swan to me. The silver shields anything hidden inside from a customs X ray. We often use that method. That ivory and onyx box in my study was a gift for you. Somehow the packages got switched. Blake never meant to get you caught up in this."

"I'm sure he didn't," Regina said quietly, remembering the sudden change of plans and the strange emotion in Blake's voice when he'd called several weeks ago. Weeks? Or had it been a lifetime? The pain was tangible as she called herself a fool for thinking he'd turned sentimental.

Monica went on solemnly. "But once all the trouble developed he decided it was best to leave the necklace hidden and let you return it to him without knowing about it."

"Which is why he told me to bring the music box to Antigua for an inscription."

Monica nodded absently. "He didn't think anyone would suspect you of having it."

Regina was just beginning to absorb the fact that her beloved Uncle Blake was little better than a thief, and that the aristocratic Monica was his accomplice. All the deceit, all those years. Her voice quivered with the impact of it. "Apparently he was wrong from the beginning. My house was burglarized the very day that package arrived. I'm sure now the burglar was searching for the necklace." And almost as sure that burglar had been Pierce, she continued silently. "But I suppose once I put the music box out with my things no one knew what to look for."

"That's why he left it in your possession during the trip. And now that he has it, your involvement is over." Monica observed the agony on Regina's face. "He *does* have it, doesn't he?"

Regina sat quietly for a few moments unable to answer as all the terrible possibilities swirled in her mind. "He may have the swan," she said at last in hardly more than a whisper. "It's missing. But the necklace wasn't inside. I took it out."

Monica shook, voice and all. "Oh, my dear."

Regina fell silent again for a long space of time, but then asked the question that had been tearing at her. "What does Pierce know about all this?"

Monica's eyes narrowed. "He's got some idea Blake's been leading me down the garden path. Blackmail or swindle. Who knows just what he thinks?"

Regina stood, no longer able to contain herself in the chair. "He knows about your arrangement with Blake."

Monica sighed with finality. "I suppose it's just as well. As long as that's all he knows."

Doubts kept Regina from telling Monica that her nephew was involved in trying to recover the necklace. Monica evidently didn't know and that was probably best. There was the question of loyalty even under these circumstance—Monica's, not Pierce's. She remembered several occasions when Pierce had professed concern for Monica's welfare. But what logical reason could he have for keeping his part in the affair from his aunt at this point? Why hadn't he warned her of the danger, unless he feared she would suspect duplicity and prevent him getting his hands on the necklace?

"Perhaps," Regina agreed, ready to leave the subject of Pierce Buchannan. She turned to another. "The man who had the heart attack this afternoon, did you know who he was?"

"One of the Frenchmen. I learned they were on the island when we went to Roseau for the festival. And of course I saw the tall one speaking to you there. The bald one had such an accent there was no doubt who he was when he spoke to me on the front lawn. They didn't say they were agents, only that they had come to see Blake. When I told them he'd left the island they seemed disappointed. I gave them punch and invited them to stay for the party. I was surprised when they accepted."

"Did you see them again?"

"I saw the tall one. He was out front. I didn't see the other one again until the ambulance came. Oh my," she said suddenly. "I'm forgetting. Dr. Williams from the hospital called you. He wants you to call him there in the morning."

About Larousse. Regina had asked to be kept updated on his condition. She hoped he was better and perhaps had regained consciousness, but she didn't hold out much hope. He'd hardly responded to her efforts to revive him. Something about that bothered her. It was almost as if she'd been fighting more than a heart attack.

She wondered, too, at the possibility that the French agents were Blake's contact, after all. Perhaps that was why they'd hung back in Antigua. They were waiting until he'd been advised it was safe to turn the necklace over to them. It was possible that was why they'd come to Whitechurch at the time Blake was to return for the necklace. If Blake had seen Larousse unconscious on the ground he might have been frightened and run, suspecting foul play.

Now she was certain. She needed to talk to Marot first thing in the morning.

"Monica," she said, feeling as if all the world weighed on her decision. "You have to tell me where Blake is. I have to take the necklace to him. Otherwise he may be in even more serious trouble."

Reluctance played with the myriad lines around Monica's mouth. Finally she spoke. "He's in the mountains. I have property there. A cabin. I'll take you to him in the morning."

"You don't have to go." Even knowing Monica's involvement she felt that was asking too much of the elderly woman.

Monica shook her head. "You wouldn't find it alone. The road is hardly more than a trail."

Reluctantly Regina agreed. "Then we'll go together. But don't tell anyone. Even Pierce." She saw that her warning hadn't been necessary. She forced a smile. "I'm going to try to sleep. I have a few things to do before we leave in the morning. Good night."

Pierce reached Whitechurch not long after Regina. Knowing how near she was and how he'd hurt her, he found himself again fighting the urge to go to her and demand that she listen to an explanation of why he was involved in a search for Blake and the necklace. But there were others involved who might be jeopardized if he didn't do as he'd been instructed.

The devil, he thought, throwing open the door to the garage. She was making him crazy. His arms ached for the feel of her, his heart felt like a solid lump of lead in his chest. He had no choice but to hope she would be willing to listen—later. The alternative chilled him.

A few clouds had drifted in and the night had turned black as the inside of a tomb. Pierce cranked the car and sped away wondering if the gloom he felt came from the darkness or his own mood.

In Roseau he parked in front of the tin-topped, wood-frame hospital and went inside. Two Dominican men waiting in the tiny lobby greeted him, then led him down the hall toward Larousse's room. The three of them talked for a few minutes, then one of the Dominicans produced the packet of personal belongings that had been taken from the patient on admission and sealed for safekeeping. With the sharp blade of a knife the man slit the packet and withdrew a wallet. Glancing around first, he handed the wallet to Pierce, who thumbed methodically through the contents.

Pierce handed back the packet. "Do you have his passport?" he asked.

"He didn't have it with him. We're checking his room."

"I doubt you'll find anything there. But in case you do..."

"We'll let you know," the Dominican finished for him while his partner sealed Larousse's belongings in a new envelope identical to the other one.

The men started to walk away. "You'll take care of things here?" Pierce asked.

He received a stony smile. "Nothing will be traced on our end."

"Good." He left as he'd come, driving the narrow rutted road at a deadly speed. One more chink wedged out and soon the entire lurid situation would topple. Only the knife twisting in his gut wouldn't still. The look on Regina's face when she'd turned and run haunted him. He knew what she thought. One more time he considered going to her room and trying to explain. Maybe there was a way to reconcile diverse paths. But he stamped down the urge with finality. He'd made a pledge to men who expected him to keep his word.

Hours after Regina had gone to bed Pierce slipped into the office. The phone dial creaked at his abuse, the transatlantic line crackled and whined. He turned off the lamp to talk in the darkness.

"Larousse is finished," he reported. "Marot is still on the island." He stretched out the cord to reach the liquor cabinet behind the desk and, opening it, poured a tall glass of Scotch. "Andrews is still in hiding. I think he has the necklace with him. He returned to Whitechurch yesterday, and I'm sure it was to get the necklace. I'd have caught him then except for the trouble over Larousse." He listened for several minutes while he drained the Scotch from the glass. "No. The niece doesn't know much, but she's getting close. I may have to get her out of the way, after all." He scowled as he listened again. "The hell with you and your orders! I'll do it my way from this point or not at all. I move tomorrow. I want it finished."

Pierce slammed the phone down and stalked out of the house and to his cottage. Regret was a bitter taste in his mouth, sleep elusive.

In the morning Regina sat a very long time in the chair by her bed considering her situation. Every line of thought brought her back to the same conclusion. She was basically alone in this. She couldn't completely trust Monica. There was always the possibility she would protect Pierce in a showdown. Monica had too much at stake to call in the local police. If Regina went to them on her own she had nothing but a story that couldn't be substantiated. She had the necklace but that proved little. She might even find herself in trouble, having brought it into the country illegally.

Accusations against Pierce might not be believed. He was known and respected on the island—even the prime minister knew him on a first-name basis. And that left her alone to find a resolution. She didn't see that she had any choice but to trust Marot. He hadn't made a hostile move, but Pierce, on the other hand, dealt with both sides of the law, whichever suited his purpose. She was certain he had a multimillion-dollar resort deal riding on successfully recovering the necklace. Men did desperate deeds for less.

She rested her head in her hands. If everything was so clear, why did she hesitate? Why did she hope Pierce would come bursting through her door to tell her this had been no more than a nightmare? She laughed bitterly at her sentimentality—this wasn't the web and film of dreams. It wouldn't disappear when she opened her eyes.

Regina forced herself to be honest. Pierce had touched her heart. Although it was difficult to comprehend, knowing that his own seemed black and remorseless.

On a rise of courage she got to her feet. Blake needed her. He was as alone as she was.

Regina dressed in white shorts and a pink cotton blouse and removed the straw hat from behind the door and put it on. It gave her a chill to know she was wearing the cause of all this heartache and betrayal. But she knew that the real cause was flawed humanity, people ruled by power and greed. People like Pierce. More despondent than ever, she made her calls from the phone in the foyer, calling the hospital first and asking for Dr. Williams.

"I'm sorry, Dr. Lawton," a nurse answered. "Dr. Williams is in surgery. Perhaps you can call back in a few hours."

"Yes, I will," Regina said, disappointed to have missed him. "Can you tell me the status of Armand Larousse?"

"One moment please. I'll check." The line went silent as she was put on hold. After a few minutes she got a reply. "Mr. Larousse's condition is unchanged."

"Still critical?"

"I think so."

"Is anyone there with him?"

"No, Dr. Lawton. He has no visitors."

Regina imagined Marot had been advised to return later. If Larousse was critical, Marot wouldn't be allowed more than a few minutes to see him.

She got the number for the hotel where Marot was staying and dialed it. Again she was put on hold, only this time it was the clack of a receiver on a table. She waited, knowing there were probably no phones in the rooms and that the desk clerk would have to send someone to get Marot. It was several minutes before he picked up the phone.

"Hello, this is Jacques Marot."

"I'm glad I reached you," she said, feeling a tremor of apprehension in spite of her resolve to remain calm. "This is Regina Lawton."

"Dr. Lawton. I've been hoping to hear from you. Have you been in touch with your uncle? Did you give him my message? His reply?"

She stopped the flow of questions. "I haven't seen him but I think I can get in touch with him." A tight lump formed in her throat. She had to stop for a moment. There would be no turning back after she asked her question. She would have put her money on Marot. "Can you come to Whitechurch so we can talk in person? I know you'll have to get a car."

"Yes." He sounded pleased. "But not immediately. I have a few matters I must clear up here first. I hope you understand?"

Disappointed he couldn't come at once, Regina never-theless assured him she understood. Undoubtedly he wanted to check on Larousse first. After a quick goodbye she hurried out to the patio, where breakfast was being served. She wanted coffee, strong and black and plenty of it. It was difficult for her to be sociable with the other house guests knowing why they'd come to Whitechurch. Soon she excused herself and left them.

Edie told Regina that Monica had awakened with a mild headache and was staying in her room for a while, and Pierce had been to the house earlier and ordered breakfast sent to his cottage. Regina hoped there wouldn't be trouble when Marot arrived. It was one complication she could do without.

After arranging for a rental car, Marot went through the lengthy process of placing a call to Paris. He couldn't see Bandy for a couple of hours yet to firm up the time for his hasty departure from Dominica.

His bag packed, there was little else to do but remove the gun he'd taped beneath the night table. He checked the cartridge and tried the feel of it in his hand. It might not be as true as he would like, but it was the best the island had to offer. He fitted it into the waistband of his trousers and pulled the tail of his shirt free to cover it. It would do.

Chapter 11

Details. The details fluttered and flew in Regina's mind like the feathery seeds of a dandelion scattered by the wind. She needed them all together, lined up where they made sense, where they could be checked off or rearranged until the answer was right. But the answer *was* right. It had to be. She couldn't fall back on doubt now. Not when she'd already set things in motion.

The trouble was she didn't want to admit she was attracted to a man like Pierce Buchannan. For the hundredth time she went over every moment they'd spent together. The attraction had made her uneasy at first. Later he'd turned on the charm and she'd felt interested. Progressing from there had been swift—straight to the heart.

Actually, attraction was a mild word for the way she felt. Love was the right one. She was in love with him. Regina shuddered at the thought. She couldn't be. She'd been a simple amusement for him in all of this, someone to get him through the waiting until he made his move. Now her logi-

cal, orderly mind didn't want to admit to having been mis-
led. So she looked for the fault in her thinking, the clue—or
the magic wand—that would make her heart right and her
head wrong.

Just as peculiarly, she still had doubts about Marot.
Nothing concrete, just that something about him still made
her uneasy. Regina shuddered once again, perplexed by the
situation. How could she love a man she didn't trust? On the
other hand, how could she confide in Marot when she didn't
trust him either?

Perhaps there was one fail-safe thing to do, something she
should have done long ago. Intent on activating her plan,
she hurried to Monica's office. She wanted privacy for the
calls she needed to make. Soon Monica's remaining guests
would be leaving for a day trip to Portsmouth at the other
end of the island. But there were still a few of them milling
around. By the time Marot arrived, however, the house
would be empty except for herself and Monica.

She'd seen Monica only briefly since talking to Marot.
There hadn't been an opportunity to explain what she'd decided to do. Observing Monica's shadowed eyes and forced
smile to the other guests, Regina preferred waiting until the
older woman was alone.

The office was unlocked. She went in, closing the heavy
doors behind her. She pushed the scattered papers aside and
sat on the corner of the big mahogany desk, picking up a
near empty glass the maid hadn't found. Scotch. Someone
had been drinking it either very early or very late. As the
operator came on the line she dismissed that from her mind.

Getting a call through was slow but she had time. Finally
the overseas operator connected her with Lieutenant Langley of the Atlanta Police Department.

"Lieutenant, this is Regina Lawton." She dreaded making this call. Maybe that was why she hadn't done it before.
"I'm calling from the West Indies."

"Well," he drawled. "Doctors do it in style, don't they?" She could picture him smirking and looking for lint on his immaculate suit.

"When we get the chance, Lieutenant," she returned, faking the lightness in her voice. "Have you had any leads on the break-in of my house?"

"None," he answered. "No more break-ins in your neighborhood, either. That makes it hard. Did you have the alarm system put in?"

"Ahh—no." She twisted a trailing strip of black silk around her finger, the weight on her head reminding her what the call was about. "But I did schedule it to be done after I get back from vacation."

"Most people are like that." He laughed but most of the sound got lost in the bad connection.

"What's that?"

"They lock the barn after the horse is gone." She heard him mumbling to someone behind him, then he was back on the line. "Dr. Lawton, is this what you called me about or should I buy a new suit and tell my wife I'm going out of town?"

She actually smiled at that. He did have a way of getting to the heart of things. "Keep your old suit, Lieutenant. I want to know if two French officers from DESE contacted the Atlanta Police shortly after you and your men were at my house."

"My tailor will be disappointed. But I won't even have to put you on hold for that. Saw them myself. Tall fellow, the other balding. Is there something I ought to know?"

"No," she answered quickly, the brief smile gone. "It just occurred to me I ought to know if they were legitimate."

"Dr. Lawton, that was weeks ago."

"I know. But I've just now come across some information I think they might be interested in. I wanted to be sure before I gave it to them."

"Okay. They were legit. They had no legal jurisdiction, of course. It was a matter of professional courtesy that they check in with us. What you tell them or don't is your business. If it's serious there are official legal channels."

"No, it's not that serious. I was just making sure. They didn't happen to tell you what they were looking for?"

"They didn't tell me and I didn't ask. I've already got enough paperwork on my desk to sink a barge. I wasn't looking for any more." He paused. "But I *did* get the impression they were looking for a man to testify in a government case."

For all his irritating manners he was sly as a fox. "Thank you, Lieutenant," she said.

"Anytime, Doctor."

Her intuition was definitely out of order. From now on she'd better rely on facts only. She was beginning to wish she'd talked to Marot long ago. Now she would check and cross-check. She'd found the card she'd passed along from Marot in Blake's room. She called the number printed on the card and heard the operator verifying the connection with someone on the other end. The voice was male, the language French. Regina could understand only enough to know she had the right agency.

"Do you speak English?" she asked, feeling a case of the jitters coming on.

"*Oui*, English. How can I be of service?"

"I would like to get in touch with Inspector Jacques Marot." She didn't know what she expected to learn, only that the mention of his name might bring something.

"Sorry, *mademoiselle*, Inspector Marot is out of the country. If you wish to leave a message, I'll relay it to him when he checks in."

"No," she answered with relief. Marot was keeping in touch with the agency. She drew in a slow breath and went a step further. "Is his partner, Inspector Larousse available?"

She detected the hesitation as the man stalled by clearing his throat. "Inspector Larousse is also away."

"Do you know when Inspector Marot will be back?"

"We expect him to return by the end of the week. Are you sure you don't wish to leave a message, *mademoiselle*?"

"No. I'll talk to him later," she said and hung up.

That cinched it. Marot *was* Inspector Marot, an officer with DESE. He was keeping the agency informed. He was acting unofficially but not secretly on behalf of his government. The facts told her she could trust him. Only knowing that seemed to squeeze all feeling out of her heart. She pulled off her hat and laid it on the desk, then dropped back limply into the big leather chair.

Why were tears stinging the backs of her eyelids as she shut them against reality? Why did she see his face? Pierce's aim had been deception right from the start. Maybe he'd had some idea about using her to persuade Blake to hand over the necklace if that had been necessary. The thought wasn't very flattering to her ego. So why did she think that if he were here right now she would plead with him to explain all this away and probably believe anything he said?

"Regina."

Her head jerked up, her eyes blinked open. "Pierce?" The next words were shaky and incoherent. "What are you doing here? What do you want?"

He shut the office doors behind him and moved toward her. His voice was low and heavy with a quality she couldn't quite place. "I don't want you looking like I'm going to murder you. I just want you to listen."

She got up and moved in a few uneven steps behind the chair where she'd been sitting. He'd come in that door almost as if he'd received a telepathic message. She was startled and a little frightened, not sure she trusted him or herself.

"I'm listening," she said hollowly.

She was shaking. He wanted to put his arms around her and tell her everything would be fine. He did neither. She certainly wasn't in a state of mind to be receptive to any comfort from him, and things weren't fine. The best he could hope for was that she would hear him out without making a dash for the door.

He let out a troubled sigh. "I'm sorry about the way things happened last night. I was mad as hell about you showing up at the shack. When I led you down to the beach I really didn't plan on anything except getting you away from Bandy and his men. I didn't mean for it to get—" he paused and searched for a delicate word "—physical, or go so far. I know that's not an excuse for what happened. It probably doesn't help to say I got swept away because I care..."

She didn't let him finish. The memories were too lifelike, too recent. Warmth and color flooded her face. "You don't have to say any more." She couldn't bear the agony of false words, not when she was already torn apart by her love for Pierce and her loyalty to her uncle. "I realize you're probably dealing with people who don't accept failure. I honestly believe that if you had a choice now you wouldn't go on with this. Somehow it's very important to me to believe that you *do* care for me—at least a little. I only wish it were enough to make you stop—"

"Regina," he interrupted, his heart severed by the pain in her face. Abruptly he moved toward her, jerking the chair away so that there was nothing separating them. Regina stiffened and her lips parted in surprise. "I'm not what you think I am. I'm not a criminal. I'm not even on the verge of being one. I'm just a man who loves you." His hands moved slowly as he talked, gripping her shoulders, pulling her tense body against his. He felt a tremble run through her, softening her resistance to his touch.

"No."

"Yes," he insisted, moving his hands up, lacing them in her hair, tilting her head back. "Yes. You feel it when I touch you." He kissed her cheek, his words coming as a warm whisper in her ear. "You know it when I kiss you." As if the world of motion had been slowed to half speed, his mouth came to hers, his lips soft and gentle.

"Pierce," she mumbled, wanting to believe him, knowing her body did. Like a heated candle she melted into him, losing all thought to the coaxing of his lips. She felt a little faint. Maybe she was wrong about him. Surely she was wrong.

At the sound of a knock, Regina jerked away from Pierce, her mind whirling in confusion at the unexpected sound. Slowly the door eased open and Edie peeped in.

"Excuse me," she said. "Dr. Lawton, Mrs. Whitechurch told me to hurry and find you. She wants to see you right away."

"Thank you, Edie. I'm on the way." Edie discreetly closed the door and hurried away. Regina turned back to Pierce. Her brain was next to useless when he was around. One touch, one kiss, and she was completely disoriented. She backed away as he came toward her again. "I'd better see what Monica wants," she said hastily. "Her headache may be worse." She started for the door but Pierce caught her arm.

"Don't run away from me again, Regina." His dark eyes held her even after he let go of her arm. "We have to talk. I'm ready to tell you the truth."

Fighting to break the sensuous bond, she averted her eyes from his. She had to get away from him. If he held her again she feared she would lose all sense of purpose. As much as her heart wished for that, she didn't dare let it happen.

"I'll just be a few minutes," she said, knowing Monica was probably growing impatient, and not wanting Pierce to get the idea of going along.

"Come to my cottage after you've seen Monica. No one will interrupt us there."

"All right," she agreed, relieved, not certain she would do as he asked. "In twenty minutes." Quickly she got her hat from the desk and hurried out, stopping along the way only long enough to ask one of the servants if all the guests were gone. He reported that the last of them had just driven off to Portsmouth.

She found Monica in her room, sitting in a wicker chair, cane across her lap, and wearing a yellow silk dress. Regina supposed the color was an attempt at cheerfulness, but the worry on Monica's face lingered.

"A small miracle," she said softly. "My headache's gone. I can be ready to leave in half an hour. I wanted you to know so you'd have time to get the necklace."

Regina nodded, tilting her hat forward as she did so. Odd, she hadn't even thought of having the necklace when she was with Pierce. What would he have done if he'd known it was there in the room with him all the time? A dark thought formed. Perhaps it was better she didn't know. She had no intention of telling anyone, even Monica, where the necklace was before she knew Blake was safe.

"It'll be a little longer," Regina said. "I've asked Inspector Marot to come here."

"Marot?" Monica brought her hand nervously to her throat. "Is that wise?"

"He's all right," Regina said emphatically, hoping to believe her words. Pierce had swayed her resolve and she needed to get rid of the thin shadows of doubt. "I've checked," she went on. "I'm sure he's Blake's contact and I think I should talk to him before we leave. There are a few things I want him to confirm. After that we'll be ready to go."

"We?" Monica's eyes widened in alarm. "You intend for Marot to go with us?"

"It's better if he does. There are others on the island who want to find Blake." Her voice shook but she couldn't reveal that one of them was Pierce. It occurred to her she ought to find a way to persuade him to leave the plantation before Marot arrived. "I can't risk anyone else getting to him first," she went on. "Marot can offer protection. Blake will need it. Until the necklace is back in France, he won't really be safe."

Monica sighed tiredly. "I'm sure you're right, my dear. I don't mean to be skeptical. It's just that everything about this affair has gone wrong from the beginning. Who could imagine a necklace could be so important?" Her papery lids fluttered. "And I haven't even seen it."

Regina refrained from offering her a look but the comment made her so conscious of the presence of the necklace that it was hard not to believe it glowed around her hatband like a neon sign.

Monica wanted to change into slacks and walking shoes, and it was agreed she would stay in her room and rest until it was time to go. Fortifying herself for another meeting with Pierce, Regina started toward the rear of the house. Before she got to the door, Edie summoned her to the phone. Thinking it might be Marot saying his business had been concluded sooner than expected, she went briskly to the nearest extension.

The caller was Dr. Williams.

"How is Larousse?" The sound of his voice eased Regina's agitation somewhat. She felt a comfortable rapport with him simply because he was a doctor.

"The patient died. That's why I called last night. I didn't want to leave such a grim message with Mrs. Whitechurch. I knew she had guests."

"Tell me what happened," she requested, finding suddenly she wanted to sit in the fan-backed straw chair by the phone. Accepting the death of a patient never got easier. And though she'd only spent a few minutes trying to revive Larousse after she found him, she took his death personally.

"He lived only a couple of hours after reaching the hospital. It was heart failure as you diagnosed. Unfortunately it doesn't appear to have been from natural causes."

"I beg your pardon." Shock flew through her. She couldn't believe what she was hearing. She'd known there was something odd about the way he hadn't responded to her emergency treatment, but she had never dreamed of this. "Please explain," she said weakly.

"I will," he said. "But it must be in confidence. The heart failure seems to have been caused by an overdose of a drug."

"What drug?" she demanded.

"Our tests are inconclusive. You must understand, Dr. Lawton, our laboratory facilities are primitive compared to what you are accustomed to. Samples have to be flown out to a larger, more modern hospital. We may not have the results for another week."

"Do you think it might have been an illegal drug?"

"I don't know. It might have been. On the other hand, it might have been an improper dose of a prescription drug. Unfortunately we don't have Mr. Larousse's medical history."

"I know he took allergy capsules. Perhaps his partner could help with anything else you need to know," she said in a nervous burst of speech.

"His partner?" Dr. Williams's voice lifted. "I haven't met him."

"That's odd." She bit her lower lip. "I know he went to the hospital."

"It isn't surprising. I've been unusually busy. The police may have talked with him. Because of the unusual circumstances of the death they took charge of the body almost immediately. I believe they are making the arrangements to ship it to France. They are allowing no information to be given out. That's why the nurse didn't inform you of his death when you called this morning."

"I see." She found reassurance in learning Marot was in contact with the local authorities. "It was kind of you to call and let me know."

"As a fellow doctor I thought I should. You worked very hard to save his life. I hope while you're here you'll visit our hospital. Perhaps you can give us some suggestions."

"Thank you. I'd like that. I'll be glad to help any way I can."

"I'll give you a call later when things settle down here. We seem to be having a rush of patients during the festival." He laughed lightly. "And I predict lots of new babies in the spring."

"I wish you luck," she said. "Goodbye, Dr. Williams."

It wasn't as if she needed more things to wonder about. But now she questioned why Marot hadn't told her about Larousse's death when she'd spoken to him earlier. She supposed he preferred to do that face-to-face. Or as Dr. Williams had suggested, perhaps he agreed not to discuss the matter.

The muscles in her neck were tight and aching. She couldn't tell Monica about this yet. She was under a great strain, and at her age she needed nothing else to worry her. Regina felt guilty even depending on her to drive into the mountains. But of course, Monica knew the tangle of roads and was accustomed to driving them. Otherwise Regina would have insisted on a map and making the trip with only Marot.

Crossing her arms and rubbing her shoulders, Regina started for the Sisserou cottage, her brow creased with worry.

The door to the cottage was open.

"I was afraid you wouldn't come."

"I said I would." Heart thumping too fast, she paused just inside the door.

"Sit down." Pierce pulled up another chair. "I want to tell you about everything."

"I know everything. I've found out on my own." She surprised herself with her next words. "I want to ask you to forget about Blake and the necklace. Things won't get nearly as bad for you if you end everything now. Think of what it will do to Monica if—"

"Damn it!" If he hadn't become so suddenly angry he could have laughed at her feeble attempt to spare him whatever fate she thought awaited him. "I *am* thinking of Monica—and of you. I'm not the bad guy in this, Regina. Can't you see that?"

His eyes reflected the quick rise of temper. "I'm sure you think what you're doing is right," she said softly.

"I think it's necessary. I'm helping out the French government with a problem. My only interest is to get that necklace back where it belongs, and I want to do it without endangering you or Monica or Blake. That's only possible if you'll help me."

Her throat tightened. She'd left the hat in the house. But was it possible he suspected she had the necklace and that he knew how compelling he could be if he took her in his arms? "How can I help you?" she asked weakly.

Hell! Frustration swelled inside him. They were communicating about as well as they could through a cement wall. He didn't have time to take a wall down block by block. He would have to hope she would listen with an open mind. "First, trust me and stay away from Marot," he said. "He's dangerous. Second, tell me anything you know that might help me find Blake or the necklace fast."

Her unreliable heart skipped a beat. She wanted to put her arms around him and tell him she would do anything he asked. Her head told her that wasn't wise. She kept telling herself Marot was the one she had to trust. Why didn't she believe it?

"All right," she lied. "Blake is to meet me at the Canefield Airport near Roseau in half an hour. He has the necklace. We were planning to leave the island together." She shook her head. "I don't know why I'm trusting you."

He jumped to his feet and pulled her into his arms. She thought his eyes lit up dangerously quick. "It's because you love me and I love you. But we'll talk about that when I get back." With a suddenness that stunned her, he brought his mouth down, not gently this time, but hungrily.

"Yes," she answered in a smothered whisper. If the room wasn't spinning, then she must be. If the earth wasn't shifting, there was no explanation for what she felt taking place inside. He seemed to have drawn out all her breath. When her lungs filled again her heart had won. She knew he loved her, and she loved him. She had to believe in that love or never believe in anything again. She had to begin by telling him she'd lied about meeting Blake.

They *had* been spinning. He'd whirled her slowly toward the back of the room. Now his kiss intensified. Regina gave herself totally to the sweep of feelings. She was only partially conscious of a few clicks behind her, then suddenly she was out of his arms and locked in a small dark closet.

"Damn it, Pierce! Let me out!" She pounded and kicked the door. "Pierce, you don't understand."

"Sorry, darling!" he shouted back. "Trust me. This is the only way I know to keep you out of danger. I've got to get to Blake. I can't take a chance on anything going wrong with you there. I'll be back," he shouted. "I'll make this up to you," he added as he rushed out the door.

It took him under two minutes to lock the cottage door and fasten the storm shutters over the windows outside. That closet door wouldn't hold her long but it would take her a while to get out of the cottage. If Marot had learned Blake was at the airport he would be heading there, too. With both of them closing in on Blake it wouldn't be advisable to have Regina around. He had to protect her.

He saw Thomas as he was getting in his car and told him not to let anyone near the cottage. An explanation wasn't necessary. Pierce knew his order would be carried out.

Canefield Airport was little more than a couple of sheds and landing strip. There was no place for anyone to hide. Blake wasn't there. When the plane he was supposedly booked on took off, Pierce had a dreadful suspicion Regina had sent him after a red herring. He made a call to Roseau.

"Marot is still at his hotel," the Dominican at the other end of the line reported. "He was on the phone and had breakfast."

"You checked with the operator about the calls?"

"Yes. He placed a call to Paris, and received one from Whitechurch."

Whitechurch. Regina. Pierce felt as if his life had been pulled out from under him. She'd talked to Marot earlier in the morning. The little witch! She'd lied like a pro and gotten him away from Whitechurch. Why? There was only one logical conclusion. Marot was going there for Blake and the necklace. Damn her! But Marot hadn't gone yet, and Pierce was about to make a change in the Frenchman's plans.

From the Reef Hotel the aroma of coffee and baking bread drifted out into the street. Pierce climbed the creaking wooden steps to the porch, crossed it and entered the lobby.

A few steps more took him to the door of Marot's room. He knocked. On his orders Marot hadn't been told of his visitor. A few words in the right ears and that was arranged. One favor begot another. A bitter taste filled Pierce's mouth. He was sick of favors. When this one was done it was his last.

"Mr. Buchannan." Revealing no surprise, Marot invited Pierce in. "You surprise me. You're out early."

"I had business," Pierce said, eyeing Marot suspiciously. Physically they were similar, no more than an inch of difference in height, a few pounds in weight. Marot would know how to defend himself, how to kill silently with his hands and feet. The look in his eye told he was making a similar assessment of Pierce.

"Am I part of that business?" Marot asked from beneath a coating of civility, offering Pierce the single chair while he sat on the bed.

"We seem to share an interest if not an intent," Pierce answered, making a circumspect glance around the room.

Marot smiled. "Intent is a such a variable. Perhaps we could reach a compromise," he suggested. His voice had changed, slightly, but enough that an edge of raw steel underneath had begun to come through.

"Maybe." Pierce's voice was harsh, too, saying far more than the simple words. "It might save us a lot of trouble and unnecessary violence."

Marot pulled a pack of French cigarettes from his shirt pocket, removed one and lit it, then dropped the pack and the lighter on the bedside table. He drew heavily on the cigarette, then blew out a breath that was all smoke. "Have you developed an aversion to violence?" His voice mocked. "That wasn't always the case. I've read your naval intelligence file, Mr. Buchannan. As I recall, you were noted for your skills in—violence.'' He followed the lifting of Pierce's brows. ''Surprised? You haven't forgotten that in our business we spend much of our time spying on our allies?''

''No,'' Pierce returned. ''I'm just surprised you'd have any interest in a file that's been inactive ten years.''

Marot laughed. ''Give me credit. The *file* has been inactive, but the man hasn't. There've been times your talents were put to use. Like now.''

''I'm impressed,'' Pierce said coolly. ''And I suppose that means you know my position now.''

Marot knew more than Pierce had guessed at first, and the man was accurate. Pierce had done a few free-lance jobs over the years, using his business as a cover. Marot's sources were good. This confrontation might not prove as easy as he'd hoped, Pierce thought, but at this point there was no backing out. He had this job to finish. He'd given his word.

''The same as that of the men you represent.'' Marot had filled the room with smoke but now he crushed out the stub of the cigarette in a coconut-shell ashtray. ''What I don't know is how flexible they might be.''

''Let's consider that at this time you don't have the necklace.'' He watched Marot's face warily.

''No.'' Marot admitted. ''But I have reason to believe it will soon be in my hands.''

''I think not. You're running out of time. You don't know where the necklace is.'' Again he read the Frenchman's face and fished. ''*I*, on the other hand, do.''

''Ahh.'' Marot's lips gave a hint of humor. ''And that is where we compromise. You get what you want, I go away and everything else is forgotten. The Thanet woman, Larousse. All that is, to use one of your American expressions, swept under the rug?''

''It could happen, if you're agreeable.'' Pierce felt a tightening in all his muscles, a quickening of all his senses. It was animal instinct but he never ignored it. Too many times his life had depended on nothing more. It was his re-action to what he saw in Marot, the narrowing of the pu-pils, the swell of the veins in his neck, the tiny twitch of his lip. He realized, too, he'd been so preoccupied with Regina at the cottage that he'd forgotten his gun. He braced him-self to take Marot another way.

Marot's smile was a cold one. "Consider it from my point of view," he said. "If I make this compromise with you, then it means I cannot be trusted to do the job. And when that happens I'm finished. It seems for me the risk calcu-lates better than the certainty of your deal."

"I'm sorry you see it that way," Pierce retorted, the fea-tures of his face stark and stone hard.

Down the block a band started to play, a few horns and a bongo drum.

"Maybe we can talk about it some more," Marot said, pulling out another cigarette and reaching toward his pocket for a lighter. When he brought his hand up a pistol filled it. Pierce lunged at him, but not quickly enough. Marot fired a single shot.

Cursing his stupidity for trying to play cat and mouse with Marot, Pierce dodged, but too late. The bullet creased his temple and he crumpled to the floor.

The band finished a tune and stopped playing. Marot laughed scornfully. "You Americans think talk is the an-swer to everything." He turned Pierce's head with his foot and seeing the blood flow freely decided there was no rea-son to risk another shot. "You'll be unconscious long enough, my friend."

Marot glanced at his watch and scowled. He was running late. He would have to spare the time to arrange for Bandy to dispose of Mr. Buchannan. A few minutes later Marot left the hotel by the back door quickly, merging into the crowd on the streets.

How long had he been lying in the darkness? Pierce opened his eyes but got nothing but blinding pain. The grogginess cleared a little. Now he remembered. A shot. He'd heard a shot and then started falling through cold, black space. His cheek rested in something warm and sticky. Blood. His blood.

Hell! It hurt to think. He wanted to go back to sleep. Sleep it off. Wake up in the morning without a hangover. But he kept thinking about Regina. Regina and Monica. If Marot got to them it would be all over.

Chapter 12

Damn him! Why had she even thought about trusting Pierce Buchannan? Regina battered the cottage door with a piece of driftwood from an arrangement, but the lock wasn't as flimsy as the one on the closet. The shutters wouldn't budge, either. She shouted until her throat ached, finally concluding no one could hear her. She looked at her watch. More than an hour had passed since Pierce left. Marot would be arriving soon.

Resting her temples on the heels of her hands, she leaned against the wall and tried to think calmly. How could she get the door open? The gun. She remembered the gun in the drawer and quickly went to look for it. It was there, but not loaded. She started a search for ammunition.

Steering the car like a drunk, Pierce somehow managed to get to Whitechurch. Marot's car wasn't there. Either he'd come and gone or not arrived. He hoped for the latter. That meant Regina and Monica would still be at the plantation.

Leaving the car out of sight behind the garage, he made his best effort at running to the cottage where he'd left Regina.

She heard the pounding of footsteps on the path and started to call out for help but thought better of it. If that was Pierce outside fumbling with the lock she'd best meet him with surprise.

Nerves. His hand shook so he could hardly fit the key in the keyhole. She had to be in there. The door was still locked. Marot hadn't gotten to her yet. With a flick of his wrist he released the lock and quickly pushed the door open. The room was dark and quiet but enough light came in from the doorway that he could see the interior clearly. Empty. He had a quick dismal thought that Marot had gotten there ahead of him after all.

"Regina!" he shouted. He rushed toward the bath, hoping she was inside. Halfway across the room he was conscious of a shadow spinning out from behind the door and through the opening. "Regina!" He whirled and started back across the room, reaching the door as the lock clicked.

"Sorry," she called from the other side.

"Regina, don't go. Listen!" he shouted, pounding the door. "Wait."

"Can't," she answered, pocketing the key that in his haste he'd left in the lock. "I've made up my mind to turn Blake over to Marot. He can guarantee Blake's safety."

"No! Regina!"

"I won't tell him you're here. I owe you that. I'll be back once Blake is safely with Marot. Then you can decide what you have to do." Fighting back tears she ran to the house.

Dr. Lawton was too damned resourceful to suit him. When he got his hands on her he would—Hell! He would make love to her. Pierce made three successive kicks to the cottage door. The lock held. The effort started his head hurting again and gave him an instant of blackness. A cold knot formed in his stomach. He leaned against the wall to rest.

Damn the woman! He'd turned into a blind blundering fool the first minutes he'd seen her. Maybe it served him right for forcing his way into her life like a bulldozer on the loose. If he hadn't fought the attraction, fought the feeling he had for her, she might not be in this desperate situation. Neither would Monica. His face was contorted with rage and frustration. He had to get out before they left. Once Marot had the necklace he'd snuff out anybody who could talk about it.

He knew that twisted mind now. An accident, three bodies off the mountain or whatever diabolical scheme he could hatch. Something staged that wouldn't shut down the island before he could get off. Pierce knew that was the only reason he was still alive. Marot had feared risking another shot and must have thought the wound worse than it was.

Another wave of blackness washed in front of his eyes. The pain came in surges. He wasn't going to be any good to himself or anyone if he didn't get control of it. A series of deep breaths eased the thunder in his head a little but had no effect on that in his heart. God! It cut into his gut knowing in a few minutes she would be driving off with Marot.

Why the hell hadn't he demanded the truth from Monica? Why the hell hadn't he told Regina just how everything stood instead of locking her in that damned closet and rushing off like Lancelot? If he'd told her what he suspected about Marot on the beach that night she followed him instead of giving in to what his body demanded, she wouldn't be with that bastard now.

Even if he got out and got there in time to save them, she would probably never forgive him. His anger, his fear, his guilt simmered inside him. He loved her. He should have made her believe that. He needed another chance. He would make another chance. Eyes clenched shut, he aimed two more kicks at the door. Once more the thunder and lightning raged in his head. Time. If only there were time.

Marot arrived just as Regina pulled on her hat and walked to the veranda. An early shower started as he hurried up the steps.

"Inspector Marot! I was getting worried."

Marot smiled to himself, shook the water off, then followed her inside. "Sorry," he said. "My business took longer than I expected."

She took him to Monica's office, where they sat facing each other in leather wing-back chairs. Marot looked as if he could use a drink and accepted her offer of one. At the liquor cabinet she poured a cognac for him but decided against having anything herself.

"Thanks," he said, his fingers by chance touching hers as she handed him the glass. She found the contact oddly alarming.

"About Larousse." She twisted her ring, an automatic gesture whenever she was flustered. It was something she'd been doing frequently lately. "I had a call from the hospital this morning. Dr. Williams told me he didn't make it."

Marot stiffened a bit and blinked his eyes a couple of times. "Oh?" he said. "You know about that?"

"It's all right," she went on, seeing his confusion. "I know that because of the circumstances of Larousse's death and the unofficial nature of the case you're working on it's to be kept confidential. Dr. Williams called as a matter of professional courtesy. He knew I'd be concerned about a patient I'd—" she hesitated "—worked with personally. Even if he had been turned over to someone else."

"I see," Marot's voice evened out. "Well, it's perfectly all right. You should have known."

"Dr. Williams was surprised he hadn't seen you at the hospital," Regina said, hoping to lead him toward some sort of explanation.

The heavy brows went up quickly and Marot's hands twitched indecisively for a moment. "It is very difficult for me, you see. Armand was a friend. And there were calls to make, to the family, the agency. I needed privacy."

"Of course," Regina said softly, her mind whirring around Marot's words. Something wasn't right, but until she put her finger on it she had to stick with her plan to trust the Frenchman.

"And," Marot said, with a sigh of mock resignation, "even with Larousse gone I am obligated to go on with my work." He lifted his lean face to hers. "That is why I'm here. I hope what you have to tell me will make all this seem worthwhile."

She stared at Marot for a moment, feeling utterly miserable. She started to tell him about Pierce but the words and the will to say them lodged in her throat. She'd made Pierce a promise.

She swallowed roughly.

"Inspector," she told him, her voice sounding as if it came from someone else, "I want you to know I checked on you through the Atlanta police and by calling your agency in France. I think you can understand it has been difficult to know who to trust since this began. For a long time I had only hints of what was going on. Perhaps if I'd talked to you sooner…"

"It might have made no difference," he said soothingly. "The important thing is that you're talking to me now and soon it will all be over."

"Yes." She sighed heavily. "I'll be glad of that." Feeling the gnawing of inner torment, she went on. Perhaps Marot could be persuaded to give more information. "I'm sure you know others have been trying to get the necklace."

Marot sat back, relaxing as if he were pleased with himself. He downed a large swallow of cognac. "Do you mind if I smoke?" he asked. He reached for his cigarettes and lighter, frowning as he realized he'd dropped them when he fired at Buchannan, then smiling as he realized that in a few minutes Bandy's crew would be dropping the troublesome Mr. Buchannan into the ocean.

"I'm afraid there aren't any cigarettes here," Regina said, noting his distress. "Monica doesn't smoke."

"It isn't important," he insisted and finished his drink. "To answer your question, yes. I am aware there are a few corrupt officials in my government who saw an opportunity to use the necklace. They hired—shall we say mercenaries—to track it down and get it to them. That is the reason Larousse and I had to pursue your uncle and the necklace unofficially. We could not afford a leak that might reach those officials."

She found little comfort in hearing that. "Then you *are* Blake's contact? You and Larousse came here yesterday to meet Blake and pick up the necklace?"

Marot, eyes glittering in triumph, nodded quickly and decisively. "Yes," he said. "We knew he would be suspicious if two DESE agents suddenly appeared and made demands. That's why we arranged for a contact he knew to tell him he could trust us." He went on to explain how important it was that Blake agree to return to France and testify. "The necklace alone is important, but we need the insurance of Mr. Andrews's account of how he came into possession of it. We have been careful not to alienate him. As you are aware, once we located your uncle we have merely stayed close, standing by until he felt confident enough to turn the necklace over to us."

That fit. Marot and Larousse could have moved in at any time trying to force Blake to hand over the diamond necklace. They hadn't. It was the others who'd used force and violence in their quest for the necklace. But she couldn't believe that Pierce was included in the group.

Her voice faltered as she started to speak again. "It was someone working for those other people who killed Larousse, wasn't it?"

"Yes," Marot agreed, frowning. "We split up while we waited. We didn't know where Mr. Andrews would be. It was the last I saw of Larousse until the ambulance took him away."

She'd put it off as long as she could. "Do you know who's responsible for Larousse's death?" Her heart sank as she asked the question. She really didn't want to hear the answer she feared put into words.

"I have a strong suspicion that . . . Mr. Buchannan overpowered Larousse and injected him with a lethal drug, hoping the cause of death would be attributed to a heart attack. You know the rest." He shrugged as if dismissing a weight from his shoulders. "You found Armand."

She felt an uneasy tingling on the back of her neck but was too overwrought to attribute it to anything but sadness. She nodded woodenly, seeing Pierce in front of her eyes, accused, condemned. A criminal. And still her heart wouldn't let go of loving him. Tears threatened to fall and she desperately didn't want to shed them in front of Marot. It seemed terribly callous to think so, but she didn't imagine he was a man who was given to sentimentality.

"What will you do about Pierce?" she asked.

Marot's eyes lifted shrewdly. "There is really nothing I can do but report him to the local authorities. I have no power to make an arrest here. It will be up to them to take him into custody before he leaves the island. There is the matter of another murder in France. Extradition papers must be filed." Suppressing a cold smile he went on. "Mr. Buchannan's fate is completely out of my hands."

Regina felt as if her pulse was slowing to a stop. Her wish was to shut her eyes and wake up in her bed back in Atlanta the day before the silver swan arrived in the mail. But that was impossible, juvenile thinking. Numbly she looked at Marot. "I'm ready to take you to Blake," she said reluctantly. Regina got to her feet feeling as if her whole body had turned to lead. "I'll have to get Monica. She'll drive us. She knows the way."

A sudden rattle at the open window of the office sent both of them whirling around. Marot's arm twisted toward the small of his back.

"Winston!" Regina said, smiling her relief at the big white Persian who habitually jumped in windows. "You frightened me."

"A cat," Marot said, his lean face regaining some of the lost color. "Never had much use for them."

Winston trotted over to Regina and made a few condescending rubs against her legs, then trotted on to the closed doors and demanded to be let out. "Just a minute, Winston." The cat dropped to his haunches and began cleaning his paws.

Marot eyed Regina as if she were deranged for explaining herself to the animal. "He looks a lot like your cat, Marley," he said absently.

"Marley?" A shadow of a lost thought fluttered in her mind with a dim image of Marot and Larousse visiting her house in Atlanta. "Yes, he does," she added quickly, remembering she wanted to find Monica. At the door she paused with her hand on the knob. "Mrs. Whitechurch is in her room. You can wait for us here if you like."

"I will," he answered, crossing the room to the desk and lifting the receiver of the phone. He started to dial. "I need to call the Dominican police and advise them of my actions."

"Inspector Marot," Regina said quickly. "Mrs. White-church doesn't know about her nephew. If you..."

He turned away from her for a moment and spoke into the phone, at the same time pushing down the button, which returned a dial tone to the line. "This is Jacques Marot," he said. "Connect me with Officer Cabot please." Turning back he placed a hand over the mouthpiece, giving Regina a look of understanding. "She won't learn of it from me," he said calmly. Regina nodded and opened the door to leave, Winston running out ahead of her. As she started down the hall she heard Marot saying, "Officer Cabot, I am at Whitechurch Plantation. I suggest you look for..."

Regina hurried away. She didn't want to hear him tell the officer to look for Pierce. Otherwise she would have no excuse for not reporting his whereabouts. Still, she didn't rush through the corridors on her way to Monica's room. Needing a few moments alone to think, she made a detour to her room.

Regina shifted the strap of her shoulder bag. Something Marot had said was bothering her, only she couldn't lock in on just what it was. Probably nothing significant, just another irrational attempt by her subconscious to find some shred of evidence in Pierce's favor. For some reason she kept wanting to postpone what was already under way.

She reminded herself Blake would be safe. According to Marot he would have to go to Paris and testify. Any charges that might be made against Blake were open to bargaining. Marot didn't foresee trouble there. Although the French government had been aware of Blake's marginal activities for some time, they hadn't considered them serious enough to pursue. The indication was Blake would be a free man once his testimony had been given.

Someone had closed the shutters in her room. It looked dreary and dim with the rain falling outside. Close to tears she paused just inside the door, but only for a moment before she was grabbed from behind and a hand clapped tightly over her mouth. Oh hell! she thought, this was becoming habitual.

"Where's the gun?" Pierce demanded. He saw her eyes go to her shoulder bag and took it from her. The gun retrieved, he let Regina go.

"You aren't going to shoot me, are you?" she asked, feeling her legs weaken.

"No! Dammit! I'm not going to shoot you. But I may hold the gun on you to make you listen to me for once. Sit down."

Regina dropped into a chair, then rose again quickly. Her hands flew to her mouth to cover a gasp. "You're hurt!" Her eyes dwelt on the crusted blood at his temple and the bruised, swollen eye underneath. She couldn't tell much about the seriousness of the injury, only that it needed cleaning.

"Sit and keep quiet," he ordered. "I'll live."

"What happened?" Her eyes widened as she saw the tendons and veins in his neck tighten and throb. She fell back into the chair, seeing that it was prudent to do as he ordered.

"Marot sent a bullet my way." His hard tone stung her.

"He shot you?" Concern rushed in before she focused on the rigid set of his mouth. The thought of him hurt, taking a bullet, made her forget for a moment that he held a gun on her, and that he might have killed people as well. She saw the dark gleam of the barrel and remembered. She couldn't trust Pierce. "I don't believe you," she said slowly.

"Why did I think you would?" he asked sarcastically as he dragged a second chair up close and sat, the gun resting on his knees. "Marot tried to kill me. He wants to kill Blake. He'll kill you and Monica, too, as soon as he has the necklace."

Her look mirrored her skepticism. "Marot is a French agent working for his government."

"He's an agent working for a radical faction within his government. His instructions are to get the necklace and leave no witnesses. He killed Larousse."

"He says you did that," she retorted bitterly.

The lines of his face hardened. Pierce swore, wincing again as pain shot like jagged lightning through his head. The blackness threatened to come but he refused to yield to either it or the pain. "How?" he demanded. "How does he say I did it?"

"An injection. You—"

Pierce stopped her and bit back his anger. "Larousse swallowed whatever killed him," he said flatly, fighting the now constant pain. "Ask your doctor friend."

So tense she barely rested her weight on the chair cushions, Regina looked him fiercely in the eye. "Will I get a chance?"

He gave a nod. This was futile. He had to find a quicker way to get what he wanted. "If you like," he answered solemnly. "Marot's waiting. He'll be looking for you in a few minutes." As he leaned forward, Regina leaned back but not far enough or quickly enough to avoid his catching hold of one of her hands.

She trembled, feeling the temperature of her blood go up a few degrees.

"Feel that," he said. "Feel what just a touch does for us."

"I don't feel anything," she insisted, denying the quick fire in her veins, trying to pull her hand free.

He jerked her to her feet. Before she could even voice a scream, he had her in his arms and his mouth sealed her lips. "You lie badly," he whispered, touching her cheek, the corner of her eye, "with your face, with your words." He touched her lips. "But your lips don't lie when I kiss you and your body doesn't, either. Listen to what's inside you, Regina. Listen to what your heart tells you. Believe in me. Trust me."

She was unable to speak. While she hesitated he brought his mouth gently back to hers. She felt her tense body going soft with the contact. What was he telling her? What was he asking of her?

With a moan her lips parted. She circled her arms around his neck, drawing him closer. She seemed to be turning to fluid, streaming, losing all resolve to resist, losing herself. Yet even dazed she was aware of every well-honed part of him fitted against her. She felt his heat, his hardness. For a crazy moment she thought if he didn't take his mouth away she would disappear into him. For another crazy moment she hoped she would do just that. Were all her instincts wrong? Could she feel so right in his arms if she didn't belong there, always?

The world became a blur, then cleared slowly as he did break away. "Pierce," she whispered, wanting to say what she'd felt.

A fingertip to her lips silenced her. Pierce fitted something in her hand and stepped back. A glance down at what she was holding brought a gasp. The gun.

"Regina, my darling," he said calmly. "You have to make a choice. I'm going to get Marot one way or another, and I'm going to find Blake and the necklace. Either you trust me and help me or—"

"Or what?"

"Or you'd better shoot me right now."

A quarter of an hour later, shaking as if she'd been put in permanent motion, Regina raced through the corridor. She found Monica and Marot waiting in the front hall.

Breathless and pale she came to a halt. "Sorry to keep you," she said, finding it impossible to stand still. "I needed to go to my room for a few minutes."

Noting Regina's evident jitters, Monica gave her a questioning look. "Are you all right?"

"I'm fine. Just nervous about Blake, about everything," Regina replied hastily.

Marot patted her shoulder comfortingly. "From this point, Dr. Lawton, let me worry about Monsieur Andrews and the necklace."

"Yes. Yes, I will." She twisted her ring around her finger. The necklace. It must have a curse. She hated it.

"I had the kitchen prepare some food for Blake," Monica said, getting her cane, then struggling with a large hamper. "Most likely the supplies at the cabin have run out by now."

Marot made a little bow and took the heavy hamper from Monica. Beside him, Regina pulled the brim of her straw hat down a little lower on her head. The necklace seemed to grow heavier every minute. But if it weighed a ton she had no intention of revealing where she carried it. She hadn't even told Pierce before... No. She wouldn't think of Pierce. He'd forced her to make a choice. She could have no regrets. No one would know where the necklace was until she'd had a chance to explain things to Blake. After all he'd been through he deserved the opportunity of placing it in Marot's hands.

Marot, beginning to look impatient, waited at the entrance. Monica paused before leaving to give instructions to Edie.

"If my nephew returns before we get back tell him we've gone to the mountain cabin," Monica said.

Marot's eyes gleamed with dark satisfaction. "And if the police arrive you may relay the same message. I've requested they come here." He glanced at his watch. "But I think we should be on our way." He started down the steps.

Regina followed, feeling guilt hit her like a load of buckshot. Her hands shook so that she slipped them into her pocket to hide them. There was no chance of Pierce getting that message.

Monica ordered a vehicle brought around front. It wasn't the one she usually drove and Regina questioned the change.

"This one has four-wheel drive," Monica explained. "I always take it when I'm going to the cabin."

"But wouldn't we be more comfortable in the larger car?" Regina asked nervously.

"No," Marot interjected, opening the driver's door for Monica. "Mrs. Whitechurch is right. In the rain, on steep roads, the four-wheel drive is best." Marot opted for the back seat. Reluctantly Regina climbed in the front on the other side.

The road wound up the mountain like an afterthought, all curves and bends seeming to crisscross back over ground already covered. Smaller roads branched out in places like threads in a spider's web. To make matters worse the rain started again, cutting down the visibility to near zero. Several times Monica had to stop and wait for the downpour to slacken so she could see the road.

"I understand what you meant," Regina said, still nervous and needing to break the long silence that had hung in the car since they left Whitechurch. "Nobody could have found the way up here without help. How did Blake do it?"

Monica spoke without glancing over, keeping her eyes on the narrow muddy road. "He's been there a few times with me. We used to grow coffee beans up here, but getting them down the mountain was counterproductive. The place is deserted now. We knew he would be safe there." She paused to take a breath. "I'm very glad, Inspector Marot, that you identified yourself to us. Otherwise I don't know what we

would have done. There's no phone. Blake was here alone
and didn't have—''

Regina pinched Monica's leg, hoping she was in time to
prevent her from telling Marot Blake didn't have the necklace.

"What's that?" Marot asked, showing the first sign of
interest in what Monica was saying. He leaned forward in
the seat to hear her better.

"Sorry," Monica said, rounding a curve sharply and
throwing Marot back against the seat. "I was saying Blake
didn't have any way of getting in touch with you himself
without coming down the mountain and risking his safety."

The look of interest fell from Marot's lean face. "How
much farther?" he asked irritably, making a surreptitious
glance at his watch.

"In this weather, half an hour," Monica responded.
"Though it's only a few more miles in distance."

"Damn!" Marot snapped, fumbling in his pocket for
cigarettes and frowning as he remembered where he'd left
them. "I'm ready to get out of this primeval place." A
glance out the window and through the thin sheet of rain
showed him the sharp drop-off of a cliff. He laughed under
his breath. It was rather ironic that his quest for Andrews
should start at a chalet in the Alps and end in a mountain
cabin halfway around the world.

Regina turned her head slowly, surprised at the hard,
grating sound of Marot's voice, surprised that hearing him
say "damn" took her on a flashback to the night of the
break-in at her house. That curse dislodged some little
fragment of memory deep in the cells of her brain. A
shadow of dread began to form there, too. She'd heard
Pierce use that word dozens of times in the past few days.
Never once had it shaken her psyche like this. Why?

She turned back to stare at the windshield, the wiper blade
zigging and zagging hypnotically over the drenched glass.

She forced herself to think analytically—to think it through as if she were making a diagnosis. In the office at White-church there'd been something else that bothered her about Marot. What was it? She went over every line of the con-versation in her head. Nothing seemed peculiar about it, but at some point she'd felt almost as she did now, that some-thing wasn't adding up.

She slid her hands up behind her neck, digging her fin-gers into the tight, tense muscles there. Maybe it hadn't been anything he said. Maybe it had been a movement, an ac-tion that seemed out of place. She tried visualizing that ex-change, the two of them sitting in the leather chairs, Marot drinking cognac. Later he'd stood suddenly. But there was nothing odd about that. They'd both been on edge and sur-prised when Winston leaped in the window. She'd jumped up herself and then Winston had walked over and tried to appease her.

Winston. That was it. The cat. Marot had mentioned that Winston looked like her cat, Marley, also a white Persian. Only Marot had never seen Marley. The cat had been locked in the kitchen when Marot and Larousse came to the house. He couldn't know what Marley looked like unless he'd seen him another time. That could only mean Marot had been the burglar who stepped on Marley's paw. Marot!

Her spine stiffened, the blood drained from her face. She felt weak, dizzy. Now the lost thoughts came pouring back as heavily as the rain. Larousse had warned her in the An-tigua airport that someone was not what he seemed. He'd meant Marot. She saw Larousse's deathly white face be-neath her own as she'd tried to revive him.

Of course. It would have been easy for Marot to have emptied out Larousse's allergy capsules and substituted a deadly drug. Why hadn't she seen it before, instead of being as compliant to Marot as a sacrificial lamb?

Her lips silently formed Pierce's name.

"We're here," Monica stated, pulling the car up a short drive to the front of an unpainted wood cabin nestled into the rain forest. The two words sounded like a shotgun blast to Regina's ears.

The rain stopped abruptly, leaving the world around them fresh and vitally alive. Golden streams of sunlight slipped through the thick green leaves high above to kiss frilly tree orchids and shiny bromeliads. A green tree frog croaked and was joined by a host of others. The wild beauty of the rain forest was apparent to Regina even as her heart thundered the beat of her fear.

Monica set the handbrake and pushed down the handle to open her door.

"Wait," Marot said. "Let me get out first."

Monica responded to the command in his voice and stayed behind the wheel. In the rearview mirror Marot could see Regina's face and read her expression. He reached behind his back and pulled out the gun.

"So, Dr. Lawton." Hearing the mockery in his voice she whirled around. His face twisted into a terrible look of humor, his lips curled back in a sneer. "At last. At last that medical mind has gone to work and you've figured it out." He pointed the gun at her head. "Really a disappointment. I wanted to make that revelation my own way. Tell me. What was it that gave me away?"

Monica took one look at the gun and started to tremble. "The cat," Regina said. Her voice rattled. "My cat."

"Ahh." He sounded his annoyance. "Your cat. I saw your cat only when I broke into your house and stepped on the nasty beast. Very clever," he acknowledged. "I'm not usually careless with details."

"No. You're not," Regina said, getting a hold on her voice, thinking maybe praise would keep him talking and give her time to think of something other than that Marot planned to go down the mountain alone. "I don't suppose you actually made that call to the police from Monica's study.''

He looked up and laughed. ''I have been extremely careful to avoid the police while I've been here. Not at all a difficult job, I'd like to add.'' Marot shook his head indulgently. ''If you're thinking Buchannan will be along to rescue you, forget it. My friend Bandy has disposed of him by now.''

Regina's face blanched. Rescue. Pierce. That's just what she was thinking, what she wanted, what would be happening if only she'd foreseen...

Monica gasped and collapsed against the seat. ''What do you mean?'' she cried.

Marot gave them a disgusted look. ''Details,'' he said. ''I dealt with him before I came to Whitechurch.''

''You killed him?'' Monica asked weakly.

Marot shook his head. ''I only started the job with a bullet. Bandy will enjoy finishing it. And that's enough chit-chat,'' he growled.

''Pierce,'' Monica sobbed.

Regina's face blanched. Bandy wouldn't have the pleasure. She'd made sure of that. Marot was inhuman. Pierce had been trying to protect her all along. Why hadn't she listened to her heart? If she'd listened and confided in him instead of getting hotheaded all the time, none of them would be in this disaster.

''Forget him,'' Marot snapped. ''Now get out of the car, both of you, and walk to the cabin.'' They did as he said. Marot fell in behind them and jammed the barrel of the gun against the back of Monica's head. ''I don't want any trouble from Andrews.''

Regina stumbled up the front steps ahead of Monica and Marot. He planned to kill them. All along his plan had been to kill Blake as soon as he got the necklace. She and Monica were just a couple of pawns clearing the way for the big move.

"Stop!" Marot ordered in a low but steely voice. "You." He nudged Monica with the gun. "Call Andrews to the door. Don't let him know anything is wrong."

Swallowing hard, Monica did as she was told. "Blake," she called. "It's me, Monica. I brought food."

"Good," came Blake's muffled reply. He jerked open the door. "I'm starving."

"You'll die hungry," Marot growled, forcing both women inside. "Find something and tie them," he demanded, waving the pistol. "And hurry. I'm running out of time."

Hands uncomfortably roped together behind their backs, Regina and Monica sat on a rough bench while Marot talked. His voice grated like a buzz saw headed at Regina. Death could be only minutes away. This was the point in old movies where the hero rushed in and saved the day. Things weren't looking hopeful for that happening here.

Where was Pierce? Back at Whitechurch she'd stalled long enough to give him a chance to conceal himself in the trunk of the car. Marot had been careful not to leave evidence linking him to his crimes. Pierce needed to catch him in the act this time. She'd agreed to help. What could have gone wrong? Why wasn't Pierce bursting in right now and stopping this?

Two terrifying thoughts occurred to her. First, Pierce might have chosen the wrong car, not anticipating Monica would take the four-wheel-drive vehicle. But in that case he'd have followed them up the mountain and should only have been a few minutes behind. Or, second, if he was in the right trunk, the rough ride up the mountain might have made him black out. He could easily have a concussion from that wound. Regina fought for control. In that case it was all up to her.

"The deal is this, Andrews," Marot said. "You hand over the necklace. I disable the car, leave the three of you tied up here. By the time you get loose and down the mountain, I'm halfway back to France. Everybody's happy."

"And if I refuse?" Blake asked as Marot pulled the ropes painfully tight on his wrists.

"Then I put a bullet through this head." He pointed the gun at Monica. "Or maybe this one." He laughed. "But what a shame to mess up that pretty face." He nodded smoothly to Regina. Her eyes filled with disgust. "I deeply regret we didn't have more time together, Doctor." He trailed his fingers over her cheek. "But..." She wrenched her head away, bringing a sneer to his lips. Angered, he turned back to Blake. "But either one would get the message across. I mean business. I want the necklace."

Blake, face drained white, looked hopelessly at Regina. She didn't really trust Marot to keep his word and spare them, but with hands tied and Pierce out of it, it seemed the only hope they had.

"It's in my hatband," she said, letting go of her terror for a moment.

Marot voiced his surprise as he snatched the hat off her head. "Well, well, Doctor. I approve. Beautiful. Smart. If you'd been only that much more clever—" he indicated an inch with his thumb and forefinger, "—you might have saved yourself." Hurriedly he unwound the unknotted the scarf, revealing the diamond necklace. The stones caught the light, sending a spray of rainbows on the wall. Marot mouthed his admiration, then pocketing the necklace, breathed out a deep sigh. "My future," he said, waving the gun carelessly. "Now out of here! All of you!"

"I thought—" Blake started.

"Obviously, thinking has never been your strong suit, Andrews. For all I know there may be another cabin over the hill, a radio. Who knows? I make it a policy not to leave witnesses. Now get into the car," he ordered Monica and Regina. The car Blake had used was nearest, Monica's parked a few yards away. Marot shoved Blake up against the trunk of his car and reached into his trouser pocket for the set of keys. Finding them, he cracked the gun handle against Blake's head, knocking him into the back seat. "That's for all the trouble," he growled.

Once they were all inside, Monica and Blake in the back seat and Regina in the front, Marot hurriedly tied their feet. A moment later he rolled up the windows and locked the doors. Blake groaned in pain.

"You won't get away with this, Marot. Remember that!" Regina shouted through the glass as she struggled to pull her hands free from the ropes cutting her wrists.

"Careful, Doctor," Marot laughed. "My esteem for you is falling by the minute." While he spoke he walked to the rear of the car and removed the cap from the gas tank. "A fitting use for your scarf, don't you think?" he shouted, seeing that she was straining to turn and get a look at what he was doing. With a stick he pushed the end of the scarf into the tank until it reached the fuel. "Silk burns fairly slowly. That should give me just a few minutes to get far enough away."

He reached to his shirt pocket for his lighter, then swore as he discovered it missing. He gave the tire a vicious kick. Still swearing in French, he unlocked a rear door, jerked it open and snatched Blake's lighter from his shirt pocket.

As soon as he turned around Regina leaned over the door lock and pulled it up with her teeth. That was all she had time to do before Marot was looking at her again.

"Au revoir," he shouted and blew her a kiss as he flicked the lighter and brought up a flame.

Chapter 13

Pierce raised his head in the darkness of the car trunk. The heavy stale air in the tight compartment combined with the jostling had been enough to make him black out. His heart lodged in his throat. The car was still now. He had no inkling how long he'd been out, a few minutes or too long to matter. Fearing what he might see, Pierce eased the trunk lid open.

"Marot!" he shouted, seeing the Frenchman holding a lighter to a strip of black cloth. He knew instantly what was happening and sprang out of the trunk.

"Buchannan!" Marot's face twisted with hatred. While Pierce covered the yards between them, Marot cursed viciously, dropped the lighter and grabbed at his waistband for the gun.

He had a chance to fire one round, the shot missing the mark and shattering the glass of Blake's car.

Pierce slammed into Marot, sheer will and purpose overriding the pain in his head. Marot took the blow fully in the chest, the impact momentarily stunning him. Pierce was on him before he recovered.

"Your aim's getting worse," Pierce shouted, grappling Marot's wrist to control the gun.

"You'll wish for a bullet before I'm through with you," Marot growled. "You have an annoying way of showing up at the wrong moment." Slinging an elbow up he hit Pierce just below the wound on his temple. The pain exploded in Pierce's head. He stumbled back, giving Marot an advantage.

His gun hand clear, Marot raised the pistol and aimed. Watching from the car, Regina managed at the same moment to force up the door handle and shove the door open with her feet. It struck Marot in the back, knocking him off balance and giving Pierce the opening to send the gun spiraling into the forest.

Regina struggled out of the car. Pierce saw her and tried to warn her back. As he spoke Marot hit him like a sumo wrestler, throwing Pierce against the car fender. Marot dived at him again. Using the vehicle for support Pierce swung out both feet, knocking Marot to the ground as if he'd been hit by a cannon ball.

Regina watched petrified, afraid a word or a move would distract Pierce again.

Marot cursed savagely. Hatred burned in his eyes. In combat stance Pierce and Marot circled each other warily, eyes locked like laser beams. Pierce studied Marot, calculating the man's strengths and weaknesses. The biggest difference was that Pierce was fighting for the people he loved. That had to be advantage enough.

Marot had the quickness of a cat and changed tactics just as often, but Pierce was just as quick, ducking Marot's punches and plowing his knee high into Marot's back.

Marot screamed a string of French profanities as his legs buckled beneath him. Face flushed with rage, he rolled to his feet. "This is starting to interfere with my timetable," he snarled.

A sweep of dizziness threatened to overcome Pierce, and he struggled with it. He might have overestimated himself. The way he saw it he had one good move left in him. It had to count. He saw Regina's face, ghostly white, and thought of what Marot would do to her if it didn't.

Whirling, he placed a direct kick to the side of Marot's head. He felt the thud as Marot hit the ground. If he'd had the strength he might have made it a certainty the Frenchman was dead. As it was he didn't. He would let the Dominican authorities deal with him.

"Sorry I'm late," he said, giving the half grin that warmed her heart as he walked painfully and slowly toward her. He threw his arms around her, holding on as if he had everything he needed within his arms. "God! Of all the stupid plans. I never should have let you get in the car with Marot. I could have lost you."

Hands and feet still bound she rolled her head back and looked up at him. "I wanted to help. I needed to. We're all safe now. Marot's finished. That's all that matters."

"Tough lady, aren't you?" He kissed her, drawing strength from her, then broke the circle of his arms and started to kneel and untie the cord at her ankles.

She shook her head. "Wait. I'm fine. Get Monica and Blake out first." As Pierce walked away Regina lowered herself to the ground to sit until he came back.

Pierce obliged her by going around the car to get Monica out first. He untied her feet, then helped her out. As he loosened her hands, Blake slid out beside them.

"Are either of you hurt?" Pierce asked as he loosened Blake's bonds.

"No. Just shaken," Blake answered as he gently touched the bump on the head Marot had given him. "And glad to see you."

"Sorry I had to put you in this danger," Pierce started. "We needed to let Marot convict himself."

Blake frowned and began to speak. "I think I'm the one who ought to apologize to—" breaking off as he saw Marot dashing toward Monica's car.

Pierce saw Blake's expression freeze. He jerked his head around, saw Marot running, but the sight that sent him into a black, helpless rage was the blaze climbing toward the gas tank of Blake's car. The bastard was going to blow them all up. He had only seconds to drag Monica and Blake over the embankment across the road, the same seconds to shout a warning.

"Regina! Get clear!" he yelled, hoping somehow she could get to her feet and out of the way enough to shield herself from the explosion.

She saw Marot running and spotted the flame at the same time she heard Pierce's warning. She heard a series of thuds from the other side of the car and hoped it meant they had found cover.

Heaving herself away from the car and rolling as best she could, Regina drew in what she believed would be her last breath. Parts of metal shot into the sky, high over the roof of the cabin. Beneath, what remained of the car crackled and roared from within an inferno of flame and smoke. Pierce climbed over the embankment and raced toward it.

"Regina!" he shouted, rounding the burning heap, his heart stopping when he saw no sign of her. Monica and Blake ran up behind him.

"Where is she?" Monica cried, tears glistening on her mud-stained face.

"She was here," he said, his voice rasping. "I don't know if..." He couldn't finish. "Regina," he called her name, hesitantly, afraid there wouldn't be an answer. But there was, from a shallow gully about twelve feet from the car.

Pierce raced to the edge. The gully was filled with mud and she was covered in it from head to foot.

Relief washed through him like a cleansing river, opening up floodgates, freeing emotions he'd had dammed up for years. She was safe and he loved her. It was simple. That simple. Smiling as if he'd just been given the world on a platter he stood above her, hands on his hips, legs braced wide apart, staring down. "Well, well. If it isn't the tar baby," he said.

Her blue-green eyes gleamed like a couple of sapphires set in a mud face. The look was pure disbelief. "Oh God! Pierce," she cried as happiness bubbled through her. Her eyes grew rounder and bigger as all the panic came back. "Blake? Monica? Are they safe?"

Pierce dropped down on one knee. "They're fine."

"Marot?"

"He won't go far." His smile deepened, actually turning up the corners of his mustache as he shook his head. "How the devil did you get from over there to this gully?"

Regina squirmed, trying to sit up in the mud. "Back rolls. Blake saw that I took gymnastics as a kid." She stretched out her tied hands to him. "Now get me out of here."

"I don't know," he hedged. "You're awfully dirty."

"You're not spic-and-span yourself." He glanced at himself. He'd picked up a little mud diving over the embankment. She shuddered and looked around at the gully. "I think there're leeches in here."

"Well, in that case..." Pierce climbed down beside her and hauled her up, then used a pocketknife to cut her free.

From the road she heard men running and knew another moment of fear. "Who is it?" she asked hurriedly.

"Dominican police, attending to Monica and Blake. They'll have picked up Marot."

Two officers appeared at that minute, spraying the burning car from fire extinguishers. Regina rubbed her wrists and ankles, then hastily wiped away as much of the mud as possible. That wasn't much. When she was done Pierce swept her into his arms. She draped her arms around his neck and he carried her into the cabin. He held her tightly, hugging her close against him before he set her down. Inside the cabin she found a towel and water and washed away most of the rest of the mud.

"Better?" she asked.

"Some," he said, shaking his head. The pain in his temple brought a groan.

Regina moved closer to him, her trained eyes following the track of the bullet. Marot's work. She insisted he allow her to clean the head wound he'd refused any treatment to before. Reluctantly he agreed now, sitting quietly as she washed away the crusty blood.

"That's a mess," she said, dabbing his temple with the wet cloth. She breathed in a long, relief-filled breath. "But there's really only a crease from the bullet under all that dried blood. You won't need stitches," she said as she gently touched the sides of the wound. "Just some quiet and rest. How does it feel?"

"Like I hit a tree at ninety miles a hour and bounced off."

"That good?" She smiled, combing his hair away from the wound with her fingers. "Well, it's no wonder the way you've been behaving since you got it."

Pierce, eyes intent on her face, caught her hands and pulled them away, holding them tightly in his. "Actually, it's down to a dull ache now."

"I'm keeping a close watch on you anyway." She tried to look serious and professional but found it impossible as she read the smoldering secrets in his dark eyes.

"Good." His voice was husky and low, his smile like the sun coming out after a storm. "A very personal physician is just what I need."

He was pulling her toward him when Blake and Monica came in a moment later, a police captain with them. Swearing under his breath, Pierce let her go and greeted Captain Sams. The officer gave him a quick report. Pierce had been right. One police jeep was already on the way back to Roseau with Marot in custody.

"Queenie! You're all right!" Blake cried, rushing toward her and wrapping her in a big hug.

The captain wanted to hear their story, so slowly and carefully each of them pieced in the details. Apparently for years Inspector Marot had been a connection within DESE for a powerful underworld syndicate. That syndicate planned to use the necklace to pressure an important French cabinet member to grant favors for their organization. When a man with Pierce's intelligence credentials had called, seeking information about Blake Andrews and Jacques Marot, the French government had enlisted his help.

In France evidence was being gathered to connect Marot to the death of Nellie Thanet. Today's activities promised to be the last of his criminal acts for a long time.

"I'd already started an investigation, thinking Blake was swindling Monica," Pierce said. "The French set me straight about Blake's enterprises. Although they didn't think he was involved in the scheme to use the necklace against the cabinet member, they weren't sure."

"I just wanted to help Nellie," Blake said. "She'd been approached about the necklace but refused to turn it over to the syndicate. She was too angry with her former lover to return it to him when he asked for it. She thought she'd earned it. In her eyes the best thing to do was convert it to cash. I took it against my better judgment, having no idea the syndicate wanted it as badly as they did. I—uhh—" He looked nervously at the police captain.

"It's all right, Mr. Andrews. We've made an agreement with the French government. What you say will be strictly confidential and unofficial."

"Thanks." Blake nodded. "I mailed the necklace to Monica to be presented to a buyer. Only my housekeeper in Switzerland made a mistake posting the packages and sent it to Regina instead. I was upset. That was an inconvenience, but at the same time I still didn't know the danger we were all in."

"Marot must have learned about the package. I was informed he'd visited your chalet in Switzerland," Pierce said.

"He broke into my house looking for the necklace but didn't find it." Voice strained, Regina glanced apologetically at Pierce. "I'm sorry. At times I was sure that burglar was you." Pierce placed his hand over hers but remained silent. "I suppose after that Marot decided to follow me, thinking I would lead him to Blake. And I did."

"Undoubtedly he was the man who broke into my hotel room in Antigua and attacked you."

"Yes," Regina said. "What I don't understand is how Larousse fit into this and just why he was killed."

Pierce broke in. "Larousse was an honest man. Somewhere along the way he realized he was being used and that Marot was working for the wrong side. Marot must have gotten suspicious and watched him closely. Larousse knew Marot could be vicious. He tried to get word to his superiors in France when they split up and traveled to Dominica separately. Larousse came posing as a tourist. Unfortunately, the message was intercepted and Marot learned of it. He killed Larousse, trying to make it look like a natural death. I learned from Bandy and his men that they'd brought Marot in illegally."

The lieutenant broke in. "Marot had little to worry about. He intended to leave the same way. If he'd been successful, there would be no way to prove he'd ever been on Dominica. If confronted he could claim his illegal entry was necessary to the case. With his credentials almost anything is possible. There would be no way to tie him with several more murders either."

"I was to meet Larousse that afternoon at Monica's party," Blake said glumly. "To turn over the necklace. When he collapsed in the garden I got scared and ran, thinking I had the necklace with me."

"Which you didn't because I'd removed it." Regina sighed. "Then Marot convinced me he was Blake's contact and that Pierce was trying to harm Blake. I'm sorry to say I believed him. Even after I agreed to help Pierce I wasn't sure about Marot. It was when I remembered about the cat that I knew what he was really doing."

"The cat?" Three male voices harmonized.

"He mentioned seeing my cat. When I thought back I knew he could only have seen Marley if he'd been the burglar. I knew then how dangerous he was."

"Nevertheless, it all worked out," the police captain said, rising to his feet. "I'll be getting back to my headquarters and on the way I'll forget everything but that I have two Frenchmen to deport, one dead, one alive."

"What about the necklace?" Regina asked.

"It will be handed over to the French consulate in Barbados. And I think a grateful French cabinet member will begin to appreciate the comforts of home. Ahhh, one other thing, Mrs. Whitechurch. I trust you will confine your business endeavors to the agricultural kind from now on." Monica assured him she would. "Then let us be on our way. Mr. Andrews, Mrs. Whitechurch, you'll ride with me. That is what you wanted, isn't it, Mr. Buchannan?" He smiled innocently.

"Yes," Pierce concurred. "Dr. Lawton and I have a few things to straighten up here."

Regina lifted her sandy brows in question. Did they?

A few minutes later Monica and Blake climbed into the second police jeep and started down the mountain.

Pierce checked the roof of the cabin for any burning debris and made sure none of the wreck was still smoldering. There was little danger of fire spreading in the perpetually wet rain forest but he preferred to be cautious. Regina stood back a few feet, shuddering as she imagined what might have happened if they hadn't been able to get away from the car.

Satisfied, he walked back to her and wrapped an arm possessively around her shoulders. "It's all over, isn't it?" she said, snuggling against him.

"It's over." Leaning down he kissed the top of her head. "Blake may have to go to Paris to settle up a few loose ends he's left there. I don't think he'll find any charges against him. This case is to be handled with the utmost French discretion." While he talked he led her back in the cabin.

"It's ridiculous," she said, pausing as he pulled the door shut. "I always thought I was an excellent judge of character. This time I was completely wrong about everyone. Especially you. I'm sorry," she said. "Really sorry I couldn't read my own emotions and know the truth sooner."

"You don't owe me apologies," he said taking a seat on one of the bunks. "But I've got a cart full for you." She started to protest but he silenced her with a look. "Let me say this, please. I told you about my marriage breaking up. What I didn't tell you was that April was pregnant at the time. I didn't learn about it until after she'd had an abortion. It was my child. For years I had nightmares about the child I'd lost."

"Pierce." She saw the hurt in his face and sitting beside him tried to comfort him with a touch. "I'm sorry."

He trembled. "I never allowed myself to care about a woman again, never met anyone who moved me. You, however, were different. You put a wrecking ball in my plans from the start. I knew I was falling in love and was too stubborn and too frightened to admit it.''

Now she *did* interrupt, not caring about the rest of his confession. "You're sure about it now?"

"I'm sure," he said. "I love you." He didn't look happy about it. The smile was haphazard on his face. "Hell! I don't know how to say this. I know I pushed you too far that night on the beach, made you do things you didn't want to do. I know you can't for—"

Regina smiled, feeling the first moment of pure relief in days. "You're wrong. I was furious at you. I thought you were a criminal. I thought you intended to hurt Blake. But I loved you, even then. I wanted you that night. That's what made me angry."

"Regina..." Unknowingly he reached for the wound at his temple.

"You're hurting. We ought to get you somewhere where you can rest," she said, reaching for him.

"I'm hurting all right." He pulled her into his arms, almost into his lap. His eyes were dark and moody. "Hurting because I've been a fool a long time and because it almost cost me the woman I love." The hurt was a slow steady ache. A man deserved to feel pain when he'd seen heaven, had it in his arms, and almost let go.

She propped pillows behind him. He fell back against them. God, he was tired, drained.

She kissed him gently on the lips. "I'll pull the car closer to the house," she said. "I think you're about to drop. We'll get going."

"No," he said drowsily. "We'll stay here."

She gave him a stern medical look. "You need..."

"A doctor, rest. There's a basket of food in the car. The captain left a first-aid kit. I've got everything I need right here."

She couldn't argue with him. He fell asleep and didn't open his eyes until sixteen hours later.

"Good morning," Pierce said, opening his eyes to find a pair of serious blue-green ones staring at him.

"Good afternoon," Regina corrected, a smile curving her lips when she heard his cheerful tone. "How do you feel?"

"Happy. Hungry. How do I look?" he asked, rubbing his day's growth of beard.

She cocked her head to one side and looked him over. "You've got a blue-ribbon shiner, a goose egg..."

He plumped a pillow and sat up. "Are those medical terms?"

"Absolutely." She kissed him lightly on the lips. "You've got no broken bones. I checked them all."

Pierce looked under the sheet and saw that he wore only his briefs. "I thought I remembered a pleasant dream."

She laughed. "I washed your clothes in a stream. Mine, too. They're dry now." She laid his dry but wrinkled clothes across the foot of the bunk, then crossed the room to the table and started removing things from the hamper.

"You sleep any?" he asked, getting up, stretching and taking his time about getting into his clothes.

"A reasonable amount." Fruit, cheese, crackers. That would do. In such warm weather she wasn't sure the sandwiches would still be good. "The captain was back to check on us this morning. I told him we'd be down later."

"Thanks. And thanks for staying with me." He joined her at the table.

"I didn't mind. Last night was the first peaceful night I've had in weeks. I rather like it up here."

When they'd finished eating, Pierce helped her clean up, insisting his head felt fine. He found Blake's razor and managed a cold-water shave.

When they left the cabin and stood on the small porch outside, Pierce eased her into his arms. His eyes darkened. "We'll come back here sometime and stay as long as we like."

"Is that a promise?" she whispered.

He answered with a kiss. And with the kiss, needs shot through him, old ones, new ones, long-suppressed ones. They were the needs he'd thought made a man weak. Now he knew they were the ones that made a man strong. Strength would be in lying beside her, in sharing her life, the joys, the sorrows, the tomorrows. He moved his mouth over hers, devouring its softness.

Her heart melted as he flowed through her like a song on a night breeze. The sweet feel of it overpowered her. When he pulled his mouth away she was breathless.

"Follow me," he said, coaxing her down the steps and into the car. He had one more important threshold to cross, committing his life and love to the woman who already held his heart. He wanted to do it right. "There's a place near here that doesn't even belong in this crazy world. I want to take you there."

He drove a few miles down the road and parked. Holding his hand, Regina trailed behind him as he started up a path so narrow it was barely discernible in the lush jungle foliage. The forest was alive and wet, seeming to swallow their tracks. A few feet into the jungle and their shoes were soaked from the leaves and vines that dripped ever-present moisture into the path. It was a pleasant, soothing dampness, almost ethereal.

Above the sunlight was a green glow in the bursting foliage. Enormous, ancient vine-laden trees and giant ferns billowing like tents surrounded them. Anthurium, bromeliads and other tropical plants filled the trees and forest floor. Deeper in the rain forest the constant dripping mist grew heavier. It was like no place Regina had ever seen, the feel of it like nothing she'd ever known. She wouldn't have been surprised if a naiad or other mythical creature appeared in the path before them.

"This is it," Pierce said, drawing her up beside him as they came to a small rocky grotto filled by a breathtakingly beautiful waterfall. Flowers, ferns and more of the magnificent trees framed the falls. Sunlight broke through where thick leaves would allow, lighting streaks in the clear green water. The scent of wild orchids clung in the air. "It's the Emerald Pool. Ever see a more beautiful place?"

"It's wonderful," Regina whispered, completely captivated by the unworldly quality. Looking at it, she thought from such a place, if not life, surely love had sprung. It invited. She didn't wait for him to lead but climbed down the rocks toward the emerald waters alone.

Pierce followed, his shirt and shoes discarded along the way. Regina tossed her shoes to the bank and dived beneath the water. Pierce followed, coming up full of laughter with her in his arms. Prisms of water slid from her face and hair and from his. The laughter echoed. It was as if there was no other place than this, no other people, no other longing than theirs.

How this place suited her, he thought. A dreamworld, a dream woman. One as compellingly beautiful as the other.

"A vision," he whispered. "I love you."

"I'm glad," she answered, lifting her fingers to stroke his cheeks. Her eyes glowed with enjoyment. "Very glad." His face was as she liked it, smiling, teasing, intriguing. Warmth flooded her skin as he touched her hair with his hands.

The slow ache had gone to his heart. "I want to make love with you," he said softly. "Here where everything seems new and fresh and full of hope." The last time they'd made love he'd demanded and taken. He wouldn't do that again. "Will you let me?"

"Yes." The sound from her lips was hardly a sound at all as she buried her face against his chest.

He pulled back only a little, enough to see clearly into those glistening crystal eyes, enough to lose himself in them. His mouth crushed against hers before he reminded himself this time he must be gentle. The pressure lightened, his lips only lingering on hers, his heart feeling as if there'd never been disharmony between them. He caught her hands, opening them, drawing them to his lips, kissing the palms, the wrists, feeding her pulse with the heat of his mouth.

Her hands were suddenly freed as Pierce plucked at her shirt in gentle persistence, loosening the fastenings, sliding it from her shoulders. His kisses were whispers on her damp skin, his words even softer in her ear. He followed a feathery path from cheek to throat, lingering in the softness there, then at the slope of her shoulder. His breath was warm against the soft swell of her breast, as he savored and tasted, circling the tight peak with his tongue.

She hardly knew when he loosened her shorts and pulled them from her. Only that as time wound around them and lights played magical colors on the water his body molded flesh to flesh against hers. She felt him against her, the hard masculine symmetry of his body. Blood pounded in her brain and ran hunger in her veins. The sensuous rush of water on bare skin intensified the feel. His hands stroked, ranging deep beneath the water, probing gently and never far enough. Her eyes were tortured with wanting, her body throbbing. Her faint moans of pleasure spurred him on.

"I want you," she pleaded, yearning for the fulfillment of having him inside her. "I need you."

"No," he murmured, feeling a ripple of pleasure run through him, finding it almost an impossibility to refuse her plea. "Not yet. I'm not done loving you this way."

His hands were hot brands in the water, boiling it around her, his mouth no less, sliding beneath the surface, touching everywhere. She was as bold, knowing all his male glory with her hands and lips. When the pace slowed it was because both were too near the peak and had no wish to hurry over.

"I want to feel you against me," he whispered brokenly, swimming up behind her and pulling her buttocks against his hardness. He enfolded her in his arms, burrowing his face into her wet cascading hair.

Wondrous tremors shook her as his hands roamed. If she never made love with him again there would be memory enough from this one time to last forever. She would remember every touch, the tastes, the smell of him, every kiss and the depths to which it had taken her.

He turned her, slowly, creating ripples on the water's surface. She watched them grow in endless rings—like her love for him. His eyes burned with passion, hers like two blue-white stars.

"Pierce, I need you..." The words fluttered between them. He caught her by the waist, his broad hands almost spanning the narrow width.

Pierce looked down at her, calling her name, speaking of love, lifting her slowly up the length of his thighs, bringing her higher. Now the water simmered, or was it her? Holding her high, he nudged softly at her femininity. She moaned and pleaded with him but he gave no more. Whimpering her need, she wrapped her legs around his hips trying to urge him forward. His face betrayed his restraint. He was near the edge, his face lit with wanting. Her mouth found his, crying her need. Her kiss was enough to snap his control.

A groan tore from him as he sheathed himself inside her. His body quivering, he lifted and lowered her as if she were weightless. The water wrapped around them, churning with their rhythm. She cried his name over and over—everything else was erased from her mind.

A hot surge of heat built inside him. He needed her now, always. He tried to tell her that she was all he wanted, as his body released its thunder.

He held her a long time, not wanting to break that special union. Eventually he eased her into the water and she splashed onto her back, floating beside him. He helped her wash and then, damp skin glowing, climb from the pool. His own body still throbbed as he rolled and rinsed in the cool water. He would never have enough of her. He didn't know how he could bear seeing her go back to Atlanta, back to her practice. He wouldn't even think of her out of his life.

"You're very rough on my wardrobe, Mr. Buchannan," she told him as she located her soggy clothing, frowning her dismay at the condition they were in.

"You don't need a wardrobe when you're with me." He gave her a sweeping glance, taking in the long silky legs, the golden curls, the full soft curves. "I like you in that," he taunted as he climbed out of the pool and started the search for his own wet clothing. He found his shirt and trousers but couldn't keep his eyes off Regina long enough to find his shoes.

She quirked a brow at him. "A lecher no less."

"A man who appreciates art and beauty." He decided his shoes had gone down the river, another pair sacrificed to passion. He couldn't stay away. He crossed the few feet of ground between them, taking her in his arms and kissing her suddenly, causing a stir of arousal she found delightful.

Before he let her go she looped her fingers in his hair, pulling his head down to be sure the wound on his temple hadn't opened up.

"It's a good thing," she told him. "I could lose my license letting a patient be so—active—with an injury like that."

Pierce kissed her again, then retrieved his trousers, wrung them out and put them on. "You have no worries. I'll give a sterling testimonial to your bedside manner."

Laughing, Regina did as he had, wringing the water out then slipping into her clothes. "Still like that, do you?"

He placed a hand over his heart. "Absolutely. I hope it's not the kind of care all your patients get."

She shook her head. "Oh, no. I save that for special cases."

"Like?" He gave up on his shirt, just wringing it out and throwing it over his shoulder.

She rubbed her chin as if she was musing over the question. "Like the man I'm going to marry."

He gave that half grin she found so endearing, and began to caress her shoulders. "I was getting to that," he said softly, but with no displeasure in his voice.

She kissed him softly. "I'm sure you were. You're very direct."

He looped his wet shirt around her, trapping her against him. "And frequently in need of a doctor."

She wrapped her arms around his waist, her eyes lifted plaintively to his. "That isn't why you're so agreeable to this, is it? You *do* get more bruises than a kid with new skates."

"Uh uh," he said, enjoying the feel of her, surprised at the sudden tightening in his loins. "I have far more pressing needs."

She moved her hands on his back, liking the solid, sinewy strength of him. "What about your business? Wasn't it in Miami?"

"I'm moving my headquarters to Atlanta." Sliding an arm around her waist, Pierce guided her away from the grotto and toward the path. Dusk was near and only thin threads of light still fell through the trees. He knew how difficult it could be to find the way out once all the light was gone.

"Won't that be inconvenient?" Her fingers linked through his, she followed when the path narrowed, walked beside him when it widened. The last few feet was traveled in total darkness but when they reached the road, a few colors of sunset, rose and amber, still remained in the sky.

"Not nearly as inconvenient as commuting to Miami every day. My nights are reserved for you."

"And all the children we're going to have," she added.

"All the children," he repeated. "I love you, Regina." He wrapped an arm around her and held her still a moment. "Every minute we have together is precious. I don't want to lose any of them."

Regina sighed as his mouth covered hers. Her senses were alive to the pounding need in his body. The sky had become black velvet, the moon a silver sphere behind a blue-green peak. She thought they would be very late getting down from the mountain.

His kiss deepened. Paradise lost. Paradise found. The memories took over—and the promises. They'd first made love in this Dominican paradise, this Eden. And afterward everything went wrong, just as if they'd taken a bite of forbidden fruit. This time she would make sure nothing did. Ever.

* * * * *

from
Nora Roberts

Skin Deep

Available September 1988

The third in an exciting new series about the lives and loves of triplet sisters—

In May's *The Last Honest Woman* (SE #451), Abby finally met a man she could trust . . . then tried to deceive him to protect her sons.

In July's *Dance to the Piper* (SE #463), it took some very fancy footwork to get reserved recording mogul Reed Valentine dancing to effervescent Maddy's tune. . . .

In *Skin Deep* (SE #475), find out what kind of heat it takes to melt the glamorous Chantel's icy heart. Available in September.

THE O'HURLEYS!

Join the excitement of Silhouette Special Editions.

Silhouette Intimate Moments

SET SAIL FOR THE SOUTH SEAS
with
BESTSELLING AUTHOR
EMILIE RICHARDS

This month Silhouette Intimate Moments begins a very special miniseries by a very special author. *Tales of the Pacific*, by Emilie Richards, will take you to Hawaii, New Zealand and Australia and introduce you to a group of men and women you will never forget.

In Book One, FROM GLOWING EMBERS, share laughter and tears with Julianna Mason and Gray Sheridan as they overcome the pain of the past and rekindle the love that had brought them together in marriage ten years ago and now, amidst the destructive force of a tropical storm, drives them once more into an embrace without end.

FROM GLOWING EMBERS (Intimate Moments #249) is available now. And in coming months look for the rest of the series: SMOKESCREEN (November 1988), RAINBOW FIRE (February 1989) and OUT OF THE ASHES (May 1989). They're all coming your way—only in Silhouette Intimate Moments.

IM249-R

Silhouette Intimate Moments

COMING
NEXT MONTH

#253 THAT MALCOLM GIRL—Parris Afton Bonds

Rob Malcolm, had been a rancher all her life, and her only dream was to have her own spread someday. Then Hollywood—and Jed Pulaski—came to Mescalero, and she fell in love with a man as different from her as night from day. Only time would tell if these two opposites could merge forever in the glory of the dawn.

#254 A SHIVER OF RAIN—Kay Bartlett

FBI Agent Luke Warren burst into Rachel's quiet life, insisting that her former husband had been a thief. Worse still, the sexy man planned to stick around until the stolen money was recovered. Soon Rachel found herself the target of the real thieves and of Luke's latest campaign—to win her heart.

#255 STAIRWAY TO THE MOON—Anna James

Ella Butler, widow of a famous rock star, was sick of publicity, and then she met Nick Manning, a prominent diplomat. His career placed him in the limelight, and she was certain they could never have a future together. But Nick would do anything to keep her—even climb a stairway to the moon.

#256 CHAIN LIGHTNING—Elizabeth Lowell

Mandy Blythe didn't want to be anywhere near the Great Barrier Reef. She didn't like the water, diving made her nervous—and she certainly didn't trust Damon Sutter. He was a womanizer, and the last man she could ever fall for. But the tropics were a different world—and paradise was only a heartbeat away.